Praise for Karmen Lee

"Brimming with heart and humor, this second chance romance has it all—rivalry, tension, chemistry, longing, and of course, more than a few tricky 7-10 splits. A breathtaking, heartwarming romance."

—Ashley Herring Blake, award-winning author of *Delilah Green Doesn't Care*, on *The 7-10 Split*

"Loaded with wit, unrealized feelings, and unresolved history, Lee's [*The*] *7-10 Split* delights and elevates a bowling rivalry between the cutest pairing with a striking side of steam."

—Kelly Cain, author of *An Acquired Taste*, on *The 7-10 Split*

"Charming, witty and full of heart, *The 7-10 Split* is second chance romance at its finest. The laugh-out-loud scenarios and snappy banter left me rooting for Ava and Grace from the start. Karmen Lee has created the perfect formula—fiery tension, palpable chemistry and the willingness to forgive—leaving readers with what we love most: The ultimate HEA."

—Author Denise N. Wheatley, on *The 7-10 Split*

Also by Karmen Lee

The 7-10 Split

Visit the Author Profile page at Harlequin.com for more titles.

KARMEN LEE

The Relationship Mechanic

HARLEQUIN

afterglow BOOKS

Recycling programs
for this product may
not exist in your area.

ISBN-13: 978-1-335-57490-9

The Relationship Mechanic

Copyright © 2025 by Kristen Rhee

Harlequin Enterprises ULC
22 Adelaide St. West, 41st Floor
Toronto, Ontario M5H 4E3, Canada
www.Harlequin.com

Printed in U.S.A.

One

"I'm bored."

Vini squinted against the glare of the sun. It was a beautiful uneventful day the same as any other. Business had been slow leaving her with the need for something, anything, to happen. She rolled her eyes at Aiden's words but couldn't deny she felt the same. Excitement was hard to come by in Peach Blossom, but even this bout of boredom was a bit much.

"Seriously, Vin. Can't you at least put a television in here or something?" Aiden's voice was starting to do her head in especially when he started with the whining. "Watching paint dry would be more entertaining at this point."

"If you're so bored," she replied, not bothering to look over at him, "why don't you organize the new shipment of parts we got in this morning?"

She knew that was a guaranteed way to get Aiden to shut up before he got on a roll of even more complaints. It wouldn't be the first time, but she didn't need his boredom to lead to her annoyance. He groaned but dutifully got up and walked to the back room where they kept the parts they needed to fix the vehicles that came in and out of the shop. Vini watched him go and almost told him she would do it instead. Organizing the stock wasn't fun, but the repetitive nature of it at least helped the time go by faster.

Music drifted through the air and Vini leaned forward, elbows on the counter as she gazed out the window. The street in front of her auto shop was clear, save a couple cars that drove by. She almost regretted relocating the shop to the outskirts of the main part of town, but the space it had afforded her was worth it in the long run. Still, it would've been nice to be able to go one or two buildings over to chat with people instead of having to walk the three miles it took to get to Main Street. Not for the first time she was regretting not buying a television and installing cable in the shop. Or at least getting a smart TV to stream something. The radio only helped so much when there was a lull in vehicles to work on.

The landline ringing shook her out of her boredom, and she grabbed for the phone hoping desperately that there was something interesting to do.

"Hey, Lavenia. You free right now?"

Vini winced at her whole name being used. It wasn't the first time Sheriff Patrick had done it, despite her insisting he was more than welcome to call her by her nickname like everyone else in town did. No one used her whole name anymore. Except her father when she was in trouble or her sisters when they were being assholes.

"Yeah. You got a job for me?"

"A car on the shoulder out on Seventy-five Southbound a mile out from exit one forty. Driver said the damn thing is a rental that just crapped out on her and could use a tow. She's staying in Peach Blossom so figured I'd call you instead of Tony."

"Good looking out," she replied pushing up off the counter. Tony Prichard ran another auto shop in the town forty minutes north of them. Sheriff Patrick usually patrolled the strip between the two towns and called in help depending on which way people were headed unless it was an eighteen-wheeler which was much heavier than any of Vini's equipment could handle. "I'll get the truck and head your way. Is it a case of the forgotten pit stop again, or do you think this is legit?"

He chuckled, no doubt remembering the last wayward tourist who had somehow forgotten to fill his tank and then was surprised when the car exhausted its fumes and refused to go a mile farther. That had been a hilarious story to relay to her family when she had gotten home that evening.

"Nah. It's a genuine one."

"Got it. Be there in twenty."

Vini called out to Aiden letting him know she had a job before grabbing her sunglasses and heading to the back lot. The air was blessedly warm compared to a few days prior when a random cold front had brought in the type of chill that had everyone in coats in the morning and short sleeves by the afternoon. Fall in Georgia was peculiar like that. But today was one of those gorgeous days that just guaranteed good things, and it put a little pep in Vini's step as she climbed into the truck and got going.

She whistled along to the radio and dropped her sunglasses over her eyes as she made her way out onto the highway. Finding the sheriff was easy enough, though she did have to go up a ways before she could turn onto the other side of the road. As Vini pulled up, she waved to Patrick. He walked over as soon as she had parked.

"Thanks for getting here so quick. I got a call about a disturbance out at McArthur Farms so I'm heading out if you're good."

Vini nodded as she looked over at the car in question. "Yeah, I should be good." As he got back in his car and drove away, she walked over to the driver's side. "You all right?"

"No," the woman said through the cracked window. She pushed the door open and stepped out. "I am so far from all right, it's not even funny. Something told me I should have gone to Italy, but did I listen? No."

Vini snorted softly at the running commentary that didn't seem to require any of her own input. She always marveled at people who seemed to be able to ramble on without needing to take a breath. Jordan, her nephew, was like that sometimes, though he was a kid, so it didn't seem all that unusual for him. "Okay. Can you tell me what happened before the car stopped on you?"

The woman waved her hand at the car, somehow look-

ing elegant even as her words came faster. Vini had to focus
hard to understand as each sentence picked up speed.

"I was just making my way down the interstate, even
though this wasn't even the car I reserved. I asked for *re-
liable*, and somehow they heard *heap of junk* instead." She
turned and kicked the tire, making Vini hide another snort
of amusement behind her hand. Dark brown eyes shifted to
her, though there was none of the anger in them that she
seemed to have for the car beside them.

"There wasn't any warning," the woman continued now
turning to face Vini more fully. Honey skin glowed with
the warmth from the sun overhead, and full lips seemed to
wrap around each syllable distracting Vini even more from
the words she needed to hear.

"So there was no sound before it stopped?" Vini asked
trying to get her mind together as she stared at one of the
most attractive women she had seen in a long while.

Those same lips tugged down before the woman answered. "I don't think so. But I had the music up, so I wasn't
exactly paying attention. I know it's not from a lack of gas,
though. I'm not that clueless." She smiled before pausing.
Vini waited to see what else she might say but was startled
when the other woman thrust out her hand. "I'm Jessica."

Vini looked down at the hand before reaching out to
shake it. "Vini."

Warmth enveloped her slightly smaller hand, and Vini
had to force herself to pull away. A thumb brushed over
the back of her hand as they separated, and she swallowed
hard. It had been a while since she had gone to the city and

flirted with anyone who would actually flirt back, but that handshake seemed to be a bit handsier than strictly necessary. Then again, Jessica was probably just happy to have someone come save her from the situation to begin with. Vini had heard enough stories about creepy mechanics, and she wasn't trying to add to them by being overly friendly.

"Well, let's get her back to the shop so I can see what's up." Vini stepped away, her mind going into work mode as she got the car hooked up. She hopped back out of the truck and called out to Jessica. "We're all set. Hop on in, and I'll bring you to the shop. Town's not too far from me so you can get there no problem."

Jessica nodded before following Vini's lead. It wasn't the first time Vini had had someone riding in the tow with her. It wasn't even the first time she had another woman there either. But for some reason, she was hyper aware of her new passenger in a way she never had been for others. The ride was quiet save for the music. Heavy bass seemed to discourage talking, though Vini figured Jessica was probably tired enough from her ordeal.

They pulled into the lot, and Vini helped Jessica out, telling her to go on inside and she would be in to help her figure out how to get to the town. There were no cabs in Peach Blossom, and the only types of car services were friends you could call to help you out. With it being the middle of the day, Vini doubted most would be available at the moment.

"So I got your car situated. I have some time this afternoon to take a look and let you know what's going on."

Jessica nodded. She was leaning against the counter when Vini came in and hadn't moved even when Vini came up to the counter as well. At some point, she had taken her hair out of the tight ponytail it had been in when Vini drove up, and it fell in dark loose spirals over her shoulders. Vini's own tightly coiled hair was kept in braids, but she currently had those in the same two braids she always wore it in when she was working.

"That would be great," Jessica replied not taking her eyes off Vini. Something about her gaze had Vini feeling self-conscious in a way she never had. Her overalls were oil-stained, which wasn't new, but she did wonder what she looked like to the other woman.

Most people Vini helped often remarked that she looked far too young to be the one in charge of the shop. A few had even tried to talk over her or spoken to Aiden instead of her. She was always quick to shut that down and felt no guilt in kicking someone out and telling them to call for someone else to deal with their bullshit. This didn't feel like that, though. Jessica wasn't looking at her with disdain or judgment. In fact, Vini couldn't read her expression at all.

"Is there somewhere you needed to be?"

The question seemed to shake Jessica out of whatever thoughts she was having, and she straightened up. "Yeah. I was coming to town to stay with a friend of mine for the next few weeks, and I was trying to make it to her place." Jessica raised an eyebrow. "I don't suppose you guys have taxis out here, huh?"

Vini twisted her lips and shook her head. "Not even one.

The main part of town is about a three mile walk which I don't recommend."

Jessica chuckled. "I wouldn't even know which direction to walk in, so no problem there." She pulled her phone out of her purse. "I suppose I can text my friend and ask her to come get me once she's off work. Hopefully that won't mess up her plans too much."

Vini meant to let her do just that, but something about Jessica made her want to help. It wasn't a helplessness. Despite clearly not being local, Vini got the sense that Jessica wasn't easily left floundering and would no doubt power through figuring things out with or without Vini's help.

"Listen, I know you don't know me," she started, her mouth moving faster than her brain could process what she was offering, "but I don't mind giving you a lift to your friend's place or into town if you prefer to wait it out. There's a diner that has pretty good food and free Wi-Fi, and there's a small bookstore a quick walk from it."

Jessica tilted her head and gazed at Vini before her lips curled up in a smile. "I would love if you could drop me off at my friend's place. It should be unlocked. She told me you guys still do the whole not-locking-your-doors thing around here, which is different in a charming sort of way."

Vini raised an eyebrow. The way she said *charming* sounded a lot like *strange*, but she appreciated Jessica's tact. It was true somewhat. They didn't just go around leaving all the doors unlocked or anything, but people in Peach Blossom were a lot more lax than in the bigger cities. If anyone did break in, chances were the whole town would know who the culprit was by afternoon.

"All right. Well, we'd better get going so I can get back here and check your car out."

"Lead the way, and I will happily follow," Jessica replied with a grin. Her voice deepened leaving Vini even more perplexed than before. Instead of acknowledging it, she gestured for her new customer to follow her out the front this time where she had her regular truck parked. She didn't quite know why she was even offering when she never had before. When Jessica rattled off Grace's familiar address, Vini tried to keep her expression neutral. She hadn't heard much about Jessica from Ava, but as she pulled out of the parking lot, she resolved to find out more.

TWO

Riding down a dirt road with the Georgia sun high overhead was not what Jessica had in mind when she'd told her parents she was going to visit Grace for the next six weeks. To be fair, the road wasn't actually dirt, and the tree-lined roads that made up wherever they were actually were charming. Add the overall-wearing cutie beside her with dark brown skin and lips made for kissing, and this was probably the best thing that had happened to Jessica in the past couple weeks.

"So Vini," she said breaking the silence that had fallen between them. She didn't know how long it would take to get to Grace's place, so she figured starting a conversation might help pass the time. "Have you lived in Peach Blossom long?"

"All my life," she replied, her eyes not leaving the road. "Born and raised here."

That was so strange to Jessica. She had been born on an

army base in Yongsan, and though she had lived in South Korea up until middle school, later she had spent years traveling around. Between her dad's army career and her mom's acting and voice-acting gigs, she never stayed in one place for longer than a couple years before moving on to the next. "Wow. So you've never lived anywhere else? Not even for a little bit?"

"Nope," Vini said lips popping around the final *p* sound in a way that caught Jessica's attention and refused to let go. "Started working at the shop in high school and took it over after I graduated and got my certificates. Been doing it ever since."

That caught Jessica's attention. She let her gaze slide over Vini's face and tried to gauge how old she was. She didn't look any older than early twenties to begin with, but the way she said that made her seem so much older. "How old are you?"

Vini's lips twitched like she wanted to smile, and her eyes finally shifted for a moment to glance over at Jessica. "Twenty-two for another couple weeks."

Relief washed though Jessica. There was still a five-year difference between the two of them, but that wasn't so bad. *Girl, what are you thinking? We didn't come here to gallivant among the locals.* She gave herself an internal smack on the back of the head for even letting her mind go there for a moment. Sure, it had been a little while since she had last enjoyed the company of someone else and stress always did make her a bit hornier than normal, but that didn't mean she needed to jump the first person who smiled at her. She wasn't desperate yet. Plus, small towns weren't always known for being the most welcoming. Sure, Grace had given the place nothing but praise since she got back, but she'd also grown up here. People always tended to have blind spots for the familiar.

It was part of the reason Jessica kept moving. If she didn't stay too long, she wouldn't start to romanticize something that wasn't even there. She preferred to have her feet firmly planted in reality.

"You're really young for working in the shop all by yourself."

Vini raised an eyebrow but didn't reply. For a moment, Jessica wondered if she had said something out of turn, but it was the truth. When she thought about mechanics, her mind instantly conjured images of thick-necked men with greasy hands and a perpetual eye for talking you into paying for things your car didn't actually need. Then again, Vini's cute baby face would probably have even more of an effect. People probably wouldn't expect to get swindled by a cherub wearing overalls.

"So will you let me know what's wrong with the car and price things out before you do the work?" Jessica asked, wanting to know if she was going to need to sell a kidney on the black market to get the rental car back that she didn't even want. If it cost too much, she was tempted to leave the damn thing here and let someone else worry about it. The tabloids could do whatever they wanted with that information, and she would still feel justified.

"Of course," Vini replied. Jessica raised an eyebrow when

she didn't elaborate but let it go. She wasn't trying to annoy Vini to the point that she dropped her off on the side of the road in the middle of nowhere Georgia.

Vini turned right, and the road got a little bumpier before a picturesque house came into view. Jessica couldn't help but be delighted by the quaint feel of the place with its long porch and old-school shutters. She didn't even know people put shutters on houses anymore.

"Wow. This place is adorable."

A soft chuckle beside her wasn't enough to pull her attention away as the truck rolled up the driveway. The two-story house was painted white with sky-blue wooden shutters adorning the windows giving it a homey feel. There were a few trimmed bushes in front and a driveway leading up to it that made Jessica wonder if at some point there had been a basketball hoop at the end of it. It reminded her of those homes she saw in the old television shows her mom liked to watch. It was all very…domestic.

When Vini pulled the truck up to a stop, Jessica almost told her to turn around. Jessica Jae-eun Miller didn't do domestic. She was a spirit that could not be tamed, especially not by a town so small it didn't even have taxis.

"Well, here you go. I can wait here if you need?"

The offer was tempting, and Jessica wondered again if maybe there was something more to it. She was absolutely down for a roll in a cornfield, but she didn't think Grace would appreciate her defiling the guest room so soon after her arrival. Jessica did have some tact.

She turned and favored Vini with a wide smile that she

had been told a few times was rather captivating. Vini's eyebrows lifted slightly, but besides that her expression didn't change. It left Jessica a bit off-kilter. "Oh, you don't have to do that. I'm sure I'll be fine."

Vini stayed quiet as Jessica gathered her things and opened the door. It wasn't until Jessica was halfway up the small stairs leading to the porch that Vini spoke up again. "Wait."

She turned when she heard the sound of a door opening, and Jessica smirked briefly before fixing a curious expression on her face and turning. Vini was only a couple steps away and she looked just as good as she had only a foot or so away inside the truck. She moved with no hesitation as she made her way to Jessica. Before Jessica could get out a word, a piece of paper was thrust in her direction.

"What's this?" she asked reaching out. Their fingers brushed as the slip of paper changed hands. She looked down at Vini's retreating fingers before jerking her gaze over to the piece of paper now in her own. "Your card?"

"Yeah. So you have my information for updates on your car." Vini pointed to the back of the card, prompting Jessica to turn it over. "That's my personal cell. I'm not always in the shop, so feel free to shoot me a text, and I can let you know when I think I'll be finished with it and how much it'll cost."

Jessica nodded slowly before looking back up at Vini. "That's really kind of you." *Damn. Cute and nice? Grace will just have to forgive me.* She gestured to the house. "Want to come inside for a bit? I'm sure I could find some coffee or a bottle of wine."

Vini shook her head. "I should get back to the shop and get under your hood. Tell Grace I said hey."

Jessica blinked quickly and tried to remember if she had mentioned Grace's name. Before she could say anything else, Vini turned and made her way back to the truck. With a little wave, she was gone, leaving Jessica confused and slightly turned-on. Without another word, she turned and tried the door, shocked—and yet not—to find it unlocked. She made her way inside, her gaze focused on the slip of paper in her hand as she wondered how soon was too soon to call.

"Where's my favorite PR nightmare?"

Jessica rolled her eyes as Grace came around the corner, but she didn't hesitate before going in for a tight hug. The rest of the afternoon had been uneventful as she unpacked her suitcase and explored the house she had only seen in pictures and over camera when they FaceTimed. It wasn't what she was used to, but there was something strangely comforting about the step back in time. Many of the rooms had been updated, and Jessica could clearly see where Grace tended to spend most of her time. The back enclosed porch was especially begging for her to grab a book and some sweet tea so she could spend some time back there like a good Southern belle.

It reminded her of her grandparents' home just outside Wonju, South Korea, with all the trees interspersed with older homes and farmland. It made her want to go exploring, but she had figured it would be better to do that with someone who was actually from here. It had been tempting to call Vini and ask her for a more personal tour around town. If not for her exhaustion and the need to call and complain to the car rental company, she might have done just that.

"I'm so glad you came." Grace pulled back and looked at her, brown eyes glassy. Jessica shook her head.

"You big sap." It had been a while since they were last together, and if not for being tired, her eyes might have been a little misty as well.

"Let me drop this stuff in the office and get changed," Grace said gesturing to her bag. "I want to hear all about your drive down here. It still sucks I wasn't able to come get you from the airport."

Jessica waved away her words. By the time Grace came back down wrapped in sweats, Jessica had gotten comfortable on the couch. There was a tray of meats and cheeses on the coffee table that she had brought as a present. She drew Grace's attention to them once they both settled in.

"So I noticed there wasn't a car in the driveway when I got in," Grace started. "Is everything okay?"

Jessica made a stack of cheese and meat on her cracker. She shoved it in her mouth, not caring how she looked. She was damn hungry after her ordeal. She wiped her hands and chewed furiously before answering. "The damn thing stopped on me."

Grace frowned as she reached for a slice of pepperoni. "Stopped on you how?"

"Like, just slowed until it wouldn't move at all," Jessica replied waving her hand. "I barely made it to the side of the highway before it did. Luckily a cop came by and pulled over when he saw my hazard lights."

"Well, damn," Grace huffed out. She popped the meat in her mouth before continuing. "So wait. How did you get here, then? And why didn't you call me?"

"Girl, you were working. Besides, it gave me a chance to meet the cutest little mechanic I have ever seen. Seriously. Normally, I'm wary of them, but she was an angel in oil-stained overalls. I almost asked her out, but I remembered that I was supposed to be on a break."

Grace shook her head but smiled. "Yes, you are. No shacking up with the locals. You're only going to be here for six weeks, and I don't want to deal with the fallout of you magicking the pants off someone and then jetting off never to return." She reached for a piece of cheese before pausing and cutting her eyes at Jessica. "Plus, didn't you *just* deal with some drama that reached the internet? You're lucky Black Twitter didn't get ahold of it, otherwise you would have been trending."

Jessica winced at the reminder of why she was spending six weeks in a rural town in central Georgia instead of an Italian beach somewhere with her parents. Her mom and dad would have been more than happy to have her come with them even after causing her mom drama, but she had known it would be better for her to take some time away to let things die down. It wasn't every day you got caught with two of your mom's colleagues. Sure, it wasn't like they were all together at the same time, but the end results of her trysts coming to light had been the two costars going at it and Jessica's face being splashed on the back pages of a few tabloids and Daum.net.

"I am rather alluring."

"Jess," Grace said, her voice full of warning. It needled Jessica to be chastised, but she knew Grace only did it for her own good. Plus, she was right. Seeing the look of disappointment on her mother's face had hurt enough. She didn't need to see the same look on Grace's face in her rearview mirror as she left town. She also didn't want to make things more difficult for Grace after she left. Things hadn't been the best when she had moved to town to begin with.

"Oh, all right," she agreed finally. It really wasn't that difficult to give in. Vini was cute, but she wasn't cute enough to risk making Grace angry. Okay, that was a lie. With a face like hers, Vini would have had no problems convincing some people to go to war for her, back in the day. "I won't cause any trouble."

Grace giggled before reaching for her glass of wine. "I doubt that, but just don't have anyone coming after you with a pitchfork and we should be fine."

Three

Vini turned off the car and paused. She knew when she went in the house she was probably going to have to deal with some teasing from at least one of her sisters. She contemplated whether she should just turn around and spend the night at the shop. It would only delay the inevitable, but at least she would have another day to think about how to spin things. Peach Blossom was a great place to live, but because it was so small, she had zero doubt someone had already seen her take Jessica back to Grace's place. She wouldn't even be surprised if she walked in the house and was immediately confronted about doing something so far out of character.

Vini Williams didn't like people. She didn't dislike them either, but she wasn't going to go out of her way to help someone she didn't know. It wasn't the *Southern way*, as her dad always said, but she figured her sisters could pick up the slack in that regard. She was kind in other ways that really mattered.

With a sigh, she took off her seat belt and left the car. She had stalled long enough. She walked into the house looking one way and then the other when she wasn't immediately accosted by either her nephew or one of her sisters. She figured their dad would be nice and at least give her time to sit down at the dining table before he started in with his questioning. She had made her way all the way into her room and changed out of her dirty overalls before she heard the first sign of the apocalypse.

"Oh, sister. I heard you met someone new today." Dani's singsong words made her freeze. She sent up a silent prayer to whoever was listening before leaving her room and coming back downstairs. The scent of fried chicken and the sound of sizzling on the stove did little to improve her thinking or make the knowledge that she was about to be presented with a firing squad any better. When she braved the dining room, Dani was at the stove. She didn't turn toward Vini, but Vini had no doubts she knew she was there. Their dad was already at his usual spot at the table with a paper open and obscuring his face. Neither of them made a move, but Vini was still on edge.

Maybe trying to be helpful would keep them from jumping on her at the first chance. "Do you need any help with that?"

Dani shook her head and waved her away. "No. I'm all good here, but if you want to go ahead and set the table, that would be great."

Vini nodded and slowly stepped away. It was weird that that was all that was said so far, but she decided not to look a gift horse in the mouth and made her way to the hutch that kept all their dishes. She resolved to keep an eye out for Ava so she didn't get rushed from behind, but then remembered that she wouldn't be in until after her hair appointment. When Jordan made an appearance, Vini let out another sigh of relief. Dani rarely talked about local gossip in front of him. That meant she was probably safe from having to talk about this afternoon anytime soon.

"Did you wash your hands?" Dani asked as she brought over the food. She set it on the table and gave him a look when he mumbled vaguely that he had. "Hold your hands up and let me smell them."

Their dad let out a soft snort on the other side of the paper, and Vini couldn't help but smile as Jordan slowly backed away from the table before turning and running out of the room. A moment later she heard water running from the half bathroom down the hall.

"It's hilarious that you always know when he's not being truthful," Vini said with a soft smile. "It always drove me crazy when Mom used to do that."

The familiar burning sensation that always accompanied talking about their mother was slow to form this time, and Vini felt another sense of relief at being able to mention her without wanting to run the other way. Dani's smile was just as soft as she looked in the direction Jordan had gone.

"Yeah, I guess it's something that just happens after you become a parent. But enough about that. How was your day?" Lulled into a false sense of security, Vini answered truthfully.

"It was fine. A little slow, but I did get a call from the sheriff of someone's car having stalled out on the highway." Thinking nothing of it, Vini sat down and started doling out food from the plates. Her father folded the newspaper and put it away as he put food on his own plate. Things were calm and normal as they all dug in once Jordan returned with his newly washed hands. It was almost enough to make Vini feel triumphant at getting through dinner without having to talk about Jessica.

It wasn't that she didn't want to talk about Jessica. The woman had been the only thing on her mind since Vini had dropped her off at Grace's house. It was new for her to feel so strongly about someone after only one meeting. Typically, if she felt strongly about someone, it was in the other direction, wishing they would never darken her doorway again. But this time was completely different.

Vini had given Jessica her number without thinking twice about it, but now she found herself glancing at her phone every few seconds, wondering if that had been the wrong move. Was she even interested, or was Vini reading things wrong? What if she didn't call? What if she did? What would they even have to talk about? Grace had mentioned little tidbits here and there about Jessica but nothing substantial. Vini didn't know much about her aside from the fact that she traveled a lot. Vini had barely gone farther than the nearest big city. Sure, she occasionally went on vacations to Savannah or Florida when she could get away from the shop, but she wasn't some profound world traveler like Jessica seemed to be. They didn't seem to have much of anything in common.

Vini did have Jessica's number on the paperwork she'd filled out for the car, but using that was overstepping professional bounds, something Vini never did. The number was given for business, not pleasure. Besides, if she had met Jessica organically like at the lesbian bar she frequented on the rare times she went up to Atlanta, it was doubtful that Vini would have had the confidence to approach her in the first place.

"Harley said she saw you driving over to Grace's place today. What were you doing out there?" Dani's words might've seemed innocent, but the tone in her voice let Vini know the question was far from that. "Did your little trip have anything to do with Peach Blossom's newest face in town?"

Thinking quickly, Vini answered and hoped that her words would be enough to discourage any interest in continuing this line of questioning.

"Yeah, the person who broke down on the highway was apparently Grace's friend, Jessica. She was coming to visit so I decided to drop her off. She seemed like the type to try to walk into town, and you know how treacherous that can be. I didn't need her getting attacked by a coyote on my conscience." She thought that sounded good, and the way Dani nodded she hoped that would be the end of the conversation. When the front door opened and closed,

Vini's hopes for getting out of this conversation unscathed plummeted.

"Oh, good. You guys are eating. I'm starving." Ava sat down in her usual chair and started serving herself some food. "What are y'all talking about?"

"Vini was just telling us how she rescued a damsel in distress from the highway."

"I was not," Vini hissed glaring at Dani over her fork. Undeterred, Dani continued.

"Harley let it slip that not only did she sweep in heroically but she also drove the poor dear into town—something we know she never does. Isn't that right, sis?"

Vini narrowed her eyes at Dani's knowing look. "I hate everything about you."

"So does this damsel have a name?" Ava asked. "And why was she driving to Peach Blossom? We don't get a lot of tourists this time of year."

Vini tried to appear unruffled. It really wasn't a big deal no matter how salacious Dani tried to make it seem. "Jessica. Apparently, she's Grace's friend." At Ava's sharp look, Vini felt her heartbeat jump. "I told her I would look over her car and let her know what's going on with it."

Ava hummed before taking another bite. She didn't appear anymore interested than normal, but looks could always be deceiving. "Is that so?"

Her question was deceptively calm, but Vini wasn't fooled. Whereas Dani might have a few questions, tease her a bit and then let things go, Ava was like facing an inquisition. If not for her being a teacher, Vini had no doubt that she would have made an excellent lawyer. Her way of asking questions back-to-back until you had no other choice but to give in and spit out the truth would have had her highly sought out. Still, Vini refused to surrender so easily. If Ava wanted information, she was going to have to work for it.

"I knew she wasn't from here, so I decided to be nice."

Their father grunted and nodded as if cosigning her words. It really wasn't that outlandish. Sure, she had never offered anyone else a ride to town before, but there was a first time for everything. And surely Ava could agree that being nice to Grace's friend was the way to go.

"Anyway, other than that, it was a boring day in the shop. Got some parts in and had Aiden—"

"Does she date women?"

Dani's question cut her off, but she continued like she hadn't heard it. "—unload them and put them in their places. I'm thinking it might be time to add onto the shop, given the last few jobs Patrick had to send elsewhere since I didn't have the equipment for them."

Her dad nodded again. "Always said you would need to add to the new place. Sounds like time to do that. We do have some money saved. Probably a good idea to look at hiring another person part-time at least."

"You should probably ask Grace if her friend dates women," Dani powered on, refusing to be ignored. "It's not every day we get some new blood flowing into town. Was she cute?"

"Anyway," Ava replied. She looked at Vini. "If it's the

same Jessica Grace has mentioned before, your best bet is to stay far away."

"Why?" Vini asked the question before she could think about whether it was a good idea to show any interest. It wasn't like it would be the first time she was interested in someone at all, but it had been a while.

Ava arched an eyebrow. "From what Grace has told me, Jessica isn't exactly known for settling down with one person. I believe the word she used was *free-spirited*, but what she really meant was *flighty*. You should probably keep away from her."

Vini frowned and looked down at her plate. She didn't doubt Ava's words. She would know more than her about Grace's friends, but nothing Jessica did had read as *player* to Vini. Then again, Vini probably wouldn't have known if she did. It wasn't like she got a lot of practice when it came to the dating game. Peach Blossom was progressive as far as small towns went, but that didn't mean the dating pool was any bigger.

"Besides," Ava continued. "From what Grace was telling me, the only reason Jessica is here is to let things die down after being caught with two of her mom's coworkers. Not exactly a pillar of stable relationships. You don't need to get caught-up with someone who doesn't plan on sticking around or being serious about you."

"Still, how often do new people come in?" Dani insisted. "She could at least ask. No harm in that."

"The harm is getting involved in someone who comes into your life and fucks everything up because she can't sit still," Ava counters. "I'm sure Jessica's a nice person, but is that really someone you want Vini to date?"

"It really doesn't matter what either of you want since, number one, I am in fact an adult and, number two, I have no plans to see her again outside of giving her the car back." Vini jumped back in when she saw Ava about to argue. "I helped her out because of her relationship to Grace. That's it."

Vini continued eating, ignoring how wrong that sentence felt. Ava and Dani kept the conversation going, but she was no longer interested. Meeting Jessica had been a fluke, and nothing would come from it. She could keep things professional, and then she would never have to see the other woman again.

Four

Walking to Vini's shop was probably not the smartest idea, but despite questioning herself after each mile, Jessica refused to be defeated. Sweat beaded across her forehead, and she sighed in relief when Vini's building came into view. The day was beautiful with blue skies and a few fluffy clouds. A cool breeze blew which was enough to keep her from being completely overheated, but the sun was enough to have her wishing for a wide-brimmed hat. At least she had been smart enough to put on her comfortable tennis shoes. She had thought about dressing to show off her best assets, but in the end, she didn't want to seem like she was coming on too strong.

The overhead bell rang as she pushed the door open. Inside, cool air rushed over her, and it took a moment for her eyes to adjust to the lower light. The place was empty with soft music playing from the doorway across from her. She walked up to the counter and paused. If she were in anyone else's place, she would have walked around the counter without a thought. But she was trying to make a good impression. Vini had been hard enough to read during their first encounter, but Jessica was pretty sure just barging in and making herself at home was not the best way to go about things.

"Can I help you?"

Jessica jumped slightly when a voice called out from somewhere deeper in the shop. She leaned over the counter and tried to see beyond the doorway that looked like it led to some dodgy back room. A figure came around one of the shelves and walked into view.

"Did you need help with something?"

The man was tall and stocky with broad shoulders that looked strong enough to do some heavy lifting. He was tan, almost tanner than Jessica, with curly dark brown hair that flopped over his eyes making him look boyish despite his size.

"I was looking for Vini. She brought my car in yesterday." That was mostly true. Jessica didn't actually give a shit about the car. She had already called the rental agency to put them on blast about the dud of a vehicle they'd given her. When she mentioned being stranded on the side of the highway, they relented and let her know they would be reimbursing her for any costs of fixing the heap of junk. "I'm Jessica."

The guy walked around the counter and held a hand out toward her. "Aiden. I'm Vini's right-hand man around here." Jessica shook his hand to be polite, though she glanced behind him. "You must be the one she dropped off in town yesterday, then. She mentioned you were pretty."

"Oh, did she?" Jessica had been more interested in finding out if Vini was around, but now that she was here, she wondered how much more information she could get out of Aiden. Vini thinking she was pretty was a nice start, but that didn't mean she was attracted to Jessica. Still, a girl could hope. "Did she mention anything else about me?"

Aiden's smile morphed into a knowing smirk. "Maybe. Why? You interested in our mini mechanic?"

Jessica shrugged, not wanting to seem too obvious. "It would be nice to get to know my savior, considering I'm going to be spending a few weeks here."

Aiden leaned closer. "Well, if you really want to know, Vini said you were the pret—"

"Aiden, did you finish getting those parts organized, or have you been standing around gossiping the whole day?"

Damn it, Jessica thought to herself. She was glad that Vini was here, but she would have liked to pump Aiden for a bit more information. She turned, her eyes once again drifting over Vini's frame as the woman walked over to them. She wasn't in overalls this time, instead sporting a tight T-shirt that showcased strong shoulders and a trim waist. Hips that had been hidden in overalls yesterday were now on clear display wrapped in black trousers that left Jessica whistling inside her head. Vini might be vertically challenged, but that didn't mean she was lacking elsewhere.

"Jessica, what are you doing here?"

Eyes snapped back up as Jessica kicked herself into gear.

It was time to turn on the charm. "I didn't have anything going on today and figured I would get out an explore a little bit. My feet led me here so I thought I would pop in and say hello."

Vini gestured outside. "I didn't see Grace's car out there. Please don't tell me you walked all the way here."

Sure fucking did, and I have the bunions to prove it. "Okay, I won't tell you I walked all the way here." Aiden's bark of laughter made Jessica smile.

"You could have texted me."

"I know. But I figured stopping by in person was a better bet." Jessica leaned against the counter as she let her gaze wander over Vini again. She was perplexed when she saw her frown. Usually, people were happy when they realized she wanted to see them in person. Never had Jessica received a frown. "Did I come at a bad time?"

Vini shook her head, though the frown still painted her face. "I'm still working on your car, but it should be ready in a few hours if you want to keep checking out the town. I have your number on file so I can call you when I'm through."

That was not what Jessica had been expecting. Nothing about this encounter was going the way she had envisioned, and now she was left scrambling to figure out how to recover. Was it possible that Vini really wasn't attracted to her? It wouldn't be the first time, of course, but it was the first time Jessica had dealt with so many mixed signals.

"That's okay. I don't mind waiting here. In fact, I sort of had a favor to ask." After a few well-placed questions last night, Jessica had come up with a backup game plan for accidentally on purpose spending more time with Vini. She figured there was no harm in being nice. And shouldn't she be trying to make friends while she was in town? It wouldn't be good for Grace's reputation if she had a friend come to town who snubbed the locals. "The whole mess with this car has shown me how little I know about vehicles, so I was wondering if you wouldn't mind teaching me a few things."

Vini's frown grew deeper. "Teaching you a few things?"

"Yeah. Grace mentioned you sometimes teach a few auto-shop classes at the high school." That had been another surprise. Vini in her twenty-two years of life seemed far more worldly than her age and left Jessica feeling a bit ashamed that she was damn near thirty and hadn't achieved half as much. "I'm lucky the car didn't crap out on me until I was close to Peach Blossom, but I hate to think about what might happen if it does that again on my way back to Atlanta."

"True," Vini agreed. She crossed her arms and looked over her shoulder where Jessica could see her rental was propped up. "Getting stuck somewhere unfamiliar with no working vehicle isn't the greatest."

Jessica nodded and kept up her earnest routine. "And if I'm somewhere with bad cell service, I might have to wait hours. At least if you teach me the basics, I can handle a few things that might happen." Vini's expression still seemed unsure, making Jessica wonder if she was pushing too hard. Maybe Vini really didn't want anything to do with her. She wasn't trying to force someone to be around her if they didn't want to be. She wasn't that desperate for human companionship.

"Never mind. It was just a thought." Jessica shrugged before moving to leave.

"Wait." Vini took step forward her expression clearing. She scrunched her nose as she looked to the side, and Jessica wanted to groan at how unfair it was for her to be that damn cute. "I'll do it. I'll help you."

"You don't have to. I can ask someone else."

Vini smirked. "You could try, but they wouldn't be as good as me."

That had Jessica raising her eyebrows. From anyone else's mouth, she would assume they were flirting with her and would respond in kind. When it came to Vini, though, the jury was still out on that one. Getting a read on her was quickly becoming one of the most frustrating games Jessica had ever played. She decided to keep it fairly neutral for now.

"I don't doubt that. I look forward to our first lesson. Will we be starting today?"

"No," Vini replied, shaking her head. "I need to finish checking out the damage, but I know it's far outside of the basics."

"Fair enough," Jessica said not doubting her expertise. She didn't know the first thing about cars, and she wanted Vini to feel comfortable so she would let her lead things. There was no point in asking for lessons and then not listening to her teacher. She looked around and spotted a small table with two chairs. Neither of them looked super comfortable but they would have to do for now. Her feet would not put up with her attempting the trek back to town on foot. "Do you mind if I post up here and get some work done?"

Vini shrugged. "Yeah, that's fine. The Wi-Fi password is *Jordan212* if you need it."

"Oh? A boyfriend's name?" Jessica breached the topic with a supposedly nonchalant question. She glanced at Vini whose face was marred by a confused frown.

"No. That's my nephew's name." She gestured to a side door that led to the attached garage. "I'll be out there working. Holler if you need anything."

Jessica smiled widely. "I definitely will. Don't worry about me. Act like I don't even exist."

Vini nodded but didn't say anything more before heading to the garage. Aiden shot Jessica a quick thumbs-up before he, too, disappeared back into the back room, leaving her in the lobby alone to pick apart everything that had just occurred. It was true, she did have some things she could work on, namely reviewing her social media for damage control. She had locked her social media profiles down as soon as the first whispers of scandal had started brewing, but that didn't mean people weren't still having a field day with the whole thing. Gossip was a favorite past time for many, and unfortunately, Jessica found herself the topic of conversation instead of just observing from the sidelines.

Her mom had accepted her apologies with the grace she always seemed to have in abundance, but that didn't mean Jessica didn't still feel bad. Thankfully, the pictures that had surfaced of her kissing her mom's castmates had been grainy, but she wasn't exactly able to blend in when she was back home in Korea. Defamation laws kept the whispers at a minimum, but there had still been talk about her mom losing the role. After having been gone from the entertainment industry for so long, this should have been her mom's triumphant return. Jessica hadn't meant for her bit of fun to affect her mom's career and had quickly decided that making herself scarce was the best solution to let everything die down while the management company did its thing.

Jessica had always been a free spirit when it came to relationships and occasionally it blew up in her face, but this was a totally new level and not one she wanted to repeat. Her sexuality had never been an issue with her parents, and for that she was grateful. They had always presented a united front which was something she envied even if she didn't like the thought of always having to compromise. Her mom had done it for the sake of her dad's army career, but Jessica wasn't sure if she could have done the same.

"Six weeks of self-imposed isolation and I can get back out there and pretend like none of it ever happened," she muttered before dropping her bag on the table. She sat down and winced at just how uncomfortable the chair was. Still, she had said she planned on waiting, so wait she would. Even if it meant getting next to nothing done as she watched Vini work her magic.

The next few hours seemed to fall away as Jessica pretended to be doing anything other than stealing glances at the woman just beyond the glass door. Vini's face was almost serene as she moved this way and that carrying tools that Jessica couldn't even pretend to know the names of. Even the sounds faded into the background as she watched Vini in what was clearly her element. The woman moved like poetry Jessica wished she understood. Every now and then, their eyes would meet, and once or twice, Vini's lips would twitch like she wanted to smile. It gave Jessica hope that maybe she wasn't totally off base. It also gave her time to think of how to use their time together to get to know more about her. Vini didn't seem to be the type that gave up personal details easily, but Jessica wasn't trying to court her like some duke in a historical romance novel. Things didn't have to get too deep to be worthwhile.

By the time Vini had the car back down on the ground, Jessica knew what her next moves would be. Keeping it simple seemed like it would be the key here. Being coy didn't appear to be the way to go. She could appreciate it in a way. Too often, the women she dealt with moved in a series of chess-like starts and stops. It was exhausting sometimes to navigate that push-and-pull dynamic. That didn't seem to be something Vini utilized, but there were other things Jessica knew she had to take into consideration. Small towns were notorious for running on word of mouth, and Jessica knew firsthand how quickly things could spread when a whisper network got ahold of them.

"Your car is ready to go," Vini said, drawing Jessica's attention again. Her once-clean shirt was smudged with grease as she wiped her hands on a towel. Her expression was even, and Jessica followed her to the counter. Neither of them said anything as Vini printed out the paperwork and handed it over. "Here's everything that was done. I know you said the rental company was reimbursing you, but let me know if they push back on anything."

"Thanks so much," Jessica replied as she looked over things. She raised her eyebrows when she saw the quoted final price. "Wow, that's much lower than I thought it would be." She kept reviewing when she heard another door open and close.

"I see you're giving her the friends and family discount."

Jessica snapped her eyes up at Aiden's words in time to see Vini swatting at him and making shushing motions. When she saw Jessica's attention, she froze.

"The friends and family discount?" Jessica asked forcing her expression to stay neutral when really she wanted to grin. "Are we friends, then, Vini?" She dropped her tone, slightly crowing internally when Vini's eyes widened. Not wanting to make her feel awkward, Jessica pretended to turn her attention back to the papers. She set them on the counter and signed without prompting. She wasn't worried about the price after her conversation with the car company.

"So are you going to the bowling match tomorrow?" she asked without looking up. "Grace said it was going to be a big one. I figured I would go to lend some moral support and cheer them on." Before she could overthink things, Jessica wrote her number and a little note telling Vini to call her on the paperwork.

"Yeah. If I don't, Ava would probably lose her shit,"

Vini replied softly. "She's my sister, so I have to support the family."

Jessica looked up in surprise but slid the paperwork across the counter with a smile. Grace hadn't thought to mention that little tidbit when they were talking last night. This would complicate things slightly, but with another glance at Vini, she was thinking it might be worth it. "Great. It'll be good to see another friendly face there." When Vini reached for the paperwork, their hands brushed against one another. "And it will be good to see you again. I'm looking forward to what you plan on teaching me."

At her words, Vini paused, their fingers still overlapping as she looked into Jessica's eyes. There was heat there, Jessica was sure of it. Vini was into it, and Jessica had to figure out a way to let her know that she was more than a little interested. Besides, when everyone was on the same page, there was nothing wrong with a fun little fling.

Nothing more, nothing less.

Five

Vini's mind was a mess of half-formed sentences and halted conversations as she made her way into the bowling alley. She had spent too damn long staring at Jessica's paperwork particularly the hastily scrawled note inviting her to connect.

Personally. Maybe biblically.

There was no way to misinterpret that. Jessica had been flirting, and she was clearly interested in Vini for reasons unknown. She wasn't trying to be self-deprecating, but Jessica was so obviously in a league of her own it wasn't even funny. Vini knew she was cute, a fact that she had made sure to check before leaving the house this evening. She had even closed the shop an hour early to give herself a chance to head home and get cleaned up before making her way to Terry's. Aiden had been a little too excited about that, but at least he had stopped the comments about Jessica for the last hour before they left. But rather than help, that had left her spinning in a maze of her own thoughts until she was so caught-up she had no way out.

"Vini, good to see you."

"Hey, Terry," she called out after pausing at the front counter. It was easy to see where the match was being held. There was already a good-sized crowd circling two of the lanes on the right side of the alley. "Wow. Didn't realize bowling would get this kind of turnout."

Terry chuckled. "You'd be surprised. Business has been jumping since the bowling team was reinstated. I think the Peach Blossom Strikers are here to stay."

Vini hoped so. She knew how badly Ava had wanted to get things going, and after the drama of her and Grace's start, she deserved things to go her way for a bit. "Good deal. I better show my face, so Ava knows I was here for sisterly support."

With a final wave to Terry, she made her way over to the group. It took Vini a moment, but she finally spotted Ava's familiar cloud of curls. She was barely taller than the students she was coaching. At Ava's nod of acknowledgment, Vini held back and observed. She smirked when she saw Grace walk over to the team and the way Ava seemed to perk up once she realized she was there. The two of them were hilarious to watch when you knew what to look for. Grace's smiles always seemed wider, and Ava's more genuine when they were together.

A pang of jealousy knifed through Vini. She was happy for her sister, but she couldn't deny her wish for a small taste of that.

"Fancy meeting you here."

Her lips twitched at Jessica's words. "I told you I would be here." She turned slightly to glance over her shoulder. Jessica was standing a short distance away. Long legs were wrapped in dark denim and a loose turquoise blouse draped over her shoulders. Her hair was down this time, and Vini couldn't deny her desire to feel the curls fall between her fingers.

Jessica shrugged one shoulder drawing Vini's eyes. "Still, I can't imagine this is your idea of fun on a Friday night."

Vini turned more fully to face her and tried not to feel self-conscious in her threadbare jeans and simple long-sleeved top. She had done more than the usual throw-on-her-uniform-and-go. Her braids were loose and adorned with gold charms that occasionally caught the light. Dani had given her a once-over with raised eyebrows when Vini left the house, but thankfully, she was able to escape without comment.

"Why not?"

Jessica arched an eyebrow as people started moving closer to the lanes and stepping around when neither of them moved. "I would assume a cutie like you would have more exciting plans. Maybe a monster truck rally or something if you really wanted to get wild."

Vini swallowed hard at being called *cute*. There was no doubt now that Jessica was smooth, but rather than wanting to head in the opposite direction, Vini wanted to lean into it and flirt back. Ava's warning was in the back of her mind, but it was easy enough to ignore it when faced with Jessica's glances and knowing smiles.

"Bowling doesn't get you excited?" Vini asked, letting her tone sound coy. She was rusty not having flirted with anyone in months, but she figured it was like riding a bike. She would hop back onto it and ride until the wheels fell off.

Jessica tilted her head, her eyes dragging down before sliding back up to meet Vini's gaze. "Balls and pins aren't exactly my thing."

Jesus. "What is your thing?" Time seemed to stop when Jessica moved. She closed the distance between them before leaning in.

"Play your cards right, and you just might find out." Her breath licked over Vini's ear making her shiver. Before she could respond, Jessica had made her way over to the crowd, leaving Vini with heated cheeks and a dry mouth. She turned in time to catch Ava's look and schooled her face into a mask of indifference. Vini could play calm and collected.

The tingles still licking up and down her spine were no one's business but her own.

Ignoring Jessica for the past two hours had been a test in patience. When the match started, Vini had moved to one of the tables Terry had set out for spectators. She had ordered a water to fix her dry mouth and nearly sucked the whole thing down at once when Jessica glanced back at her with a look that was pure heat. Vini was surprised none of the people between them burst into flames. She had slowly been warming up until she damn near had to fan herself to cool down. It wasn't until a cheer went up in the crowd that she was able to snap her attention away from Jessica.

"Who won?" she asked a woman standing close to her. Vini didn't know much about bowling, but it didn't seem like the scoring was as straightforward as basketball or football. She had given up trying to follow it many throws ago and instead cheered distractedly whenever the Peach Blossom Strikers got a strike.

"St. Mary's."

Vini sucked her teeth in annoyance, but Ava and Grace were smiling like they had won. After the pressures of the season, they probably felt like they did. Fixing a smile on her face, Vini moved closer to congratulate the team.

"You guys bowled a good game."

"The girls bowled a great game," Ava enthused her lips spread in a wide smile as she high-fived the girls. Grace stepped closer as the crowd dissipated. A warmth washed over her back and without turning, Vini somehow knew it was Jessica.

"That was a close match. For a team that only started this year, you all are amazing." Vini glanced over at Jessica as she took up space beside her. She didn't know how Jessica could tell it was a close game, but she wasn't going to say anything to contradict that. "Congratulations."

Grace pulled her into a quick hug. "Thanks, friend. I'm glad you were able to come see the team play."

"Of course. I wouldn't have missed it for anything," Jessica replied. She stepped back. "Plus, I was able to meet Ava.

You've talked so much about her that it's great to finally meet her in person."

Ava arched an eyebrow. "Oh? What has she been saying about me?"

"Perhaps we should head out to celebrate," Grace interjected quickly. Vini snorted softly at the slightly panicked look on Grace's face. She didn't know why. Everyone knew the two of them were together. Playing it cool was pointless. "I know I would love to celebrate a successful season."

Ava stepped closer to Grace, her smile morphing into a smirk. "And how would you like to celebrate, dear co-coach of mine?"

"Well," Grace started leaning into Ava before realizing they still had an audience. "I should probably get Jessica back to the house, and then we could—"

"Actually," Jessica interjected, "I booked myself a suite at the Blue Bell Bed and Breakfast. I figured win or lose, you two would want some time to yourselves."

Vini had to fight hard not to smile at the impressed look on Ava's face. Grace looked grateful before trying to push back, but Jessica was having none of it.

"But you rode with me here. I can at least drive you back to the house to get some things."

Jessica waved off her words. "Already done. I stashed a go bag in your trunk."

"At least let me drive you—"

"I can drop her off," Vini volunteered before she lost her nerve. She knew she needed to add more, based on the surprise on all their faces. Well, all except Jessica who looked like she knew exactly what was running through Vini's mind, which would have made one of them at least who knew what she was up to. Vini didn't have a clue. Ava's previous warning was still in her head, but the volume of it was growing ever quieter by the second. "I was planning to grab some things from the shop, and I can drop Jessica off on my way there."

She didn't have any reason to stop by her job, but she figured with the way Ava always got onto her about working too much, it might take some suspicion off or give her something else to focus on. Her bets paid off when Ava spoke up.

"Seriously, Vin. You better not be working after hours again."

Vini shrugged. "I make my own hours, but no. I promise I'm just grabbing something and then heading home. Well, I might grab a drink at Janie's before that, but either way, no working tonight."

Vini could have continued, but the looks Ava and Grace were giving one another let her know she didn't need to. When they headed out to the parking lot, she and Jessica followed, and soon enough they were alone again with nothing but Vini's nerves and the center console of her truck keeping them apart.

"You know, I wouldn't mind a drink myself," Jessica said once they were on their way down the road. Vini squeezed the steering wheel as the leather under Jessica squeaked with her shifting. It was difficult to pretend she was just another stranger when she was so close and yet so far. "Mind some company?"

"That's fine."

"Or," Jessica said leather creaking again until a soft touch landed on Vini's upper thigh. She glanced down and swallowed hard at the sight of Jessica's hand cupping her leg loosely. "We could grab a bottle and share it somewhere a little more private."

Was she saying what Vini thought she was saying? It sounded like an offer to join her in her room. Was Vini really about to spend the evening with someone her sister had warned her against getting involved with? That last thought annoyed her. She didn't need Ava's approval to spend time with someone, and she certainly didn't need her approval to have sex. If that was where this was leading. No, it was exactly where things were leading, and Vini was more than a little excited. Just because there was attraction, that didn't mean she would get attached. People hooked up all the time, and sure, maybe Vini hadn't after being so busy with getting the shop up and running as it should, but that didn't mean she couldn't now.

Jessica was interested, and so was she. They were grown-ass adults. They didn't need anyone else's approval. Decision made: she placed a hand over Jessica's and squeezed it gently.

"Sounds like the perfect plan to me."

Six

The streets were quiet as Vini steered them through town. Jessica had been surprised how quickly Vini agreed to moving things to a more intimate location given how hot and cold she had blown before. They had stopped at a small package store to grab a bottle of wine, though if she had her way, not much would be consumed. Jessica had no desire to get sloppy. She liked her partners fully ready to say *Yes*. Or *No, don't stop*, depending on what they enjoyed.

Jessica opened the door to her room and took a few steps in before pausing. The room was softly lit by a lamp on the table by the door making it warmer and more inviting. The room was large with a door to the right leading to the quaintest bathroom Jessica had ever seen, right down to the claw-foot tub that she would be taking advantage of. The walls were a muted green that normally would have Jessica gagging, but with the gold-plated bedframe and neutral bedspread, it surprisingly worked. It was old-school for sure, yet in a way that tugged at nostalgia rather than looking tacky.

"Wow. If you put this anywhere else, it would probably have me running in the other direction. But it's actually really cute."

"Yeah. Diana has an eye for decorating."

Jessica turned and watched Vini glance around the room. Her lips were turned up in a soft smile that had Jessica smiling with her. There was still a thrum of tension just below the surface, but it was easy enough to let it simmer. They didn't need to rush things. As much as Jessica wanted to see just what Vini had been hiding underneath her overalls, she didn't feel the need to push.

"Do you know everyone in town by name?" Jessica asked as she walked over to the bed. She dropped her bag on the floor before plopping down on the bed and looking up at Vini. "Am I in an old-school TV show where people smile and wave every time you walk by?"

Vini chuckled. She closed the door behind her, throwing the lock. The click of it sounded so final, but all Jessica could feel was anticipation. She leaned back on her hands and crossed her legs. She knew how the position lengthened her torso. When Vini's gaze shifted traveling the length of her until their gazes met, Jessica felt the air in the room warm a few degrees. She was hot now like she had been as they glanced at one another over the crowd of people at the bowling alley. It had been hard to keep from going to Vini's side then, if only just to ask her more questions.

"I don't know everyone by name. The town isn't that

small, otherwise we would all be inbred," she answered, finally walking closer to Jessica. She stopped close enough that if Jessica reached out, she could pull Vini to her side. As tempting as that was, Jessica decided to let Vini come to her instead. She had made her interest clear, and if Vini didn't want to do anything more than have a glass of wine and talk, Jessica would oblige her.

When Jessica opened her mouth to suggest opening the bottle, her words were stolen by lips pressing against hers. The aborted sound was loud to her ears until the pressure pulled away and Jessica saw Vini's shocked expression from inches away.

"Well, that was certainly...surprising."

Vini straightened jerkily. "Shit. Sorry."

"Oh, no, don't misunderstand me," Jessica said standing and reaching out to rest a hand on Vini's hip. "It was a good surprise, but maybe we can try it again when we're both ready for it."

Vini's eyes widened, but she didn't move as Jessica moved in. This time, the press of their lips was smoother, and a thrill ran down Jessica's spine when she finally had those plush lips under hers. Vini's mouth moved in aborted gestures as if she were trying to figure out the best way to get closer. Jessica brought her free hand up to cup Vini's cheek and angle her head. The movement had their mouths sliding together more fully, and Jessica felt more than heard Vini sigh.

Hands came up and clutched at Jessica's shoulders. There was a deceptive strength in that grip that had her mind cycling through all the possibilities—possibilities that flew from her mind when a tongue parted her lips, sinking between them with unerring accuracy. Jessica groaned softly, thrilled at Vini taking the initiative. With how standoffish the other woman had initially seemed, she worried that it would have taken days if not weeks to get her to realize Jessica was interested, but with her being Ava's sister and Ava dating Grace, they had the perfect reason to be around one another. Jessica would play her cards right this time. Everything would be laid on the table so that feelings never came into play. Sex was fun, and with the right attitude, no one had to get hurt with unmet expectations.

"Jesus," Vini panted out when their lips briefly separated. One of her hands was clutching the fabric of Jessica's blouse while the other had slipped around to cup the back of her neck. "If Ava knew I was here doing this with you, she would freak out."

Jessica cocked an eyebrow but didn't draw away. "Your sister?"

Vini nodded. "She said you were trouble."

"She's not totally wrong," Jessica conceded with an amused snort. It rankled that not even a full week in and already she was being put on blast. Still, Vini didn't seem to share the same thoughts, so she could let it go. "But only the good kind of trouble."

"The good kind?"

Jessica let her smile go wicked as she leaned back in brushing her lips teasingly against Vini's. "The best kind. The kind of trouble that keeps you coming back for more."

She gripped the loops of Vini's pants and pulled her along with her until Jessica could sit back down on the bed. The height difference put her perfectly where she wanted to be, and Jessica shifted to grip Vini's shirt.

"Do you mind if we take this off?"

Vini hesitated for only a moment before she let go of Jessica and took a step back. A bolt of disappointment lanced through Jessica for only a moment before she realized Vini was only giving herself space. She gripped the bottom of her shirt and pulled it up over her head. She looked around for a moment before flinging the shirt toward the small dining table and chair in front of the curtained window.

She was exquisite. Her skin was rich and drew Jessica in like the sun. When she nuzzled Vini's stomach, the skin there jumped slightly. Jessica brought her hands back up before looking up at Vini from beneath her lashes. She knew from experience that it was a look that got people going, and Vini seemed to be no different. When she reached for the button of her jeans, Jessica stopped her.

"You don't want me to get these off?"

"Oh, I do," Jessica confirmed. "But I'd like to be the one who does that."

Vini's hands fell to her sides, and Jessica slipped the button out of its hole before sliding the zipper down slowly. She was in no rush.

"Can you…" Vini's voice trailed off when Jessica looked up. "It feels a bit weird being the only one getting undressed."

A tendril of pleasure wrapped around her as Jessica

smiled. She obliged Vini's wish, standing up and pulling
her own shirt off. She let the momentum carry her until
they were both in nothing but bras and panties. Not wanting the awkwardness to return, Jessica coaxed Vini to the
bed until they were lying on their sides, lips slowly moving together in a dance that ignited a hunger in Jessica that
she wanted to quench. She shifted the hand that had been
cupping Vini's cheek until she could grip the back of Vini's
neck. The resulting groan had her smiling.

"How far do you want this to go?" She asked pulling back
so they could both draw in a breath. Vini raised an eyebrow.

"A bit of a weird question to ask when we are already in
bed together."

"Not at all," Jessica countered before leaning in to brush
her lips over Vini's. She lost herself in the feeling of them
again and only came back to her point when she realized she
had her arms wrapped around Vini. Their legs were tangled
together, and Jessica had to fight not to ride the thigh that
was so close to where she wanted it to be. "I don't want to
assume and get it wrong. I don't mind taking a little direction if it means we both enjoy ourselves."

Vini paused before her lips spread in a smile. She didn't
answer, instead leaning in again. Mouths opened almost at
once, and Jessica held back, letting Vini take the lead. Her
tongue dipped between Jessica's lips until they were tasting
one another in stops and starts. Jessica carefully brushed her
hands up Vini's back, ending at her bra strap. A short nod
had her hands moving to undo the clasp and let the mate-

rial fall away. She nipped Vini's bottom lip before drawing away again and feasting on the sight before her.

"You just going to stare at me the whole time?"

"I might," Jessica shot back before guiding Vini over and onto her back. She lifted up on her knees before curling fingers around the small scrap of light blue fabric in front of her. Vini lifted her hips, and Jessica wasted no time sliding her panties down shapely legs and over almost delicate ankles before letting them fall somewhere behind her. She reached behind to unclasp her own black bra. Before she could get to her panties, Vini sat up and wrapped her arms around Jessica's waist. If Jessica had thought Vini was a talented kisser, it had nothing on the sinfulness of her mouth against Jessica's nipples.

Sighs of pleasure fell from Jessica's lips as her right nipple was surrounded by supple heat. Teeth gently worried her nub as fingers encircled its twin, sending shocks of electricity through her. She always did like it when her partners took initiative, and when another hand gripped at her ass, she gave Vini her props letting herself be turned until her back was against the bed. She ran her fingers over Vini's skin as her panties were slid down, and when heated breath fanned over her pussy lips, Jessica didn't even attempt to stop the moan of want that bubbled up from her chest.

Hands gripped the bottom of her thighs pushing her legs apart and she let them fall until her knees hit the bed, opening herself up to everything Vini wanted. What she wanted was clearly to drive Jessica delirious, and she was doing an admirable job of it. Jessica had never been particularly vocal in bed, but her soft huffs of pleasure were soon interspersed with even softer cries. She lifted one leg letting it fall over Vini's shoulder and tried to hold on. Vini's mouth was wild. Her tongue thrust deep as if trying to burrow its way through her and out again. Hands weren't idle either with one coming up so Vini's thumb could encircle her engorged clit.

"Fuck," Jessica grit out as her hips took on a life of their own shifting and pressing up to get more of that decadent pleasure. "God, I can't—"

Voice cut off, Jessica instinctively gripped the back of Vini's head pressing her tight as she rode the waves of her release. Everything was shivery as her body tried to come down from being so high. She loosened her grip as her body relaxed onto the bed and Jessica cupped Vini's cheek. Dark eyes gazed up at her leaving her mouth dry at how sexy Vini was without even trying. Jessica had slept with more than a few people in her life, and by now she could tell when someone was posing. Vini wasn't doing anything close to that, and yet she had Jessica's mouth watering at the thought of getting between those thighs and tasting a little payback on her tongue for such an earth-shattering orgasm. When feeling returned to her limbs, she decided to do just that.

Vini yelped as their positions were abruptly reversed. When Jessica settled between her legs, she giggled making Jessica chuckle as well. "Not happy to be on the bottom?"

"I'm happy enough," Jessica replied before placing a sucking kiss on Vini's inner thigh. "But now it's my turn."

Seven

Vini woke slowly. The light was all wrong. She scrubbed a hand across her face before she was jerked into full wakefulness by the alarm on her phone. She scrambled to sit up, grabbing the damn thing before it vibrated off the table and woke up the whole house. It took her a moment to realize that she hadn't needed to worry, because she was not in fact at home. When the bed shifted beside her, she turned, her eyes widening when she found a sleeping Jessica beside her. Memories of last night flooded her brain, and she felt her cheeks heat.

"So much sex," she whispered looking down. She was wearing a T-shirt that didn't belong to her so it must be Jessica's, but the sheets bunched beneath her made it clear that was the only stitch of clothing she possessed. Her thighs were tacky with sweat and probably her own juices, so she slowly made her way out of the bed. Each step she took had her holding her breath as she gathered her clothes from last night. The room smelled like sex, and she didn't doubt that she smelled the same. Before she could second-guess it, she darted into the adjoining bathroom and locked the door behind her.

There was no way she was going to be seen sneaking out like this. It would be just like the universe for her to get caught looking disheveled like she'd just gotten her back blown out for hours. *But you did.* She shushed her inner voice and turned the shower on. Just because she had had mind-blowing sex with a woman clearly out of her league didn't mean she had to look like it. She would wash the night off, get dressed and walk out of the bed and breakfast with her head held high, damn it.

She could play it cool.

Her plan lasted the time she spent getting cleaned up and dressed. She had her game plan, and she knew how to play it. That didn't explain, then, why her mind was filled with static when she opened the bathroom door and Jessica was sitting up in bed facing her. Vini had thought she'd gotten her fill of looking at her, but Jessica barely awake and still soft-looking from sleep was something totally new to behold.

"Was it any good?"

"Any good?" Vini swallowed hard. Dear Lord, were they about to actually talk about last night? She needed like two cups of coffee and a week or two before she was ready for that. She opened and closed her mouth twice not knowing how to respond. "What do you mean?"

Jessica waved her hand before her mouth parted on a yawn. "The water. In there. Is the pressure good?"

"Oh! Yeah, it's totally fine. It felt really good when I did it." Vini winced at the vomit of words. "The shower. The shower was good. You should have one."

Thankfully, the flood of words didn't seem to have any effect on Jessica. She yawned again before moving to stand. Vini's eyes widened as the bedsheet fell away, but Jessica had apparently pulled on pajamas before falling asleep herself. The shiny fabric of the camisole and shorts covering her drew Vini's attention, and she felt equal parts relieved and disappointed at not getting another peek of that smooth sand-hued skin.

"You leaving?"

"Me?" Vini jerked her gaze up and caught Jessica's. There was no inflection in her voice, and her gaze was aggravatingly blank. It left Vini unsure of how to answer. She didn't regret last night. It was hard to when it all felt so damn good. And they were both adults. They hadn't done anything that they needed to feel regret for. "Yeah. I need to open up the shop this afternoon so…"

She didn't know what else to say. Vini wasn't completely naive, but she had never had a one-night stand like this. Usually, she wandered up to Atlanta, made out a little, and then booked it back home before they got to the main event. The last time she had sex, neither one of them had been particularly knowledgeable, and while it had been overall fun, it was nothing compared to last night. Last night was next-level action.

"Sure I can't interest you in one more round?"

"What?" Thoughts came to a halt as Jessica's words sank in. Vini was rooted to the spot as she watched Jessica move closer until they were once again pressed together. A sigh left Vini's lips before she instinctively gripped those hips that had drawn her in last night. They felt just as good in her hands now as they had then, and Vini was helpless to do anything but kiss back when Jessica's lips pressed against hers.

Any thoughts of last night being a fluke flew out the window as their tongues tasted, morning breath be damned. Vini wanted to pull some of those same noises that had blessed her ears under the cover of night. If not for her phone blaring from her pocket, she might have never stopped. Reluctantly, Vini pulled away.

"I wish I could," she replied, eyes darting down when Jessica licked her bottom lip. A shiver wracked her frame as the hunger built again. If she was going to leave, she had to do it now. "Plus, it's early enough that people might not catch me coming out of your room. Unless you want people to know we spent the night together?"

Jessica paused her dark brown eyes fixed on Vini. Truthfully, a part of Vini didn't care who knew. If not for Ava and her penchant for being too damn overprotective, she would have happily crowed to the world that last night happened.

"You're right. We probably should keep things quiet," Jessica conceded finally. "I'm not trying to get on your sister's bad side already. But if you aren't going to follow me to the shower, then you better go."

That sounded so much better than the day of work that was waiting for her. Vini let herself indulge in one last kiss, groaning when Jessica opened up so easily. She had to fling herself out of that sinful embrace just to leave the room. When Vini shut the door behind her, it took her far too long to step away.

This was hell.

Working over the weekend with the taste of Jessica still seared into her brain had been hard enough. When the scent of her finally faded from Vini's skin under the smell of oil and grease, she almost screamed. The memory of lying wrapped in Jessica's arms was all she had left to get her through today's shift, and she was struggling.

Vini hadn't run into anyone once she left the bed and breakfast, and even once she got home, there was no welcoming committee there to greet her. The weekend had passed easily enough, and when Ava came home Sunday afternoon, she hadn't said anything to Vini about Jessica. The smile on her face had made it clear why and left Vini practically vibrating with jealousy. Still, she counted her blessings and kept quiet only talking about the shop when asked. Now it was another shitty morning with too much time and not enough to do to keep her mind occupied.

"Hey, boss. We got another shipment late last night, but I'm not sure where you want me to tag them," Aiden said poking his head out of the back room when she walked into the shop ready for another day of work. Normally, she wasn't reluctant to come into the shop. It had always been her happy place, especially when her mom's health had taken a turn for the worse. Now, though, the thought of being behind these walls instead of out and about had her wanting to turn the other way. It had nothing to do with a certain woman she hadn't seen for the rest of the weekend, though.

She was probably just in need of a vacation.

"Just leave them where they are, and I'll take care of them."

"Procrastinating already?"

Vini jerked around nearly colliding with the counter. Her heart raced, beating a furious rhythm against the back of her rib cage. She hadn't seen anyone when she came in, but there Jessica was calmly sitting at the small table in the corner as if it had always been her place. As Vini tried to find some chill, she wondered what it was like to just feel so at ease in your own body that you didn't bat an eye at someone being startled by your presence.

"Jessica. What are you doing here?"

Jessica stood up. "You said you would give me lessons. Remember?"

Lessons? Plenty of lessons had gone on a couple days ago, but it hadn't been Vini who was the teacher. She racked her brain trying to come up with something, *anything* that would jog her memory. As it was, all she could remember was warm skin, wandering hands and the hit of salt on her tongue as she tasted just where those lines and curves of Jessica's body led. None of those would help her now in the light of a new day.

Swallowing hard, Vini leaned back against the counter

and did what she always did when she was caught unawares. She made shit up. "I'm surprised you remembered, considering I didn't see you all weekend."

Jessica raised an eyebrow. "Were you looking for me?"

Damn it. That had not been what she meant, but she would have to go with it. "I didn't say we had to start our lessons on a Monday. We could have started sooner."

"That eager to see more of me?" Jessica's tone was even, though her expression said more than her voice ever could. Those brown eyes that had haunted Vini's dreams were now just as heated as she remembered, and they were moving closer as Jessica walked over to her. She paused when they were only inches apart, and Vini knew she should do something to move away and regain the casual indifference that would show her as unaffected, but the warmth curling toward her kept her firmly in place.

"Yes," she whispered. It was not what she had meant to say, and it clearly had taken Jessica by surprise as well, if her widening eyes were any indication. Seeing her surprise helped kick Vini's brain into gear, and she finally recalled their agreement. "But as much as I would enjoy taking more of your money in car repair bills, I would prefer you didn't get stranded anywhere else. Follow me."

It took an extreme act of will, but Vini managed to turn away from those enigmatic eyes, gesturing for Jessica to follow her into the back room. Aiden looked up from behind a stack of boxes when they walked in. When his eyes landed on Jessica, he smiled.

"Hey, stranger. What brings you 'round again?" He nodded at Vini. "Did the boss lady fuck up your ride?"

Jessica laughed and shook her head. "I think the bastard was a lost cause to begin with, but it's running just fine."

Vini narrowed her eyes at his insinuation that she hadn't done a perfect job fixing Jessica's car. "The car is fine, asshole. I promised I'd teach Jessica some basic car care."

Aiden nodded. "Makes sense. Peach Blossom is pretty chill, but you don't want to get caught out in some of these other small towns. Not all of them are as friendly to outsiders."

That was putting it lightly in Vini's opinion, but she stayed mum about that as she led Jessica to the smaller back room that served as her makeshift office. There wasn't a ton of room in it, but there was just enough space for her desk, a couple chairs and a small hutch that she kept extra clothes in. When the front lobby door chimed, she gestured for Aiden to take care of it.

"Come on in here and get changed."

Jessica looked down at her clothes. "What's wrong with what I'm wearing now?"

Vini looked her up and down, trying her hardest not to let her gaze linger more than necessary. "Nothing, if you were relaxing at a café. But when you're working in the shop, you can't have anything loose or dangling. That includes jewelry, clothing and hair."

"I didn't bring anything else with me," Jessica replied. "Should I head back and grab something different to put on?"

She probably should have said *yes* if only to give herself more time to handle the fact that she was going to be spending more time with Jessica than she had planned. It wasn't unwelcome. Far from it. She just needed more time to prepare. Imagine her shock when her mouth answered for her. "No. I have some clothes in here that should fit you."

Vini opened the small closet before she lost her nerve, grabbing a clean shirt and pair of pants. The pants would probably be slightly short given their difference in height, but they would have to do.

"If you wanted to see me naked again, all you had to do was ask."

Vini almost dropped the clothes at the sound of that voice whispered so close to her ear. A shiver ran through her, but she forced herself to turn slowly. She shouldn't have been surprised at how close they were, and yet somehow she was. Jessica hadn't waited before sliding her loose blouse over her head. Curls tumbled down over her shoulders, making Vini's fingers itch to reach out and take hold.

"I didn't bring you back here for this," Vini replied truthfully forcing her gaze to stay locked on Jessica's. Thankfully, the door behind Jessica was shut hiding them away from prying eyes. It also left her reeling at how much privacy they had. The room wasn't soundproof, but they could be quiet. It might even be more fun to try. "I just didn't want you to ruin your clothes or sue me when you got stuck in a car part."

Jessica chuckled softly before taking a step forward. She reached out her hand. "Well, in that case, I'll get dressed. Sorry for the misunderstanding."

Vini looked down at the outstretched hand. She could pass the clothes to Jessica, and they could put this behind them, or she could take advantage of the privacy. Clearly, Jessica was open to another hookup between them.

Was Vini?

"Vin?" Jessica's voice was soft and her expression open. There was no smirk on her face as she watched waiting for what Vini would do. "It's really okay. I can get changed, and we can—"

Vini moved then, dropping the clothes so she could take Jessica's face between the palms of her hands. That earnest expression and her own desire had done her in. She wanted this, and there was nothing else holding them back, so why not? Vini had always been so good, holding back and making sure everyone else was taken care of. It was her turn to have something she wanted, and right now, she wanted heated kisses and blunt nails digging into her skin.

Jessica's lips were just as addicting as she remembered, and Vini fell into them with relish. She backed them up until she felt Jessica hit the door. When arms wrapped themselves around her waist, she groaned, letting her desire unfurl. The office was small enough that in moments the air was heated. Jessica's hands gripped Vini's back, pulling her in farther until there was no space between them. It was a wildness Vini had never experienced or imagined. Whenever she had thought about sex, she had pictured soft kisses and sweet giggles. This was all that and more. Teeth dug into her bottom lip, making Vini groan, and a tongue sought entrance into her mouth that she granted willingly.

"Should we be doing this in here?" Jessica whispered, her lips forming a smile against Vini's as they sucked in air.

"Not at all," Vini replied with a smile of her own showing how little she cared about that fact. "This is probably a really bad idea, but I don't give a fuck."

One of Jessica's hands came up and cupped her cheek. Her eyes had gone dark as she looked down at Vini's lips. Vini licked them, loving the burst of heat she could see in those mocha depths. A thumb traced her lips, and she didn't hesitate to suck it in, letting her tongue bathe it with wet heat.

"Such a dirty mouth for such a pretty girl," Jessica breathed out before leaning in to taste from Vini's mouth again. Her words set Vini's blood aflame, and she parted her lips readily.

Everything was slick and hot. Vini trailed her hands over Jessica's shoulders gripping for a moment when Jessica's tongue traced the sensitive roof of her mouth. When it toyed with her own, she carved her blunt nails down Jessica's back, enjoying the moaning vibration her actions brought. She was about to move her hands to Jessica's bra strap when a knock came from the other side of the door making them both freeze.

Eight

Jessica ground her teeth at the disturbance. Things had been progressing so nicely. She hadn't shown up with the intention of being sandwiched between a door and Vini, but she wasn't about to turn down the gift that was that deliciously petite frame pressed against hers. When the knock came again, she leaned her head back with a silent groan.

"Yeah?"

"Sorry to interrupt boss, but we have a code douche."

She lifted her head up as a giggle lodged in her throat. *Code douche?* "What the fuck is a code douche?"

Vini glanced at her before shaking her head and stepping back. Cool air rushed between them, and Jessica had to fight hard against the desire to pull her back in. She didn't want to seem too pushy, considering she hadn't even planned for this in the first place. She stared as Vini smoothed her hands over her shirt and pants, hating the fact that she never got to see them come off.

"Means there's someone asking for the master mechanic and refusing to listen to Aiden."

"So basically they are asking for the manager."

Vini glanced up at her lips stretching in a wide smile. "Pretty much. Aiden knows what he's doing, but occasionally we have people who take one look at that damn baby face of his and try to go above his head. We both usually enjoy their reactions when they see me walk in."

Jessica let that sink in as she reached down and picked up the borrowed shirt. She shrugged it on, letting it settle over her shoulders. "You mean they weren't expecting a woman to come in?"

Vini snickered before reaching forward. Her fingers curled around Jessica's ear, and Jessica froze as a wave of arousal so strong welled up threatening to pull her under. She had never been so thoroughly attuned to someone like this before. A simple touch like that shouldn't have been enough to almost undo her resolve to not push, but damn did it come close.

"That, and someone shorter and younger than him." She shrugged like it didn't bother her. For all Jessica knew, it might not. If Vini had been running this place as long as she said, then she probably had dealt with a lot of bullshit before now. Jessica had seen that kind of bullshit sexism at play so many times when her mother was in the role of director and not just actress. It has always made her bristle at the dismissive attitude, but her mother had always handled it with the type of grace Jessica only reserved for pets and children. Young children. Teenagers could suck it.

"I should get out there," Vini said gesturing at the door.

The door that Jessica was still standing in front of. With a twisted grin, Jessica stepped away, though her eyes never left Vini as she walked by. Her scent, warm and citrusy, tickled Jessica's nose, making her draw in a deep breath. For as messy as Vini's work got, she smelled so refreshingly sweet that Jessica's teeth hurt with the need to taste.

"Change into those pants and then come on out when you're ready," Vini threw out before she left the office and closed the door behind her.

Jessica stared at the closed door wondering how the hell she had gotten herself into this mess. She had spent most of the weekend relaxing in her suite and fielding questions and concerns from her parents and brother, Jason. She felt enough guilt about the whole mess with her mom's costars, but then the guilt set in from refusing to join her parents in Italy. She knew they just wanted to make sure she was okay. Well, her parents wanted to make sure. Jason probably wanted to hear the whole sordid story as fodder for his addition to drama. Still, Jessica hadn't been able to stand the thought of hearing firsthand about the increased scrutiny her mom was under. Especially when it wasn't even her fault.

Things had been all fun and flirty when Jessica first got involved with Jang-Mi. They had kept things quiet and just made it seem like two friends enjoying one another's company, and despite their nighttime fun, neither had mentioned feelings or going beyond a casual and fulfilling friends-with-benefits situation. When Jang-Mi had fallen off the grid for a couple days, Jessica had chalked it up to the good times coming to an end. She hadn't even thought twice about her mom's other costar, Irene, showing up out of nowhere declaring that Jang-Mi had slept with her girlfriend. Said girlfriend being Jessica. The shock had left her frozen until Irene launched into a loud tirade and the cell phone cameras came out.

When the inevitable fallout came, the scrutiny of flashing lights and ruthlessly dedicated paparazzi had become too much. Jessica had felt bad about fleeing, but she hadn't signed up for that kind of drama when it was all supposed to be no-strings-attached fun. She had sent both of them one last text before blocking both their numbers and going on a social media blackout. It had been Grace who suggested coming to Peach Blossom, and Jessica hadn't thought twice about it. A small town where people probably didn't know her mother and definitely didn't know her was perfect.

Or had been until now.

She didn't think this thing with Vini would draw in such a crowd of spectators, but she also was happy enough to find someone to help keep her mind off her six-week self-imposed isolation to begin with.

"Just got to keep it from going too deep," she whispered to herself as she pushed down her wide-legged jeans and slipped on the slacks Vini had left for her. She didn't want to make it seem like she was just waiting for Vini to get back, so she opened the door and headed back to the front of the shop. When she stepped through the doorway, immediately, something set her on edge.

Vini was standing behind the counter with Aiden a rigid

line by her side. Across the counter, another man stood, eyes looking hard as he looked back and forth between the two. Jessica tentatively walked forward but jerked to a stop when the man turned to look at her.

"Oh, great, another chick," he spit out before stabbing a finger at Vini. "I don't know what kind of shit you're trying to pull, but I want to speak to the master mechanic, now."

"And I told you," Vini replied, her voice hard in a way that had Jessica standing straighter, "I am the master mechanic and the owner. If you have an issue—"

"My issue is the quality of you people's work," he bellowed, cutting her off. A flush rose from his neck sliding up his chin. "I don't know what kind of town doesn't have a proper auto shop, but I will not have you fucking up my car."

Jessica was shocked. It wasn't the first time she had seen someone act a fool over customer service whether they were justified or not, but she hadn't expected to see it here. Peach Blossom so far had seemed so wholesome and nice, proving that at least here, the stereotype of Southerners being uber friendly was true. She didn't know if this guy was a local or what, but his behavior seemed so at odds with what she had experienced so far.

"Fine."

When Vini spoke, her voice was even with not even a slight rise in volume. If it had been Jessica being yelled at, she would have already been over the damn counter ready to fight the guy, size difference or not. Still, she stayed quiet. This wasn't her fight, and Vini didn't need her to begin with. If she needed backup, Aiden no doubt would have jumped in without a moment's notice. Jessica took her cue from him, hanging back and letting the boss handle it.

Vini's concession seemed to confuse the man, and his mouth opened and closed a moment with no sound coming out. Clearly, he was just as confused as Jessica about what would come next.

"If you're concerned with the quality of our work, you're more than welcome to find an alternate place for your vehicle." Vini moved then, not waiting for him to respond. She picked up the phone and dialed. Jessica waited like the other two men. She didn't know what was about to happen, and the sense of anticipation threatened to undo her. "Hey, Tony. I got a guy here looking to get some work done on his 2018 Benz C-Class."

"It's a 2019," the man barked out.

Vini didn't do much but raise her eyebrow. "Sorry 'bout that. I meant a 2019. He's real concerned about the quality of the work we do 'round here, so if you would be so kind to tow him to yours, I know he would appreciate it."

Aiden turned as if to sneeze, but Jessica saw what could only be described as a shit-eating grin on his face. When he saw her looking, he winked before turning back around.

"Thanks, Tony. Tell the wife and kids I said hey." Vini chuckled before hanging up. When she spoke to the man again, her voice lacked the warmth it had previously had. "Tony is en route and will get you squared away."

The man nodded sharply. "Good." He looked around

before frowning again. "Where's the lounge where I can wait?"

Vini's smile went sharp. "I'm sorry, sir. The lounge is for customers only, and seeing as you aren't a customer, it is not available for use."

He frowned, expression falling. "But the—"

"Tony will be here in forty minutes, so if you need a place to sit other than your car, there's a bench right outside." Vini turned dismissing him. "Have a wonderful day."

The man stood there for a moment, fists balled at his sides, but as if realizing there wasn't much he could do, he turned on his heel and yanked open the door sending the bell clanging wildly as he stomped outside. For a moment, the only sound was his footsteps crunching on the gravel, but slowly it was replaced with a soft giggle. Jessica raised an eyebrow when she saw Aiden lean over and prop himself on the counter as his laughter slowly gained momentum. She saw Vini grin at him and wondered what the hell she was missing.

"What?" she asked, wanting to be in the know. "Why are you laughing?"

Vini thumped Aiden on the back before gesturing for Jessica to follow her into the garage area. Jessica glanced back at Aiden and saw him slowly rise before he gave her a big goofy grin and a thumbs-up. She shook her head with a smile. There was something she was missing, as had the asshole who wasted their time.

When Vini paused beside a car, Jessica stepped up to her

side. "Seriously," she said getting Vini's attention, "what am I missing here?"

Vini looked more amused than angry as she glanced up at Jessica. "That guy was complaining about a woman being a master mechanic."

"Yeah, I heard that part. Is that what the douche code is about?"

She nodded. "*Code douche*, yeah. We don't get them too often, thankfully. Apparently, he was on his way to Florida when his car started making some clunky noises, so he stopped here."

Jessica was relieved then to know the guy wasn't local. She still didn't understand why Vini and Aiden were so amused by the guy requesting to be towed to another shop. "So were you laughing because the guy now has to wait outside for almost an hour to get his car towed?"

Vini snorted. "No, although it was nice to tell him to take hike. We were laughing at the thought of him realizing that Tony is short for *Antonia*." Her eyes crinkled at the sides when she delivered that bit of news.

It took Jessica a moment to understand what she meant before it hit her. She widened her eyes before letting out a bark of laughter. "Oh, shit. No wonder you were so quick to offer him up to Tony."

"Yup. And if he thinks he's going to push her around, he's got another thing coming," Vini added. "She and her wife were pro wrestlers at one point, and Tony is still more built than most men. Add to the fact that I interrupted her first cup of coffee, and he better learn to shut up real quick."

Jessica let her laughter overtake her as she pictured the moment Tony, or Antonia, stepped out of her tow truck. She glanced at the open garage door. "I need to see this go down. Will we be able to see her from here?"

Vini's smile went wicked. "Absolutely." That look did something to Jessica that made it damn unfortunate that they were out in public where anyone could just walk by. She would have loved to pull Vini in and taste how spicy that smile was. Instead, she contented herself with the knowledge that she would soon see an asshole get his comeuppance.

"Now," Vini said grabbing her attention again, "let's start with your lesson for the day."

It was on the tip of her tongue to say something about lessons after dark, but Jessica kept it to herself. She would be good...for now.

It was only two hours and a sweaty T-shirt later that Jessica wondered if she might have chosen the wrong plan for getting close to Vini. Her skin felt tacky as she brushed her forehead with the back of her hand. People had always talked about late fall and early winters in the South being pleasant, but right now she felt like she was about to melt into her clothes. The temperature in the garage had started out fine, but gradually it had warmed until not one part of her remained unaffected and her back ached with all the bending over.

"So tell me what is wrong here," Vini said as she leaned back and observed. Jessica looked down at the car, or more specifically the engine. That was the one thing that she could label so far even with Vini repeating the other parts multiple times. Jessica could memorize dialogue for a script no problem, but when it came to trying to memorize the parts in this car, she continuously drew a blank. It was like Vini was speaking French and Jessica was speaking Korean. They didn't even have roots in the same language.

She looked down at the stick in her hand and then back up at Vini. "The stick isn't wet?" Jessica couldn't help but phrase it like a question. She knew there was something important here that she should have seen, but she wasn't completely sure. She didn't want to make it seem like she wasn't paying attention to what Vini was saying. She totally was. She just didn't get it.

"Yes, and why is that a bad thing?"

"Because anytime you put a stick in, it shouldn't come out dry," she said unable to keep the smirk off her face. To her relief Vini chuckled.

"Well, you're not wrong. That's how you check your oil level, and it definitely shouldn't go in dry and come out dry." She raised an eyebrow. "And you're right. That's not good in just about any situation."

Jessica nodded and handed the stick over to Vini. She got that much at least, but she wasn't sure what else she should be getting. The engine looked like every other engine to her, as in it looked like a mass of winding metal that she didn't know the beginnings of how to make sense of.

"How did you get into cars and things? I mean, it isn't something that I think most girls grow up with."

Vini shrugged before turning and placing the stick onto

the rolling tray that she had brought over to hold an assortment of other instruments Jessica couldn't even begin to name. "The shop has been in my family since my grandfather settled here. My dad ran it when I was a kid, and in high school, I took a couple auto-shop classes and loved it." She shrugged again. "I think I've always loved cars."

"Oh, really?" None of the schools Jessica had gone to had auto-shop classes. At least, she didn't think they did. She had never really cared about cars, so she hadn't paid attention.

"Yeah." Vini paused for a moment before her gaze shifted to the side. "When I was in elementary school, my mom got really sick. Cancer. My older sisters were usually out of the house doing whatever, so my dad would bring me into the shop with him."

Jessica swallowed against the knot in her throat. It wasn't pity she felt as she thought about a miniature-sized Vini following her dad around like a little lost kitten. She always found she had to push hard when emotional topics were brought up. Usually, she attempted to avoid them altogether. But she found herself swaying toward Vini, wanting to learn more about what made her tick.

"So you decided then to take the place over?"

Vini shrugged. "Sort of. I would help out here and there, sweeping the floors or organizing the small things. When I was in high school, dad got injured, so I sort of acted as his temporary hands. He had a couple employees then, younger guys that got married and moved away after a while. He taught me more, and when he mentioned potentially having to sell the place, I realized I didn't want to let it go."

Vini rubbed a hand over the frame of the car. Jessica's breath caught when she saw Vini's lips curve up into a soft smile. It was so content and tranquil in a way Jessica didn't think she had ever experienced. It made her want to reach out and taste it so she could greedily gather some of that feeling for herself. She had to say something if only to bat away the alien thoughts in her head.

"So you went straight from high school to taking over the shop?"

"No," Vini said, shaking her head and blinking slowly as if she had just awoken from a deep dream. "I graduated a year early and enrolled in an automotive technology program. Spent a few years observing some of the guys and apprenticed with Tony until I felt ready to take things over. Actually, I met Aiden in school. He was a year behind me, and I promised him a job when he graduated. Thankfully, he took me up on it."

Vini's smile was wide and obviously proud. Jessica could understand why. Here Vini was just shy of twenty-three and she already had her shit together better than most thirty-year-olds Jessica knew. Hell, Vini had things better together than Jessica. It was so different from her experience in life, but she couldn't help but be impressed by the fact that Vini seemed so secure in what she liked and what she wanted to do even at a young age.

At twenty-two, Jessica had still been questioning if her literature major had been a good idea, and that was after she had already graduated. Even now at twenty-seven, she was only just starting to understand what she might want in life.

"That's impressive, like seriously," she replied. She leaned against the car and crossed her arms as she observed Vini and tried not to let the lingering tendril of insecurity get to her. Everyone moved through life at their own pace. It was something she always told herself when she got another Facebook message about one of her old classmates getting married or having a baby. Jessica had plenty of time. She didn't need to have everything figured out before thirty. Thirty was still young.

She caught sight of Vini's bashful grin and clung to it. The way Vini reacted to praise made her want to do it more. Especially when it was well deserved. "You are absolutely adorable."

When Vini scowled, Jessica threw her head back and laughed. The expression looked so ridiculous on her face that Jessica knew she didn't do it often. Vini had lips made for smiling: thick and eye-catching. She found it hard to look away even as Vini crossed her arms over her chest looking like a petulant child.

"Puppies and babies are *adorable*, not grown-ass women," she replied. "You could at least call me *gorgeous* or something."

Jessica laughed before leaning closer. "But you are adorable," she replied ignoring the scowl. She took the chance to cup one of Vini's cheeks. "You're also gorgeous and sexy and amazingly accomplished for your age. Hell, for any age, really."

Her words seemed to soothe Vini's ire, and her hands dropped down until they fit themselves over Jessica's hips.

She pulled her closer, and Jessica willingly went, not even sparing a thought about resisting.

"Well, I guess when you add everything else to it, being called *adorable* isn't so bad. You should tell me what else you admire about me."

"And inflate that ego any more than I already have? I don't know if that's such a good idea," Jessica teased before leaning in. She brushed the tip of her nose against Vini's, enjoying the way her eyes fluttered closed. They had been so good for the past couple hours keeping things strictly professional minus the moment when Tony had showed up in all her statuesque goodness and hauled Mr. Grumpy's Mercedes off with only a head tilt and a smirk in their direction.

They had spent a few minutes laughing hysterically at the man's face, and Vini had even called out for a celebratory pizza to be delivered. Aiden had come out to eat with them for a bit, enjoying the wayward customer's just deserts before disappearing again into the back room. Vini and Jessica had eaten and then continued with the lesson. Despite the fact that Jessica still wouldn't be able to tell the difference between a carburetor and a transmission, she found Vini's way of speaking engaging, and she hadn't been able to keep herself from staring. It had been clear that she truly loved what she did, which couldn't be said by everybody.

Now though, the semiprofessional mood had been replaced with the fun, flirty side that Jessica had greedily gobbled up glimpses of. She was quickly growing addicted to the way Vini's eyes would widen and then go heated. It left her blood singing and the hairs on her arms standing up ready for what would come next.

"I think I've complimented you enough after today's lesson," Jessica continued. "I should save some of them for next time."

Vini smirked. "Or maybe you should say all of them every time. Flattery is a powerful motivator."

"I don't think motivation is something you lack."

"You may be right. Especially now," Vini said, her voice taking on a breathy quality that had Jessica shivering as the feeling of it washed over her. The hands on her waist tightened pulling her in farther, and she found that she didn't care that the garage door was open, leaving them in plain view of anyone who might happen to walk by.

Nine

Vini sighed as she pulled the hair tie from her braids. It had been a long day, though she remained strangely energized. Maybe it was because Jessica had shown up again for the third day in a row with the flimsiest of excuses about observing Vini work. Aiden hadn't even bothered to comment on Jessica's presence, especially when Vini brought him a coffee from the new café that had recently opened up in town. Winning him over had never been that difficult, not in college and especially not now. Not that she could talk. She had been won over damn near the day she and Jessica had met.

Normally, Vini would have been annoyed to have someone so close in her space. She occasionally had students from the high school come to the garage and learn about car maintenance, but even then, there was always a moment when she had to deal with getting used to them being there. She hadn't felt that way with Jessica, and it was blowing her mind. There were even times when she needed space from her sisters, but she found herself craving Jessica's familiar warmth each day. It was as unnerving as it was enjoyable.

"I'm home," she called out, her mind still preoccupied with the conundrum that was Jessica and the low-key arousal Vini always seemed to get when she was around. They hadn't yet had a repeat of the office incident, but they had taken to driving off for lunch and spending time fogging up the windows in Vini's old truck. The fact that they hadn't been caught yet was a miracle. Clearly some deity was watching over her, keeping her from hearing an earful from Ava about who Vini decided to fraternize with. Ava generally didn't make it a point to interfere with Vini's life, but she was always overprotective when it came to her lackluster romantic entanglements. Not that there had been very many. Still, this thing with Jessica was something that was wholly Vini's, and she was loath to share any information about it with either of her sisters.

Dani popped her head through the doorway that led to the kitchen. "It's about damn time. Go wash up so we can eat. Food's ready."

"Sorry," Vini replied before ducking into the half bath in the hallway. She quickly scrubbed her nails to remove any lingering oil and bits of dirt under them. She usually did this before leaving the shop as well, but Dani was always adamant about her washing up again when she got home. It was annoying as hell, but given she worked in medicine, Vini usually gave her a pass.

Hands newly washed, Vini walked into the kitchen. Everyone was there already, which was a surprise. Ava had taken to eating dinner with Grace more often than not, but now that she thought about it, she did remember Jessica saying something about her and Grace catching a movie.

"About time you showed up," Ava remarked before reaching for her plate. "I almost told Dani that we needed to start without you."

"Rude," Vini replied. "I would have called if I wasn't going to show up. Unlike someone who just flits in and out whenever she feels like it."

Ava arched an eyebrow. "I have a girlfriend. Of course I'm not always going to be at home."

"And I have a life." Vini grabbed her own plate and started serving herself. "I have things I might be doing as well. You could always call if you think I might not be around."

Dani cleared her throat as Ava's mouth opened no doubt to retort. Ava paused before rolling her eyes and digging into her food. Vini forced herself not to roll her eyes, but she did snicker softly when Dani smiled. Beside her, Jordan was shoveling food in his mouth like he hadn't eaten all day. Dani's gaze followed hers.

"Slow down, Jay. We have plenty of time before we need to head out." Dani shook her head. He looked up at her before nodding and swallowing the wad of food in his mouth. When Vini asked Dani what that was all about, she chuckled. "There's a new librarian that started an evening e-sports class at the library. Jordan signed up at school, and the first session is today at seven thirty."

Jordan nodded quickly looking like the world's most hilarious bobblehead. "Only ten kids could join, and I was picked. They talked about even starting a team to play for real." His excitement was infectious. Vini had never really been into video games even at his age, but she had never seen him so enthusiastic about something and didn't want to put a damper on his joy.

"That sounds awesome," she replied not having to fake her excitement for him with how wide he was smiling. Even Ava's lips were turned up in a small smile as he launched into the games he hoped they would play. None of it was familiar, but if it had him this happy, then clearly it was worth it.

Dani turned back to Vini and pointed a fork at her. "I heard you had some excitement at the shop this week too."

"Me?"

"Yeah, you," Dani replied before scooping up a forkful of turnip greens. "Tony popped into the clinic today for a checkup and told me all about the Mercedes guy."

Vini shrugged. It had been a few days since then, and the guy hadn't returned so she figured all was well. "Not much to say there. He was an ass, but nothing we couldn't handle."

Dani nodded. "She also told me you had a new cutie with you that she hadn't seen before." Vini froze. She had introduced Jessica to Tony, and they had chatted briefly before Tony had hauled the guy and his car away. There hadn't been any indication that Tony was more curious about Jessica than she was about anyone else. Then again, it wasn't often new people popped up at Vini's shop.

Of course, that would be the moment Ava decided to pay attention to them again. "What new cutie?"

Vini took a silent breath and prayed to whoever was listening. "There was no new cutie. She met Jessica when she came by."

Ava's expression didn't change, but Vini knew that didn't mean anything. She was a teacher. Remaining expressionless was something she was trained to do. "And why was Jessica at your shop? I thought we decided to stay away from her."

"*We*," Vini said, "didn't decide anything. You were talking, and I let you. Who I hang out with is my own business."

Their dad chose that moment to speak up. "Well, if she's a friend of yours, you should invite her over here so we can meet her." He didn't look up from his food, so he missed Vini's wince and Dani's smirk. Inviting Jessica to the Williams' household seemed like a recipe for disaster, but he clearly didn't get that memo because he continued. "Thanksgiving is in a week, and we already invited Grace. What's one more mouth to feed?"

Ava frowned. "We don't even know her."

"All the more reason to invite her," Dani replied. "Plus, she's here to visit Grace. How are you going to invite her friend for Thanksgiving and not her? That's so uncouth."

"The hell did you just call me?" Ava asked voice rising.

"Girls," Richard interrupted, his voice pitched the same way it always was when he knew there was about to be an argument. Vini bit her lip to keep from smiling as Ava and Dani stared at one another a beat longer before looking away. He turned to Vini. "Let her know and see if she wants to join us. It's good to see you making new friends. I worry about you always being cooped up in the shop by yourself."

Vini warmed at his concern but pushed back. "I'm not alone. Aiden is there pretty much every day."

He nodded. "True, but you're so young. Maybe it's a good thing for you to be hanging out with someone else that isn't an employee. Most kids your age are out traveling and seeing the world beyond their hometown. I don't want you to feel like you missed anything."

"Dad," she whined, not wanting things to move into the direction it always did when he mentioned her not having as much of a social life as he wanted. Vini knew he worried about her, but she was fine. Sure, she didn't hang out with too many people outside of her sisters, Aiden, and occasionally Tony and her wife. But she was fine with that. If she ever felt pent-up, she could always head up to Atlanta and be more social then.

"And anyway, Jessica is at the shop because I am tutoring her on car maintenance. Nothing more, nothing less." That seemed to satisfy Ava more, because she nodded. It aggravated Vini that Ava thought she had any say in who Vini spent her time with, but she didn't feel like getting into it. It was no one's business what she and Jessica did.

"Just…be careful," Ava said looking pointedly at Vini. "I'm sure she's nice, but it wouldn't be smart to get attached when she's just passing through."

Vini brushed off her words and changed the subject. There was nothing to be careful about. This thing with

Jessica and her wasn't long-term. It was just something fun for now to pass the time before Jessica flitted off to her next destination and Vini got back to the norm of everyday life.

Vini was ready to pull out a braid or two. Fridays were usually busy, especially when it was before a holiday, and today was no different. Many of the usual suspects from town had scheduled their oil changes in advance to prepare for heading out of town for the upcoming holiday, but a few hadn't, leaving them with too many cars and two few hands. Aiden's off-key rendition of Dolly Parton's "9 to 5" wasn't helping. Dolly didn't deserve to have her song butchered nor did Vini deserve to be subjected to it.

"Fucking hell. Someone put him out of his misery, please."

Vini almost banged her knee on the car bumper in front of her when Jessica's voice came from right next to her. She glanced over her shoulder with a glare. "I'm going to put a bell on you so I can hear you next time."

"Oh, sounds kinky," she replied, not sounding at all repentant for nearly giving Vini a heart attack. "Make sure it's purple. That's my favorite color."

"Just for that, I'll make it black like your soul," Vini countered.

"You say the sweetest things."

Vini straightened as she shook her head. She wasn't really angry. Not with how damn pleased she was to see Jessica in the first place. Jessica hadn't come by the shop yesterday, and Vini had wondered if that meant she'd lost interest. Vini found cars interesting, but she knew not everyone did. She covered her excitement at Jessica showing up by grabbing the closest rag and wiping her hands.

"What are you doing here?"

Jessica held up a bag. "Figured I would bring you guys some lunch. Grace mentioned a really good diner in town that Ava's friend owns, so I went by to check it out."

"Did you say *lunch*?" Aiden piped up from the other side of the garage. Vini would have told him to go back to work, but now that he had stopped singing, she was in a much better mood. Aiden quickly rushed over, holding out his hands and making a grabby motion. "If that is a sandwich from the best diner in town, I will love you forever."

"Not that you aren't cute, but penis isn't exactly my thing." Jessica opened the sack and pulled out a smaller bag and handed it to him. Aiden danced around like a kid who just found his favorite comic, and Vini couldn't help but chuckle.

"I guess that means it's lunchtime," she replied, not the least bit upset about stopping now. She held out her hand. "I'm assuming you brought one for me as well?"

"I did, but I thought we could take ours to go and enjoy some sunshine." Jessica glanced at Aiden. "Unless you're too busy."

She probably should have said she was swamped with work given the number of cars in the garage and waiting outside, but she was helpless in the face of Jessica's hopeful expression. Besides, taking breaks was necessary, especially when it came to eating. She tried not to look too eager when she told Aiden she was going to step out for a bit, but she knew from his knowing expression she hadn't covered it well. Still, a few minutes later, she and Jessica were headed down the road, the bag of food sitting on the console between them.

"So where did you want to head to? There's a small park not far from the main square that shouldn't be too crowded right now." From the corner of her eye, Vini could see Jessica watching her, and for a moment she wished she was telepathic so she could sneak a peek at her thoughts. Jessica looked ahead again before answering.

"Is there anywhere we can go to just park and be alone?"

Vini swallowed hard. That sounded like a wonderfully terrible idea. They never seemed to keep things casual when they were alone together. It wasn't that Vini didn't want to be alone with Jessica. It was that she did. Sneaking around should have been off-putting, and yet that didn't explain why she found it so damn addicting. She shouldn't be able to recall a few places that fit that description perfectly, and yet she didn't hesitate to turn the car in the direction of one such place.

Neither one of them had come outright and said they were keeping things quiet, but she knew Jessica hadn't mentioned their trysts to Grace. If she had, Grace would absolutely have told Ava who wouldn't have let Vini out of her sight. Vini didn't know Jessica's reasons for keeping things super down-low.

When Vini glanced over, she found Jessica once again looking at her. "What?"

"Nothing," Jessica replied. "Just wondering if we are headed toward town or…"

Vini didn't wait long to confirm. "No." She slowed and turned down a dirt road. Not many cars came down here. It was a path mostly used by ATVs and bikes, but Vini's truck could handle it. She had spent many a time driving out this way when she was younger and needed to be alone. The road grew bouncier, and Vini couldn't help but smirk when Jessica grabbed for her hand squeezing it tightly until the road evened out again and the ride smoothed. Vini slowed to a stop under the cover of large trees, their branches reaching out and hiding the truck under shadow.

"You couldn't have warned a girl?" Jessica asked with a raised brow.

Vini smirked as she put the car in park and cut the engine. "Where's the fun in that?" Jessica shook her head, but her smile didn't wane. She gazed out the window for a moment before fixing her gaze back on Vini.

"So you come here often?"

"Used to," Vini replied looking around at the familiar outcropping of trees. They weren't that far from town. In fact, if she drove through the field, she would reach the edge of her friend Jane's land.

"Alone or cuddled up with someone?"

The question sounded nonchalant, but it still had Vini warming at the thought that Jessica might care. She pushed the center console up leaving only an empty seat between them. "Jealous?"

Jessica looked at her for a moment before unbuckling her

seat belt and moving across the space. With each inch that disappeared between them, Vini's heartbeat sped up until she was sure the thrumming sound would fill the cab of the truck. When Jessica's hand finally reached her, Vini almost fell into her orbit.

Their lips met with a hunger that couldn't be settled with food. Vini had never been particularly needy when it came to touch like this, but she was quickly finding herself lost without it. She gripped Jessica's shoulders as if afraid she would move away leaving Vini unsatisfied.

"You know, I never actually brought anyone here for this," Vini whispered when they separated briefly. It was a confession that cost nothing but gained her everything as Jessica smiled and pulled her in again.

Jessica's lips pressed and pressed again leaving Vini dizzy with arousal. The air grew damp with their kissing until the window behind Jessica's head started to fog. Vini didn't doubt her own was the same, and a thrill ran through her. She really hadn't brought anyone back here for hooking up. There were places around town that her friends and classmates had utilized at different times as a make-out spot, but Vini had never been particularly interested. That had all changed now. She wanted to take Jessica to each place and make memories that would live in her fantasies after she was long gone. There was only so much time. She wanted to do everything.

When Jessica's hands gripped Vini's belt, she pulled away. "You okay with taking this further?"

Vini's head was full of stuffing. She didn't know what

further meant to Jessica, but she wasn't going to say *no* if it got her more pleasure. "Anything you want."

Jessica's smile was sharp, but she didn't respond. She shifted, getting her knees on the seat before guiding Vini's legs up to the seat as well. Shoes were discarded, and between one kiss and the next Vini found herself bare-assed in her truck for the first time. There would have been a slight chill in the air if not for the heat between the two of them. Vini should have felt embarrassed being left in only her work shirt while Jessica was fully dressed, but it was thrilling. Illicit. All the things Vini had never had before.

"Are you going to take yours off too?"

Jessica leaned over brushing her lips over Vini's heated cheeks. "Maybe. If you're good."

"Haven't we established that already?" Vini asked before cupping Jessica's cheeks. They were flushed slightly and made Vini want to touch. Before she could pull Jessica back into a kiss, she shifted down Vini's body. With wide eyes, Vini looked around. She knew they were alone, but if anyone happened by, they would know exactly what was going on. "What are you... Here?"

"Yes, here," Jessica replied as she shifted Vini's legs up onto her shoulders. The cab wasn't as comfortable as a bed, but it was wide enough. Vini reached up and gripped the door behind her. "I brought you lunch, and now I will have mine."

Vini opened her mouth to speak, but before she could get a word out, Jessica's tongue laved her pussy lips, parting them slightly as it slid up toward her clit. A squeak was the only noise she could make even as the sensation washed over her. Vini was no virgin, but before Jessica, sex had been few and far between. It had been years since she had done anything more than solo, so having someone so clearly dedicated to getting her off was new, hooking her in and not letting go.

"Fuck," Vini breathed out as she reached out and brushed her thumb over Jessica's cheek. She could only hold on as Jessica repeated her motion, tongue slipping deeper between the folds of Vini's pussy as if trying to rearrange her from the inside.

Vini's breaths came faster as she followed Jessica's rhythm. Wet slurping sounds filled the cab, interspersed by Vini's moans of pleasure. She reached her other hand down to grip one of Jessica's squeezing tightly with each wave of pleasure that crashed over her. When Jessica's tongue darted over her hole, she hitched a breath only letting out when she was breeched. That slide in was debilitating, and Vini couldn't stop herself from arching into it and groaning deep. She tossed her head to the side ignoring the dull pain from thumping it against the door when a finger entered along with it.

"There you go, baby," Jessica exhaled hot breath hitting Vini's cunt and making her twitch. "Just enjoy it."

"I am," Vini panted. "Fuck, I am."

"Love it when you curse," Jessica said her voice full of amusement and barely contained heat. It had deepened and slid over Vini's skin lighting her up and pushing her arousal higher. Jessica's normal voice wasn't particularly deep, but now when it was full of want and barely contained desire, it was music to Vini's ears. When Jessica leaned back in, pressing her tongue deep again, Vini cried out softly before clutching the back of Jessica's head as she tried not to come apart.

Time meant nothing. Daylight could have passed completely and Vini wouldn't have noticed. All she knew was heat and slick pleasure as Jessica ate her fill, her tongue pressing along with her fingers until Vini didn't know what it was like to be empty. When those wicked fingers twisted, Vini clenched and sucked in a breath. As much as she wanted to hold on, there was no way to fight her release when Jessica's other hand came up and her fingers brushed across Vini's engorged clitoris.

Back strung tight as a bow, Vini lost all sense of meaning. All she could hear was the muted sound of her own cries over the rush of blood in her ears. When she finally collapsed back against the seat, it took her a moment to realize she had closed her eyes at some point. Her face was dotted with sweat and Jessica was no longer down between her legs but instead leaning over her while whispering how good Vini was and how sexy she sounded when she came. If not for having just had her brain leak out of her ears, Vini would have been able to say something sweetly sensual in response. Instead, her mouth chose that moment to send it all crashing down.

"My dad invited you to Thanksgiving."

Ten

Jessica was stressed. No, she was more than stressed. *Stressed* was when she had to show up with her mother on the red carpet and she knew people would question why a grown-ass woman was still tagging along with her mom to work.

This was beyond that.

Maybe it wasn't the smartest to keep this thing with Vini going. Sure, it had helped to pass the time the past two weeks, and she had yet to get bored around the other woman, despite still not being able to answer how much oil a car should have, but still. The multiple orgasms couldn't make up for the fact that Jessica had been invited to a holiday with the family of the woman she was secretly boning. This had to be the Guinness World Record for the Worst Idea in the History of Bad Ideas. Yet, it still didn't explain why Grace was trying to rush her along to get dressed. Was Jessica being punked?

"Why the hell are you still in pajamas?"

"Because they're comfortable." Jessica gestured to her frame and the dark gray sweats and top she had on. "Plus I look good in gray, and you know it."

Grace waved her off before walking over to Jessica's suitcase and flipping it open. "You look good in everything. Still doesn't explain why the hell you aren't dressed." She lifted a teal blouse out of the suitcase and tilted her head before throwing it Jessica's way. "Put this on. It looks good against your skin."

Jessica caught the garment with a huff. "I know it does. That's why I bought it." When Grace threw a pair of dark-wash jeans at her, she snatched them out of the air before they could hit the floor. "What the hell, Grace? I hadn't planned doing much of anything today so I could rest up for our trip to Miami this weekend. What's the big deal?"

Grace turned to her, hands planted on her hips. Her expression was one Jessica was sure her students saw a lot of. It said *no nonsense*, but Jessica had always been a terrible student. She tossed the clothes onto the unmade bed. Grace's eyes glittered as her lips turned down in a scowl.

"Pick up those clothes, take a shower and get your ass dressed. You are coming to this meal if I have to carry you out myself."

"You can't possibly expect me to go," Jessica said her voice rising slightly. When Vini had mentioned it to her last week, Jessica was shocked. She had mumbled noncommittally before diving back into a kiss to keep Vini from mentioning it again. They had seen each other every other day since then, but Vini hadn't brought it up again, so Jes-

sica took it as a fluke. It wasn't that she wasn't apprecia-
tive. She was. Southern hospitality had definitely been a
real and present thing since coming to Peach Blossom, and
if the invitation had come from any of the other random
townspeople, Vini would have entertained it in the spirit
of niceness it was offered. But this was Vini. She and Vini
were casually fucking. There was no way she could show
up to Vini's house and sit there in front of her family like
she didn't know exactly what it sounded like when Vini
cried out her name or the way her eyelids fluttered when
she was about to come.

No, showing up could only lead to trouble.

"I don't even know them," Jessica emphasized. This
wasn't like hanging out with Grace's parents. She had
known them for years, and they always invited her to spend
time with them when she was stateside. The only thing she
really knew about Vini's family was that they didn't really
know about her and that they were all overprotective. "Isn't
it rude as a guest to invite a guest?"

"You were invited already," Grace countered.

"But I didn't say I was going," Jessica pointed out, hoping
that would be enough to end the conversation. Her hopes
were dashed when Grace's phone rang and she answered it.

"Hey, babe," Grace said her dark brown eyes never leaving Jessica. "Yeah, I'm here picking her up. She's stressing
out about what to wear."

Jessica could faintly hear laughing on the other end of the
line followed by some muffled words. She could only assume Grace was talking to Ava. Knowing that Vini wasn't

the only one asking after her was enough to make her feel slightly guilty. She had been operating off the idea that Vini was only inviting her because of their meetups. But what if it wasn't even her to begin with? What if her family was genuinely trying to be nice? Jessica knew it was rude to not accept kindness when offered, especially given she was alone in town. Maybe Vini's family just didn't want to leave her at the inn.

Grace's chuckling brought Jessica out of her head and dropped her arms by her sides. "All right, I'll tell her. We should be there within the hour. Yeah, you too." After Grace hung up, she raised an eyebrow at Jessica. "See? The Williamses want you to come. Ava said they felt bad since they had invited me and didn't realize you would have been all alone for the day. They're good people."

"I never said they weren't," Jessica protested. She turned and looked out the window as she tried to figure out what to say that wouldn't give away the real reason she was so resistant to going. "I just didn't want to overstep."

Grace shook her head, her smile small and gentle. She walked over to Jessica and put her hands on Jessica's shoulders. "You wouldn't be. And besides, you would be doing me a favor. This will be the first holiday I've spent with Ava and her family. Having you there would keep me from being so nervous."

That was news to Jessica. She hadn't realized that she might not be the only one worried about the dinner. When she looked closer, she could see the strain in Grace's face: she was worried. Jessica didn't understand why. From everything Vini had mentioned, Grace was well-liked by her sisters and dad. But, if it made Grace feel better to have her there, Jessica could suck up her discomfort for one night. It would probably keep her mother off her back too if Jessica told her she was spending Thanksgiving with a family in town rather than in her suite by herself.

With a groan of defeat, Jessica gave in. "You so owe me for this."

Grace smiled wide. "Do this for me and you can have my first born."

"Absolutely not. I demand gold bars and diamonds for my service." Jessica shrugged her hands off and grabbed the clothes from her bed. Grace's laughter followed her into the bathroom, cutting off when she pushed the door shut behind her.

It wasn't until they were pulling into the Williamses' driveway that Jessica felt the cold grip of panic set in again. With each crunch of rock under her footsteps, she felt more and more like she was being escorted to her doom. Vini's sisters would take one look at her and know that Jessica had been tapping their sister. She could already hear the accusations now. She braced herself as Grace rang the doorbell.

The door opened, and Jessica looked down at the child who welcomed them. He was a cute kid, coming up past Grace's waist. His skin was a deep brown, and his eyes were familiar. He was dressed down in a Black Panther hoodie and jeans, making Jessica feel more comfortable about her own outfit. He darted forward giving Grace a tight hug before pushing them into the house.

"We're waiting for you guys," he said. "Mom wouldn't let me grab a bite, even though Grandpa snuck a roll already."

"Dad."

"I was hungry." An older man shrugged before standing up from his chair and walking toward Grace and Jessica. "Good to see you again, Grace." He enveloped her in a hug, and Jessica tried not to stare around him to where Vini was sitting at the large family dining table.

Grace hugged him back before pulling away and gesturing at Jessica. "Mr. Williams, this is my best friend, Jessica Miller. Jessica, this is Ava's dad, Mr. Williams."

He shook his head. "I told you to call me Daniel. *Mr. Williams* makes me feel old." Jessica snorted before her breath was stolen when she was pulled into a strong hug. Daniel didn't look a day over forty with his deep brown skin and close-cut ebony beard. He was tall and broad, which meant Vini must have gotten her slight stature from her mother. When he took a step back, his smile had a boyish quality that Jessica found charming. It made it impossible to not smile back.

"Thank you for the invitation, Mr. Williams," she said before holding out a bottle of wine. "I appreciate it."

"Seriously, you two," he retorted before waving them to the table. Jessica nodded at Aiden before taking the offered seat beside Vini. She knew it would look weird to not acknowledge the other woman, so she nodded and smiled.

"Hey, Vini. Good to see you again."

Vini didn't seem the slightest bit bothered. "Hey, Jess. Glad you decided to join us."

Jessica nodded at Grace who sat down across the table from her. "That one wouldn't have let me stay away as it is. She practically busted down my door and dragged me out by my toenails."

Ava cocked an eyebrow at Jessica's comment, but the last unfamiliar woman laughed before introducing herself. "That was probably my fault. I'm Dani." She held out a hand and Jessica shook it. "I chewed her and Ava out about inviting someone who had a guest and not inviting the guest. It's not how we do things around here."

"I never said I wasn't going to invite her," Ava shot back. She looked back and forth between Jessica and Vini, but Jessica kept her expression neutral. She could handle dinner. Hell, she had gone to acting classes for years. She could play it cool. She was a goddam ice cube. "But I am glad you came. Any friend of Vini and all that."

Jessica nodded. "Vini has been a great teacher. I think I might actually be ready to change my own tire."

Everyone else paused for a moment before laughing. Jessica glanced at Vini who was covering her mouth with her hand. She wasn't sure what the hell was so funny, but whatever it was seemed to break the tension, and Dani lifted the first serving dish, passing it to Jessica.

Conversation was relaxed as they loaded their plates with heaping spoonfuls of corn-bread stuffing, turkey, macaroni and cheese, and some type of green that Jessica couldn't identify. She'd had plenty of Thanksgiving meals, but usually they were small affairs with her and her parents going out to eat in whatever city they lived in, or visiting Jason and hoping he didn't get put on call for a shift. She couldn't remember the last time she had a home-cooked Thanksgiving. At least, not American style. She tried to get back to Korea each year for Chuseok to spend time with her maternal grandparents and cousins, but she usually didn't help prepare anything. This was a whole new experience for her.

"So Jessica, what is it that you do?" Daniel asked.

"Right now, I'm between contracts, but I do some voice-acting for television shows, commercials and audiobooks." He nodded, but internally Jessica was waiting for the usual questions of what that meant and if that was really a job. It was usually what her other family members asked as well when they realized she wasn't on-screen like her mother.

"Sounds like that could be a really interesting job," he said before taking a bite of turkey and leaving Jessica off-kilter. "Do you do any podcasts?"

She blinked quickly, trying to cover her shock at what seemed like genuine interest in her work. It wasn't that no one was ever interested. It was just that his acceptance came so easily. When she felt a warmth press against her leg, she glanced over. Vini was smiling softly as she looked down at her plate. No one would have been able to see anything, but that was the unmistakable heat of Vini's hand on Jessica's thigh. It didn't seem to be a move to arouse, and to Jessica's surprise it didn't.

It was a comfort. She felt comforted by Vini's presence, and before she could second-guess herself, she moved her hand down. She covered Vini's hand with her own and squeezed in thanks. Her eyes drifted away and to her own plate as she covered her smile by taking another bite of food. Despite her initial misgivings, the dinner turned out to be comfortable and easy. It had been a long time since Jessica had ever relaxed with a group of people she hadn't known closely for at least a few years beforehand. She was so busy musing on it, she didn't come up for air until she realized she had been conned into washing dishes with Vini standing quietly at her side.

"So...that was a thing," Jessica said slowly broaching the topic of her presence. "Dinner was pleasant. I enjoyed it."

Vini glanced at her. "Yeah? It wasn't too weird for you?"

"Not at all. That was top-five easiest of all dinners I have been to in a long while." Jessica passed the last dish before rinsing her hands and drying them. She turned and leaned back against the sink as she watched Vini let her words sink in.

She didn't look at Jessica when she spoke. "This is the first time my family has ever met anyone I was...with." When she looked up at Jessica finally, her lips were twisted. "Sorry if it seemed so sudden. Dad really was curious to meet you."

Jessica waved away Vini's words. "It's all good. Parents love me." Vini's chuckle was soft, and Jessica let it wash over her. She really did enjoy that sound. "Your dad seems like a great guy."

"He is," Vini agreed. She finished drying the last plate and set it on the rack beside her before turning to face Jessica fully. She looked soft and relaxed today in jeans and a butter-yellow T-shirt. Her braids were pulled back in one large loose braid, giving Jessica a view of her elegant neck.

Jessica's lips twitched with the desire to brush over that skin just to hear those deep, breathy noises she so loved. "What about your parents? Are they sad you couldn't go see them?"

The last thing Jessica wanted to do was talk about her parents, but when the sound of laughter drifted in from the other room, she conceded that pulling Vini into a dark corner or an empty bathroom was probably not the best idea.

"Not really," she replied squeezing the counter in her grip. "I love my parents, but they aren't really much for holidays. We probably would have ended up eating out or ordering in. This was a much better use of time."

Vini moved closer, leaving Jessica confused. They both knew that they shouldn't do anything that might give away what was going on between them, but her ability to deny Vini was rapidly retreating with each inch that seemed to disappear between them. If not for Grace abruptly interrupting their stare-down, Jessica would have taken one for the team.

"Hey, Vini. I think everyone is ready for…" Grace trailed off when Jessica and Vini moved away from one another "…ice cream."

"Perfect," Vini said, her voice higher than it had been a few moments before. She walked over to the freezer and pulled out a large tub of Neapolitan ice cream. "I've got this and the spoons if you guys will bring the bowls. Grace should know where they are."

Jessica nodded. "Got it." She gave Vini a thumbs-up and kept up the pretense until she left the kitchen. "Jesus,

Grace. A little warning next time you decide to barge in at a moment's notice."

"Warning? Are you kidding me?" Grace's voice was slightly hysterical, and Jessica waved her arms telling her to quiet down. "What were you two doing, and why were you so close?"

Jessica rolled her eyes and turned to the cabinets to start searching for the bowls. There were only so many places they could be, and it would give her time to figure out what to say to Grace that wasn't a total fucking lie. She didn't like lying to Grace, and so she wouldn't. But she knew she needed to play things just right to keep her high-strung friend from stringing herself into the sky.

"We were just talking," Jessica replied. She knew Grace would be annoyed at her vague explanation, but she figured it was best to start small and work her way up to the whole truth. "I was thanking her for inviting me, considering the fact that they don't know me."

Grace stared at her for a moment, and Jessica could see thoughts swirling behind those dark brown eyes. Jessica knew Grace would eventually realize what was going on, but she wasn't about to make it easy on her. If she wanted the information, she was going to have to work for it.

"Okay, fine. That still doesn't explain why you two were standing so close to one another." Grace paused before her eyes widened. Jessica could see the inevitable end barreling down on her like a locomotive. But she was stuck, nowhere to go even if she wanted to. "No. Jessica."

"What am I, a dog?"

"No, no, no," Grace repeated slapping Jessica's hands away when she tried to quiet her. She grabbed Jessica's hands and held tightly. "Do not tell me that you have been having sex with Vini. Ava's sister Vini. Ava's baby sister Vini."

Jessica tried to pull away but eventually gave in with a sigh. "Fine. I won't tell you that I have been having sex with Vini." When Grace gasped, Jessica sighed again. She really didn't understand what the big deal was.

"Why the hell would you do that?" Grace hissed, swinging her head around to scan the doorway before looking back at Jessica. "Ava is going to kill me when she finds out."

"There's no reason to tell her. Vini and I agreed we want to keep his quiet and just between us," Jessica insisted, pulling Grace back to her when she made like she was going to leave. It wasn't a complete lie. They hadn't totally defined things, but it was more so an understanding between them. "For fuck's sake, Grace. Vini and I are just having some fun. We won't even be in town over the weekend, so you can spend that time forgetting all about it and we can move on."

Grace scowled. "It's all fun and games until someone gets hurt."

Jessica rolled her eyes. "No one is getting hurt. We are two grown-ass women who decided we wanted to spend some time together. No fuss, no mess."

Grace glanced at the doorway when another round of laughter came. "You say that, but I know you. You leave a string of broken hearts wherever you go."

That stung a little, but not as much as the idea of Vini and being brokenhearted in the same thought. There was no need for all that. She and Vini were on the same page about this. "Not here," she replied firmly. Jessica paused for a moment before trying another cabinet in her hunt for bowls. She let out a triumphant noise when she saw them and pulled enough out for everyone.

"Jessica—"

"No," she snapped, clenching her jaw. Jessica could understand why Grace was hesitant, but this didn't involve her. "Vini and I just want some low-key, drama-free time. That's it. In four weeks when I leave, we will both part on good terms. I promise you, it's fine."

Grace didn't not look convinced, but Jessica would just have to prove to her how relaxed they were about all this. She and Vini were good. Grace had nothing to worry about.

Eleven

Vini woke slowly. Normally, she would be up and out of bed as soon as she cracked her eyes open, but it was the day after Thanksgiving, and the shop was closed. She could afford to take her time and relax a little. She had survived the dinner from hell with no bruises to speak of so she was going to celebrate her win.

When Jessica had walked through the doorway, Vini hadn't been sure how to act. She had extended the invite in a moment of vulnerability, but when Jessica hadn't responded, Vini hadn't known how to bring it up again. She thought for sure she had overstepped things. They were meant to be having some fun, and although their interactions also included a fair bit of getting to know one another, that didn't mean that they had a relationship where family was involved. So color her surprised when Jessica had shown up to dinner the night before. Vini had tamped down her smile and forced her expression into indifference just to keep from making it obvious how excited she was to see Jessica.

And that, of course, led into the next problem. Her excitement to see Jessica. She could have chalked it up to the sex being fire if not for how often Vini felt the desire to just talk to Jessica or ask about her favorite foods. Seeing Jessica's head thrown back in pleasure was just as much of a turn on as hearing her satisfied groan when she ate something good. And her laughter. Vini couldn't even think about Jessica's laugh without smiling.

"You're still in bed?"

With a sigh, Vini rolled over. Dani was in the doorway still pajama-clad and looking far less awake than Vini felt.

"It's a holiday," Vini replied. "I'm giving myself the space to rest."

Dani nodded. "Sounds like a perfect plan. Scoot over." Before Vini could respond, Dani had already made her way across the room and was lifting the blankets. Vini could have protested and pushed her away, but that would have made her get louder, and Vini didn't want to wake up the whole house.

"You do have your own bed."

Dani's smile was soft and still fuzzy-looking from sleep. "Yeah. But yours is more comfortable."

Vini frowned as Dani settled in, tugging the blankets around her shoulders until only her head was left exposed. It wasn't the first time Vini's bed had been invaded, but usually it was Jordan making an appearance when Dani had to work a late-night shift. When they were children, Dani,

Ava and Vini often did share beds, but it was a practice that had stopped years ago.

"What's with the sudden need to be in my bed?" Vini asked as she rolled over onto her back. She stared up at her ceiling, its bumps and ridges familiar to her, as was the glow-in-the-dark stars that she had put up when she was in middle school. Some of them had fallen off over the years, but many of them remained glowing faintly in the dark of night.

Dani was quiet for a moment, and when Vini glanced over, she saw Dani's eyes were closed. She was startled when Dani finally spoke.

"Yesterday went well." When Vini hummed noncommittally, she continued. "Dad seemed to like Jessica."

"That's good," Vini replied tentatively. She wasn't sure what Dani was trying to get at, so she thought it best to play it safe. "I know Grace probably felt more comfortable with a friend."

Dani snorted but conceded the point. "We can be overwhelming at times. But beyond Grace, it seemed like Jessica enjoyed herself. Have you talked to her since?"

Vini shook her head. "When would I have had the time?"

"Last night after she left maybe. It seemed like you two were getting along well, and people have seen her at your shop more often than not."

Vini turned her head. She knew now where this conversation was going, and she wasn't in the mood for it. Especially not when she was still trying to figure out how she felt about the whole thing. It had been three weeks of her and Jessica sneaking around and finding snatches of time to be together, and yet she still didn't feel any closer to understanding who Jessica was. She knew she was a great kisser. She knew that one heated look could have Vini's knees quaking with the need to bend. She knew that she loved to feel Jessica's skin on hers and how she searched for traces of Jessica's scent long after she was gone.

But she didn't know how Jessica liked her eggs or what she'd wanted to be when she was a kid. Hell, she didn't even know which college Jessica had gone to, and it was quickly becoming a problem. She wanted to ask all these questions and more, but would that be too much? Jessica asked plenty of questions about Vini, but she always seemed hesitant to answer Vini's own curiosity about her life. Everything seemed to stay frustratingly surface-level and one-sided. Vini didn't know how to approach things, and when Jessica was right in front of her all Vini could do was breathe.

"We don't talk that often unless she's coming to ask questions about car maintenance," Vini said wincing at the slight whine in her voice. That wasn't totally true, but she was trying not to spill the beans so soon. "We aren't that close."

Dani nodded. "Well, maybe you should change that." Her response surprised Vini. Dani had been nice enough to Jessica, but she hadn't paid more than the usual amount of attention to her. Dani opened her eyes, gaze locking on Vini in an instant. "What?"

"Ava warned me to stay away from Jessica, and yet here you are telling me I should, what, befriend her?" The whole thing was confusing. "Make it make sense."

Dani rolled her eyes. "Ava is a bit overprotective. We both are when it comes to our favorite baby sister."

"I'm your only baby sister," Vini pointed out. "That still doesn't explain why you think I should get closer to Jessica."

"She seems nice," Dani replied. "And as much as I know you enjoy your work and life here, I worry about you. Dad was right when he said most people your age go out with friends or vacation. They go dancing and drinking and make bad decisions. You have Aiden, sure, and he's a great person, but other than him, you're usually alone."

Vini swallowed hard at how serious the conversation had gotten. "I like being alone."

"But you don't have to be," Dani replied. When Vini didn't respond, she scooted closer and wrapped an arm around Vini's waist. Vini let herself be moved until she was tucked into Dani's chest like she used to do when she woke up from nightmares she couldn't name. Dani's cheek pressed against the top of her head, and Vini felt herself relax.

"What if she doesn't want to get to know me?" Vini asked before she could talk herself out of it. It was a question that had been floating in the dredges of her mind and now that it was out there, she felt a little lighter. "I'm not that exciting of a person."

"Then, she's a fool. You're awesome, and I should know because I'm the oldest and what I say goes."

Vini laughed softly. So many arguments had been ended that way, but this wasn't one where she wanted to argue back. Not when she so desperately wanted Dani to be right.

★ ★ ★

Vini stared at her phone. She had spent most of Friday turning over her and Dani's conversation in her mind. Ava hadn't said much about Thanksgiving beyond moping around now that Grace was gone to visit her mom. It had left Vini with time to come up with a strategy.

She and Jessica had exchanged numbers, but beyond a text here or there, they hadn't really talked. Now that Jessica was out of town with Grace, Vini planned to rectify that and see if they could hold a conversation when clothes weren't coming off. Before she could second-guess herself, she hit Jessica's number and held the phone up to her ear as she waited. Each ring seemed to mock her, and she tapped her blunt nails on the counter in a staccato rhythm as she waited. When the line finally clicked, she almost hung up.

"Hey, Vin. What's up? Everything okay there?"

"Yeah," Vini replied. She looked around the shop as she tried to think of what more to say. It was quiet even for a Saturday after a holiday. Aiden had taken the morning off, so it was just Vini alone with her thoughts for another couple hours.

"Aw, do you miss me?" Jessica's voice was teasing, but her words sent Vini into a tailspin. The truth was she did miss Jessica, but that wasn't something she could admit. Could she? That was probably a step too far too soon.

She knew she needed to keep it casual and ease into conversation. "I wouldn't go that far. Especially not with the way you still can't figure out the difference between a wrench and a screwdriver."

Jessica's laugh was carefree and open, and it had Vini smiling at the phone. She pulled it away from her ear and put it on Speaker as she walked into the garage. "So how's Miami?"

Jessica launched into a summary as Vini got to work. She let the sounds of Jessica's words carry her through the first oil change of the day and into the second. As Jessica spoke, it was almost as if Vini could taste and hear the sights she described. Occasionally, Grace's voice would filter over the line, but not once did Jessica mention needing to go. It wasn't until Aiden walked in that Vini realized she and Jessica had been talking for more than two hours without a single lull in conversation.

"Who are you talking to?" Aiden called out, interrupting Jessica's story of backpacking through Thailand with literally only a backpack of belongings. "Is that Jessica?"

"Aiden! Are you taking good care of my girl?"

Aiden's smile then could only be described as catlike as he wagged his eyebrows at Vini. "Only until you get back here and take of her yourself."

"That didn't sound right at all," Vini replied making a face. Aiden laughed before making his way back into the lobby. Vini sighed and grabbed a rag to clean her hands. Her stomach growled, protesting a lack of food. "I should probably go grab some lunch before my stomach decides to eat itself. When do you and Grace get back in town?"

More sounds started filtering in across the line. "Grace has to be back to work on Monday, so we get back tomorrow afternoon." The sounds of people talking grew louder, as did the sound of upbeat music. Vini knew she needed to push through and say something before she lost her nerve.

"There's a drive-in movie in the next town over that I planned on going to tomorrow night. Thought it might be something new for you if you want to join me."

"Drive-in movie? Like, the type of drive-in you see in old movies with the cars and big screen and everything?" Jessica's disbelief was clear in her voice. "I thought those things had gone the way of the dinosaurs."

Vini shook her head. "No. I mean, not completely, I guess. This one happens once a month, and I try to catch it when I have time. Last time Dani and Ava joined me, but Dani has a shift and Ava will probably be sucking face with Grace."

Jessica laughed. "You're not wrong. Grace has mentioned Ava like once an hour since we left. If it wasn't so cute, I would strangle her." Vini chuckled not surprised in the slightest. If not for Ava having been gone and hanging out with Brad, Vini would probably have the same problem. "Also, what makes you think I won't try to suck your face at the drive-in? Isn't that what the cool kids do?"

Heat scorched through Vini at the thought. It would be a lie to say she hadn't been hoping for it, but she also just wanted to spend some time with Jessica at one of the places she enjoyed. "I don't know about the cool kids, but this drive-in has caramel popcorn that is guaranteed to turn you on."

"You had me at caramel. I'm in." Grace's voice suddenly cut in loud and frantic. "I have to go. Grace is freaking out about finding her parents and not missing lunch. Our flight lands at two so we should be back to town around four."

"That's fine," Vini replied quickly. "I'll come pick you up around five when I get off. The movie starts at six, and we want to get there early to get a good parking spot."

"Sounds great. Have a great rest of your day, Vin. Talk to you later." Jessica's phone disconnected before Vini had a moment to answer, but even so, the smile didn't leave her face even when Aiden dropped a box of supplies.

Twelve

Being back in Peach Blossom after a weekend in Miami was like night and day, but the weirdest part wasn't that she missed Miami. It was that she *didn't*. Jessica had gone with Grace to see Grace's parents for the holiday weekend, and things had gone just as well as they always did when she went home with Grace. They ate a ton of food, Cuban this time, did some early Christmas shopping and generally people-watched. Rather, Grace people-watched, and Jessica added much needed commentary to round it all out. What had been different were the texts and phone calls Jessica exchanged with Vini.

It wasn't that they were chatting nonstop. That would have been rude, after all. But when Jessica was strolling down the beach admiring the way the sky was unblemished by a single cloud, the picture she snapped wasn't just for herself. When she settled into the guest room in the evening, it wasn't her mom she had called to talk about her day. The fact that it hadn't seemed out of pocket to her was what left her mildly concerned that something had changed that she was unaware of.

Her phone rang, jarring Jessica out of her musings. When she saw who it was, she groaned and counted to five before connecting the call.

"It's about time you answered the damn phone. I thought you were going to send me to voice mail."

She smiled down at the phone. "That would probably have been what you deserved. As it is, I can't believe I'm finally hearing from the famous Jason," she teased. "How the hell are you?"

It had been a few weeks since she last talked to him, what with his busy work schedule and the time difference of him being out on the West Coast. When he had announced he was going to medical school, Jessica thought he was kidding. As a kid, he had taken after their mom with the acting gene and had starred in a couple popular sitcoms. His calling it quits at twenty to instead become a doctor was a pivot that had happened faster than Jessica had been prepared for. Now though, it was like he had been born to be a doctor, and the days of acting for anyone other than his patients were probably far behind him.

"Living the dream, sis. How's Mayberry and cow-tipping?"

"You are so fucking old," she replied with a laugh. "Please tell me you've watched a show younger than Mom in the last month or so."

"No can do. My love for the classics will remain unde-terred."

Jessica shook her head. "It pains me to realize we're re-lated." She walked over to the recliner that sat in front of the window and dropped down, getting comfortable. She had spent most of the day sitting and watching people from her vantage on the second floor. It was quickly becoming one of her favorite pastimes outside of finding her place be-tween Vini's legs and in her arms.

"But seriously," Jason continued, "how are things going there? Has the heat died down enough for you to come out of self-imposed isolation? Are you still trending on so-cial media?"

She snorted. "Not even close. Honestly, I haven't even been online at all lately." That was odd too. While Jessica didn't live and breathe social media, she still tended to check up on it. She hadn't banned herself from going onto any of her usual platforms, though she had banned herself from posting anything that might give up her location.

"Wow. Mayberry must be amazing if you haven't been paying attention to the Gram or Book of Faces."

"Oh my God, it's Peach Blossom, you ass," Jessica finally corrected. "And I've been busy with other things. I've actu-ally made some friends here. I'm going to a drive-in movie tonight with one of them."

Jason was silent for a moment. Both of them had grown up moving around so much, and even now Jessica contin-ued the tradition. While Jason was more stationary because of his school and career, like her he was not a fan of small towns. When he had heard that she was planning on stay-ing in Peach Blossom for six weeks while the drama sur-rounding her latest relationship escapades died down, Jason had proclaimed that she would no doubt be bored out of her skull and on a plane to Italy within twenty-four hours. It was amazing how wrong he was.

It was also amazing how much she liked it here. Jessica wasn't just realizing it now. It had been a slow trickle of re-alization that, even without Vini and her gloriously heated kisses, Peach Blossom was actually a really nice town. Sure, there wasn't a ton of things to do. But everyone had been welcoming and made Jessica feel like she was one of them and not some weird transplant who had shown up to buy their land and kick them off it.

"You're going to a drive-in? I didn't even know those existed anymore."

"I'm sure some hipster out there has announced he rein-vented them or something and is charging admission. You could probably find one there if you really tried."

"Probably," Jason conceded. "So who is this mysterious friend who is taking you under their wing? I notice you haven't named them, but I know Mom and Dad have been talking about some mechanic you've been hanging around."

Jessica's heart jumped, and she scowled down at the phone. "They are the biggest gossips, I swear."

"Spill it. Is it serious?"

She swallowed hard at the thought of being serious about anyone. She was seriously having a good time. Wasn't that enough? "Her name is Vini, and she's just a friend. She rescued me from the side of the highway when the shitty rental car I got crapped out on me."

Jason made a noise that had her rolling her eyes. Anytime Jessica mentioned another woman, Jason immediately went to trying to figure out a way to get her to settle down with them. It probably had a lot to do with him being in a relationship with his high-school sweetheart. The two of them had been a thing since before Jessica even realized she liked women. It would be so cute if it wasn't so damn nauseating.

"And besides, I don't do long-distance relationships. You know that."

"Sadly, I do. Despite your commitment issues, the fact that you are getting out there and making friends is a good thing. Maybe small-town life will rub off on you and you'll want to stay forever."

Jessica almost gagged at the thought of being in one place forever. She was a rolling stone. A whisper on the breeze. She could not be held down.

Not that she even wanted to.

"But don't do it until after we all meet up in Italy," he continued. "I'm bringing Alicia, and I plan to propose to her while we are all there. I want to make it special."

"It's about time," she exclaimed. "The poor girl has been hanging on by a thread for damn near a decade."

"Seriously? I would have married her years ago, but she refused. What is it with all the women in my life being so stubborn?"

Jessica chuckled. "You're just lucky, I guess." She glanced at the clock. "Listen, I have to go get ready for tonight. Just because I'm out in the sticks doesn't mean I plan to dress like it."

Jason's laughter rang out over the line. "I find it very interesting that you are insisting this isn't a date, and yet you're getting ready hours before you leave. But hey, what do I know. Let me know how it goes."

He hung up before Jessica could counter his comment, leaving her staring in silence at the phone. He didn't know what he was talking about. Jessica always got ready ahead of time. She liked to put extra thought into her outfits no matter who was going to see. So what if she normally didn't get ready this early? There was nothing else to do.

She tossed the phone onto the bed and stood up. Jason was just being a little shit. There was nothing wrong with pampering yourself, and that was just what Jessica planned to do.

"I can't believe these exist."

Vini laughed as she pulled the truck into the lot. Jessica's mouth hung open as she looked at the number of cars already parked in a row. The sun was just starting to set, and yet there were at least twenty cars, some packed with families as they waited for the show to begin. Seeing it all was like traveling back in time, and Jessica couldn't help but be charmed by it all.

"How often do you come to these?"

Vini shrugged. "Whenever I can. They do this every weekend during the summer and once a month when the weather gets cooler. I missed it last month, though."

Jessica followed Vini's lead, hopping out of the truck once they had parked and then heading to where there were a couple tents with delicious smells wafting out of them. She had expected to see the usual fare of popcorn and oversize boxes of candy, but Jessica was surprised that there was so much more offered.

"Get whatever you want," Vini said, waving her hand at the menu in front of them. "Seriously. My treat since this is your first time and everything."

"Really?" Jessica wanted to be sure before she went hog wild. "I might legitimately get one of everything, and I'm not trying to blow your budget."

Vini's hand landed softly on Jessica's back before she guided her forward. "For the privilege of popping your drive-in cherry, I will gladly pay as much as is needed."

Jessica laughed and gave Vini a soft sock on the arm before letting go of her worries. When it was their turn to order, Jessica ordered a bucket of homemade kettle corn popcorn, a pulled pork baked potato and cotton candy.

"You want anything to wash all that down with?" Vini's amusement was clear, but Jessica only nodded enthusiastically and happily ordered a sweet tea lemonade. Vini's smile widened with each item that filled her hands, and when they settled back in the truck, the previous space that had been between them had shrunk until Jessica could feel Vini's warmth on the other side of their food trays.

The setting sun bathed the car in deep oranges and gorgeous reds painting intricate patterns across Vini's skin. It made Jessica want to reach out and touch to see if the colors felt different beneath the whirls of her fingertips. They weren't alone here, though. They were parked in the middle with cars surrounding them on all sides. There was a good bit of space between each vehicle, enough to be able to open doors without fear of dinging someone's car, but it still meant that if they decided to take advantage of being so close, they would be spotted easily. Peach Blossom seemed open, but Jessica knew that not everywhere was like that, and she wasn't trying to get caught out among an angry group in a town she didn't live in.

Still, as the sky darkened and the movie screen lit up, she shifted over until they were nearly thigh to thigh. Vini didn't make any acknowledgment of the dwindling space, her eyes glued straight ahead as previews danced across the screen. When everything but the popcorn had been eaten, and the trays discarded on the dashboard, Jessica found herself pressed tight with Vini heating a line down her side. They shared the single tub of popcorn, and though Jessica's attention was mostly on the screen, it shifted each time she felt their fingers brush with only the slippery butter between them.

This feels like a date. The thought was unexpected, but really it shouldn't have been. By anyone else's standards, this would have been a date. They were at a movie, Vini had bought dinner, and though they hadn't held hands or kissed, there was definitely a feeling of *something* in the air. If Jessica were looking for that kind of thing, this would have been perfect. But she wasn't. This was just Vini being nice and showing her around. She probably had heard that

Ava and Grace were planning to spend the night together and decided to be nice and invite Jessica out so she wouldn't be lonely. It was a sweet gesture and one that even Jessica could appreciate.

"So what did you think?" Vini asked. They were close, closer than Jessica remembered. Vini's face was cloaked in darkness with only the light from the end credits illuminating her. Her eyes were wide and her lips so easily within reach. All Jessica had to do was lean forward a few inches and they would be kissing. Her lips tingled at just the thought of it, and she knew they needed to go somewhere fast before she kissed Vini in clear view of anyone. She didn't doubt that there were probably people from Peach Blossom here, so that would be the opposite of keeping things under wraps.

Jessica licked her lips and tried to ignore the heat that flared in her when she saw Vini's gaze follow that motion. "It was great. I wish I had known about these sooner." Her enthusiasm wasn't fake. The whole concept was amazing, especially with the food that they had gotten. There was no way she would be able to go to a regular movie theater with its lackluster dining fare ever again. "My parents would have loved it too. They always complain that going to the movies these days is so annoying because of people texting or talking. Relaxing in the car is the way to go."

Vini's smile was dazzling even in the dark. "Yeah? You should bring them out here sometime. You could even get in touch with the city and see if they would put on one of your mom's old movies."

Jessica cackled. "She would absolutely die if I did that. Other than during premieres, Mom rarely watches anything she's been in. She says it weirds her out."

"I can see how it would," Vini replied. They sat quietly for a moment, gazes still caught and the air between them growing heavier with tension. It wasn't too late, but Jessica wasn't hungry. They had gotten another bucket of popcorn after the first one ran out, so she was really and truly stuffed. Going to get coffee was probably out as well. It was the weekend, but she doubted there would be too many places still open at this time of night. It was a drawback of small towns.

"I should get you home," Vini said, breaking the quiet they had fallen into. She looked away before scooting over to her side of the car. Jessica frowned as disappointment swept through her. She knew Vini was probably right, but she wasn't ready to end the night just yet. Not without at least acknowledging the tension that had steadily grown each time their fingers tangled or their eyes met.

"Or, if you don't think anyone will miss you, we could go back to mine?"

Vini paused, her bottom lip pulled between her teeth, and Jessica gave her time. She didn't want to be pushy. If Vini wanted to go home, that was totally fine. They would probably see one another sometime later that week as it was. But time was steadily ticking away, heralding Jessica's departure from the town, and as much as she looked forward to making her way back to a larger city, she couldn't deny that something inside of her was saddened by it. Peach

Blossom truly had been wonderful so far, and as much shit as Jessica talked when it came to small towns, she couldn't have chosen a better one.

"If you need to get home, that's oka—"

"Yeah," Vini cut her off. She started the car, and Jessica tried to keep the smile from falling from her face. "I mean, yeah, let's go back to yours."

Vini was smiling again, but this time there was something heavy there that called to Jessica. It was the same look that Vini had been giving her lately when they were alone, away from prying eyes. It was a look that had Jessica wanting to find a dark room to pull her into so they could fall together with no cares. It made her stomach clench and her pussy tighten. It was want, pure and simple.

Jessica smirked before reaching for her seat belt. "Well, I'm ready when you are."

Thirteen

The night had been a success. Vini was going to go ahead and call it. That didn't mean it was over. Not by a long shot. She hadn't invited Jessica out for any reason other than wanting to show her some of the great things that small-town living had available. Okay, that wasn't totally true. She was hoping that Jessica would be at least slightly impressed. Even Vini knew that drive-in movies were mostly a thing of the past. Peach Blossom was just lucky enough to have one not too far from it. Vini had many fond memories of visiting as a kid, back when things hadn't been so hard or so upside-down. Coming back with someone she was sort of, maybe seeing was a whole new experience.

Sitting in the darkened truck with only a tub of popcorn between them had been a test in patience. Jessica didn't seem to feel it as she munched away on the sweet, salty kernels that always made Vini's mouth water when she caught a whiff of them, but Vini had been more than a little aware of the tension rising between them. There had been a few looks shared between them and a lot of accidental finger brushes when they reached for the same kernel. If not for the reminder of the crowd of people around them, Vini would never have made it past the damn previews. As it was, when Jessica suggested taking things back to her suite at the bed and breakfast, it had taken everything in Vini to respond casually instead of immediately throwing the car into Drive and leaving a trail of spitting gravel in their wake.

Now though, she was almost nervous as she followed Jessica down the familiar hallway to her room. The air was quiet with only the occasional sound drifting in from outside the windows. No one had been up front to greet them, which wasn't unusual but was helpful for keeping the knowledge of Jessica and her relationship on a need-to-know basis. When the door snicked shut behind her, Vini took a deep breath before turning to face Jessica.

The light was soft, making her tawny skin glow. Jessica's eyes were half-lidded, giving her a sultry look that had Vini swallowing hard. How this woman had fallen into her lap was anyone's guess. Vini still pinched herself on the daily to make sure she wasn't perpetually walking around in a dream.

"Did you want—"

"Trust me when I say *I want*," Jessica interrupted. Vini's cheeks heated, and she kicked herself at her own internal responses to Jessica. She was grown, damn it. She shouldn't still be responding like it was her first crush. Deciding to take charge before her nerves got the best of her, Vini covered the scant few inches that had been between them. When she reached for Jessica, there was no resistance.

They fell together, mouths already parted to allow entry. Jessica kissed like a storm, her touch laying claim until Vini's mouth tingled. Somehow her hands had found purchase on Jessica's hips, tightening and releasing with each hit of arousal. Vini's tongue slid forward, tangling with Jessica's as she pressed and until there was nowhere left to go and Jessica's back hit the closed door. It was thrilling to have her so close, and Vini wanted to take advantage of every moment.

"You are so fucking beautiful." She hadn't meant to sound so breathless, but it was the truth. Jessica was almost hard to look at. Sometimes Vini found herself without words when she caught sight of Jessica, her head thrown back in laughter. Reaching up, Vini cupped Jessica's cheeks between her palms, enjoying their warmth. She brushed a thumb over Jessica's kiss-swollen lips. They were lush and pillow-soft. It was damn near impossible to do anything but lean back in for more kisses.

Hands roamed and groans passed back and forth between their lips. Vini groaned when Jessica's hands gripped her shirt but took a step back to free herself from it. That triggered something, and before she could pause to think, they both moved frantically, stripping their clothes before falling back against the door together.

Skin-to-skin was exactly where Vini wanted to be, and she moaned when their nipples brushed, hard with arousal and standing up in twin peaks. She kissed a fiery trail down

Jessica's neck, savoring each burst of salty flavor on her tongue. Hands cupped the back of her head, not guiding but simply holding steady, and Vini smiled. She continued her path, placing sucking kisses in the valley between Jessica's breasts before sliding over and covering one nipple with her lips. She tongued the dips and ridges around, loving the texture and flavor that was uniquely Jessica. The groans that rained from above her spurred her on, and she sucked lightly before switching to treat its twin with the same fervor.

"Jesus, Vini," Jessica panted out. Her back arched up pushing into Vini's touches until Vini wasn't sure if she was even still touching the door. "So good, baby."

Vini shivered at the pet name before starting downward again. She had a destination, and her mouth watered just thinking about it. When she reached the dark curly hairs that framed Jessica's cunt, she paused and took a deep breath. Food had nothing on the distinct flavor that could only be found in one place. She gripped under one of Jessica's legs and guided it up to her shoulder so she could have more space to work.

"Shouldn't we move to the bed?" Jessica huffed out. She went with Vini's motions resting the back of her knee on Vini's shoulder. "I don't want to fall on you."

"I would consider it a well-deserved death," Vini replied, eyes zeroing in on the lips she wanted to kiss next. They were plump and inviting, and she gladly went to them. The heat of them on her tongue was almost as good as the taste. Almost.

Jessica's loud moan almost made Vini rethink them being against the door. It was thick but probably not thick enough to muffle all the noises if someone walked by. The thought of that shouldn't have been as thrilling as it was, and yet it had Vini pressing harder and faster, plunging her tongue between those heated lips as she chased the source of Jessica. She wanted to hear more of that siren song.

"Fuck. Deeper." One of Jessica's hands curled around Vini's shoulder, gripping it tightly as the other pulled her face closer. Everything was wet and hot as Jessica's hips began to lift with each flick of Vini's tongue. "Your tongue…" Her head leaned back against the door with a thump.

With a smirk, Vini leaned back, enjoying the shudder that followed her tongue sliding between those moist folds. "My tongue what?"

"Oh, God, why are you stopping?" Jessica's voice cracked on the last word, and Vini had to fight hard not to laugh at how offended she sounded.

"You said 'my tongue.' My tongue what?"

Jessica stared down at her for a beat before her lips quirked up. "Are you fishing for compliments when your face is buried between my thighs?"

Vini shrugged. "Now seems as good a time as any." She leaned forward with faux nonchalance and huffed a breath over Jessica's lips. This close, she could see the sheen of spit and slick on them, and she licked her lips to chase the flavor of them from her lips.

Jessica chuckled before trailing fingers over Vini's still-sticky lips. Vini chased them, sucking a couple into her mouth and giving them the same treatment she planned to continue once Jessica told her what she wanted to hear.

"I can't believe I thought you were sweet and innocent."

Vini snickered. She didn't know what the hell about her screamed *sweet and innocent*, but she made a note to make sure to do the opposite of whatever it was. "I don't know what to tell you. Now, about my tongue."

"You have a one-track mind."

"Only when I really want something, and right now, I want you to finish your sentence so I can go back to finishing you."

Jessica groaned and leaned her head back against the door again before looking back down at Vini. "Your tongue is fucking amazing. That's what I was going to say, okay? It makes me lose my fucking mind, and then I can't think about anything else but having more of it." She cocked her head to the side. "Now, can you please get back to tongue-fucking me so I can come? I've been ready for this since you started licking popcorn butter from your goddamn fingers."

With a soft cough to hide her laughter, Vini made good on her promise to get back to it now that she knew exactly what Jessica thought about her tongue. In the back of her mind, she knew she was going to exploit that information somehow, but right now, she just wanted to see Jessica fall apart.

"Yes," Jessica hissed loudly, her grip on Vini's shoulder tightening. Vini didn't plan to waste any more time. She hiked Jessica's leg higher spreading her more for her ravenous mouth. Her tongue curled and darted back between

Jessica's lips loving the way the walls of her cunt trembled. She put everything into it, bobbing her head forward and adding a couple fingers to push Jessica higher.

The nails scraping her back was her warning before Jessica slapped a hand against the door behind her and arched again. Vini didn't let up, thrusting her tongue and fingers forward until Jessica's body jerked and she gently pushed Vini's head away.

"Jesus. I think I saw heaven." Jessica smiled wide as her eyes continued to flutter. Vini helped guide her leg back to the floor. They were nowhere near done, but moving to the bed probably was for the best. Vini didn't intend to let up until both of them were exhausted.

She stood up and smiled when Jessica reached for her. They kissed again, Jessica's tongue darting forward as if chasing the taste of herself from Vini's lips. Vini opened and let her taste her fill as she guided them toward the bed. They fell upon it, legs tangling until Vini wasn't sure where she ended and Jessica began. When fingers brushed against the short hairs that framed her own pussy, Vini groaned.

"You didn't think we were done, did you?" Jessica asked, eyes hooded as she gazed at Vini. The heat there matched the blazing inferno that was Vini's own arousal.

"Not at all. Just wanted to give you a chance to catch your breath," Vini teased. When those fingers continued on brushing lightly against the hood of her clitoris, Vini didn't even try to hold in her gasp. She was engorged and sensitive with the need to be touched. She let Jessica push her leg up until Vini was spread enough for her hand to move.

"How sweet of you." Jessica's voice was like syrup, but her smirk had Vini snorting in amusement.

"There goes that word again," she replied before leaning in for more kisses. "I don't think that word fits me at all."

"Oh, I don't know," Jessica started. She slid a finger between the lips of Vini's pussy before Vini could reply. Her finger moved easily with Vini's own juices that had gathered as she enjoyed eating Jessica out. "I'm pretty sure there's something sweet about you."

Vini watched enraptured as Jessica lifted her hand, her finger glistening with Vini's slick. Without waiting for her to speak, Jessica drew that finger into her mouth, sucking the fluid off and pulling her finger out again with a loud pop.

"You taste sweet to me."

"Fuck." There were no other words left to say. Vini reached, then pulled Jessica to her and captured that wicked mouth again. She knew she should probably get home, but all thoughts of the time vanished under heated groans that tumbled from their lips.

Fourteen

"Ava is coming to dinner tonight."

"Uh-huh," Jessica hummed in acknowledgment. She didn't understand why Grace thought this was news. She and Ava had been attached at the hip from what Jessica had seen over the past four weeks. It was why she spent so much time at the bed and breakfast and had extended her stay there through the next two weeks. It had only taken her one time to walk in on some very not-wanted noises to realize that staying elsewhere was the better plan.

"Jess."

She looked up. Grace was frowning for reasons unknown to Jessica. They had been having a good afternoon since Grace got back from work. Jessica had been out of school for years, but even she could recognize the excitement that loomed before a long holiday. Christmas was right around the corner, and Jessica was a little sad that she wouldn't be here to see how Peach Blossom did Christmas. The lack of snow notwithstanding, there would probably be some sort of parade or outdoor thing the town put on. At least, that's what Hallmark always portrayed.

"Jessica."

"Grace." Jessica stared, not sure what her friend was trying to say. Her silence seemed loaded but with what, Jessica didn't have the first clue. "Girl, can you just let me know exactly what you're trying to say, because these hints are not working."

Grace sighed before she crossed her arms. "You know exactly what I'm trying to say."

"I promise you I don't."

"What I'm trying to tell you is that I don't know how long I can keep this secret from Ava when you guys are going to be in the same room. I don't understand why you don't just stop since it's not serious with Vini. Right?"

Something about that sentence didn't sit right with Jessica. She normally would have no problem agreeing, and things between her and Vini weren't serious. If Grace had been this gung ho about her not sleeping with anyone else, Jessica wouldn't have a problem. It had happened once or twice over the course of their friendship on both of their ends. Jessica was quick with the *hell, no*s if Grace showed interest in someone who Jessica felt had bad energy. Grace might have been a little less firm about it, but she was never shy about giving her own two cents' even if she said it a little nicer. She usually had great reasons too, and she never objected frivolously, which is why Jessica didn't understand why she was so resistant now.

The idea of not talking to Vini, or seeing her in those overalls that were too damn cute they should be illegal, didn't sit well in Jessica's soul. She didn't get it. It shouldn't have been a problem to call it quits and go on about her day. But she was known for going with her gut, and right now her gut was saying *hell to the no.*

"Sure, things aren't serious between Vini and me like they are with you and Ava, but I'd still like to think that she and I are friends. Is that not a good thing to be friends with someone just because their sister or brother might object?"

"I'm not saying you and Vini can't be friends. I'm just saying do you guys really have to have sex?"

Jessica snorted. "Well, no, but the sex is fire. I mean the things that girl can do with her tongue…"

Grace held up her hands and shook her head. "I don't need to know any details. Like ever. Seriously. I will throw you out."

Jessica chuckled. "Don't worry. I have no desire to share anything with you if you promise the same."

"You don't have to worry about that," Grace said. "But seriously, Jess, I don't like hiding things from Ava. Especially since this involves her sister."

Jessica could understand that, but at the same time was this really any of Ava's business? "You're not hiding anything, considering it doesn't have to do with you. I can absolutely get along with Ava while she's here. I got along with her before, didn't I?" She hadn't actually been around Ava more than a day or two over the past few weeks, but she survived Thanksgiving with the whole Williams clan. She could handle this.

Grace nodded although her expression made it clear she was still thinking about the situationship Jessica and Vini had stumbled into. While Jessica was curious what was going through her mind, she was also growing tired of this entire conversation. She was ready to move on, and she wanted Grace to move on too so Jessica could stop mulling over why this whole thing with Vini felt so much different than her previous friends-with-benefits relationships.

"Like I said, I'll be gone in two weeks anyway, and then you won't have to worry about it. We set an expiration date for a reason, okay? No one's getting hurt, and no one's feelings are getting smashed on."

Grace still didn't seem convinced, but when the doorbell rang, she thankfully dropped the subject and Jessica got ready to play the part of the benevolent best friend. What she wasn't ready for was the Williams clan to troop into the house already in the midst of what seemed to be a spectacular argument. Ava led the group, hand-in-hand with Grace as she looked over her shoulder. When Vini walked into the room, Jessica's eyes immediately saw no one else. Even with her frown, Vini was cute. Jessica almost wondered why she looked so murderous until the argument continued and she realized what was going on.

"Please tell me you guys haven't been arguing since you left the house," Grace said, giving all of them a knowing smile. Jessica was trying to continue playing the good friend who definitely didn't egg on drama, but she was very intrigued. She knew how sibling arguments could get between her and Jason, and she always enjoyed observing someone else's when she had no stake in the game.

"Now, do you really want me to lie to you?" Ava asked with a smile even Jessica could admit was charming. It certainly had an effect on Grace who folded faster than a lawn chair.

"Not really."

"Then, I won't answer that question." Jessica smiled when Grace and Ava kissed briefly, both of them looking like they would have liked to extend that display further. Blessedly, it was Dani that spoke up, keeping things from becoming awkward.

"Well, now that we are all nauseous at your disgusting display of love to remind us that we are all tragically single, can we get back to the matter at hand?"

Ava rolled her eyes, but she and Grace separated. "Fine. It would be good to have some impartial parties weigh in on this."

Vini scowled, and Jessica wondered what that was all about. It wasn't like she had never seen Vini frown before, but usually that was reserved for shitty customers or Aiden's off-key singing. When Dani and Ava turned to look at her, Jessica almost jerked to attention. Having those piercing dark brown eyes collectively looking her way was like doing a presentation in front of a class and realizing you were naked. It wasn't often that she felt like that, but something about these Williams sisters kept throwing her off.

"Wait. Are you two asking for my opinion?" When they nodded, Jessica felt even more on edge. "Okay...well, I would kind of need to know what the whole thing is about before I can weigh in on it."

"Seems fair," Ava replied. "It's about Vini. She—"

"I love how y'all talk about me like I'm not standing right here," Vini cut in. "This is really unnecessary. I hope you know that."

Vini's declarations did nothing to placate Jessica's curiosity. In fact, now she absolutely needed to know what was going on; whether she gave her own two cents' about it or not was irrelevant.

"What's unnecessary?"

Vini's mouth opened and closed a few times before she crossed her arms with a huff. Jessica raised an eyebrow at the uncharacteristic behavior. Now she had to get to the bottom of things to satisfy her own burning curiosity.

"Please, continue. I would be happy to offer my opinion."

Dani laughed, and Jessica was surprised to see even Ava fighting not to smile. Dani walked over to the couch and sat down beside Jessica, wrapping an arm around her shoulders as if they were old buddies. Jessica went with it. Whatever was going on seemed to have something to do with Vini and her surly expression.

"Well, someone is having a birthday next week and refuses to tell us what she wants to do." Dani spoke softly as if no one else were aware of just what they were talking about.

"Oh, is that so?" Jessica gave Vini a pointed look. She

remembered asking Vini about her age, but it had slipped her mind that she would be turning a year older so soon. Birthdays were something Jessica took great pleasure in celebrating regardless of if it were her own or someone else's. If she had remembered, she would have started preparations already to do something, no matter how small.

"Yes, it seems like our pint-size princess is under the impression that if she doesn't acknowledge that her birthday is coming, we'll just let it quietly squeak on by," Ava added. She and Grace stood over by the large window, and with Dani and Jessica on the couch, it left Vini standing in the middle of the room facing off against everyone like she was on trial.

"Well, that's not happening," Jessica blurted out before she could stop herself. She saw Grace raise an eyebrow, but she didn't say anything when Dani and Ava agreed. She quickly continued before they got the wrong idea. "Birthdays are meant to be celebrated."

"Exactly," Dani agreed. "Plus, it will be so much better if you just go ahead and tell us what you want to do instead of just begrudgingly going through with it and then complaining about it for weeks after."

"Let's not have a repeat of last year," Ava piped up. Jessica wanted to ask about what happened last year, but she figured pushing for something this year was a much better use of time.

"I don't know why we have to plan anything anyway," Vini bit out finally. "It's not like it's a big birthday. I'm turning twenty-three. There are no big milestones at twenty-three that need attention drawn to them."

"Oh, I disagree," Jessica countered. "Every birthday is one more year that you've survived on this big hunk of rock. I think your sisters are wise to plan something for you if you don't want to celebrate yourself. In fact, I would happily help."

Vini's scowl lessened, but she didn't look completely convinced.

"See? I knew it would be a good idea to come over to Grace's," Dani replied, smiling widely. She shook Jessica's shoulder. "I think that planning something big is a perfect idea. You're usually so wrapped up in work at the shop that I think it would be a good idea for you to chill out for a night or two. Act your age and all that."

Vini rolled her eyes again before dropping into the oversize chair. "Something big like what? There aren't big things out here."

"Why not go up to Atlanta?" Jessica said before she could second-guess herself. "I've got some contacts that owe me favors. We could have a nice dinner and then maybe do some dancing."

"That does sound like fun," Grace said, speaking up for the first time since her living room was invaded. She looked down at Ava. "It's been a while since we had a night out like that too."

"Great. Leave it all to me, then." Jessica stood up and clapped her hands together gleefully. She was excited, not just to do something for Vini but also to feel like she was useful again in some way. She wasn't bored per se in Peach Blossom, but other than finishing out some contracted audiobook work, she didn't have much to do, and it left her feeling a bit out of step. This would give her a chance to show Vini a little of her world.

It was time for Vini to be impressed.

Fifteen

Vini wasn't sure how the hell she had gotten herself into this situation, but she was pretty sure pinching her own arm wouldn't do anything but annoy her. The few times she had spared a thought about her birthday, she had considered maybe inviting Jessica over to the house and having dinner. Thanksgiving had turned out well enough, so it wouldn't have been too much of a stretch. She had thought Dani and even Ava would probably okay it, given how little Vini usually cared about celebrating her birthday. But this... this was so far out of the realm of what she had imagined.

Being sandwiched between Dani and Jessica while Grace drove them all to Atlanta had not been on her bingo card, that's for damn sure. It was taking everything in her not to slap her own cheek on the off chance that she was stuck in one of those dreams that felt too real.

"So how do you know about this place, Jessica?" Dani asked, leaning over Vini's lap. Vini tried to lean back and away. The move only served to move her farther into Jessica's heat, which created a whole other problem that she also couldn't address without drawing attention to herself.

"I lived in Atlanta for a few months while I was working on a show." That piqued Vini's interest. Even when they were alone, Jessica didn't talk a lot about the work she did. Vini knew she had to have some type of money to afford a suite for this long at the bed and breakfast and be able to spend so much time at the shop. She had listened in on Jessica and her dad's conversation at Thanksgiving, but as always, Vini was still ravenous for more information.

"I didn't know that," Dani continued. "I thought this was your first visit to the South."

Jessica shook her head and leaned into Vini. "I've been to Atlanta a couple times, but never anywhere else. I mean, everyone jokes about Florida being its own entity."

"Which is true," Ava spoke up. She turned around in her seat. "Florida is its own breed of Southern that has nothing to do with us. I mean, falling iguanas. Enough said."

Vini choked back a laugh but didn't dispute Ava's words. She sucked in a sudden breath when Jessica shifted again, pushing the side of her leg more fully against Vini's. They had decided to take Dani's SUV, though Dani had no desire to drive. Grace had thankfully offered to pilot, and Ava of course took the front seat beside her.

"So what kind of job were you doing?" Dani asked, bringing back the former conversation. "Do you act, like your mom?"

Jessica shook her head. "Not really. I never really wanted

to go into that, though I have done a few commercials and had some minor roles when I was younger. I like voice-acting much better. Less about me and more about the words I'm recording and the feelings I can convey in my voice."

"That's cool." Vini found herself speaking up before she decided what to say, but when those dark brown eyes looked over at her and the sides crinkled up with Jessica's smile, she couldn't regret it.

They talked casually as the miles ticked by. Traffic grew heavier as they made their way closer to the city limits. It was a Friday and rush hour, which meant they weren't going anywhere fast. Vini had slowly relaxed the longer they were all cooped up together until she finally got used to the hot line of Jessica's shoulder against her own. It was a comforting heat, even if she wasn't able to wrap herself in it like she wanted.

"Anyone want to stop for a snack before we check in?" Grace asked as she navigated through the stop-and-go traffic. "Dinner reservations aren't until eight, so there is plenty of time."

"If not, there's a restaurant and bar in the hotel as well," Jessica chimed in. "I figured if it got too cold for us to want to go out later, we could at least go downstairs and celebrate."

"Good thinking," Dani agreed.

They continued on, pulling into the hotel valet before making their way inside. The hotel was gorgeous, and Vini's breath caught as they passed through glass doors trimmed in gold. The lobby was massive with dark marble floors and mirrors galore that made it appear even bigger. The lights were dim, creating a mysterious atmosphere, and Vini could see the restaurant and bar were similar in ambience. She was glad she had a few clothes that might work for the night. Even so, she worried that she would be slightly underdressed.

Jessica strode up to the reception desk. Seeing her like this, confident among the opulence around them, had Vini's mouth going dry. She was used to Jessica coming in and taking up all the air in the room, but this was on another level. For the first time, Vini truly started to understand the idea that she and Jessica lived very different lives.

"All right, I got us three rooms," Jessica said holding up the key cards. She handed one to Grace and winked. "I figured you and Ava would probably want some alone time."

Grace bit her lip, but her smile looked pleased. Vini smirked at Ava's expression. Neither one of them were the slightest bit subtle when it came to exactly what would be going down in that room. She could only hope that the walls were thick and the soundproofing was on point.

"I couldn't get all the rooms on the same floor unfortunately," Jessica continued as she led them to the hallway where Vini presumed the elevators were. They hadn't brought much luggage, just a small tote each. Tonight, they had dinner planned together and then out for drinks. Saturday, they would do some shopping and catch an Atlanta Hawks game. How Jessica had managed to get tickets to that on such short notice was anyone's guess. Vini had been more than a little excited with that particular reveal. She had thrown her caution to the wind, dragging Jessica to the office in the shop to thank her properly, and they had barely made it out of the shop's back room before another customer came in.

"It'll be fine," Ava said. Vini was happy to see her warming to Jessica, though she doubted Ava would be so welcoming if she knew what Vini and Jessica had been getting up to when all eyes were turned elsewhere. She knew she should just come clean and tell Ava to mind her business, but something still gave her pause. She knew things could get awkward given Jessica's status as Grace's friend, but the two of them had been sleeping together for weeks and everything was fine. Jessica was leaving soon, and Vini didn't want to spend what little time they had left dealing with an overprotective Ava. When she dug her heels in about something, it was hard to get her to deviate.

They piled into the elevator, and Vini found herself breathing deeply to calm the rapid pulse of her heart. The elevator doors opened, and Ava and Grace said their brief goodbyes. Vini shifted slightly when the doors shut, and the elevator continued its way up. The silence that fell was thick, and she glanced over at Jessica. She swallowed hard when Dani's gaze met hers. There was an awareness there that Vini didn't quite know what to do with. She held her breath when the elevator slowed to a stop.

"Which of the rooms has only one bed?" Dani asked.

Jessica frowned. "Both only have a king bed. Did you want—"

"Great." Dani grabbed one of the keys from Jessica's hand.

"You crazy kids have fun. I'll see you downstairs in a few." Before Vini could say anything, Dani flitted through the doors and disappeared down the hall. Shock had Vini frozen in place, and it wasn't until the doors closed that she realized what Dani had implied.

"So…" Jessica said. When their eyes met, Vini saw that Jessica was just as surprised as her. "That means she knows, right? She wouldn't have said something like that if she didn't know. Right?"

Vini slowly nodded. When the elevator stopped again and the doors opened, she followed Jessica out. They made their way down the hall, neither of them saying a word. The lush carpet beneath their shoes muffled any sounds, and the dim light from downstairs was the same here in the corridor. Jessica stopped in front of a room door and unlocked it. She didn't hesitate to walk in, but Vini had to take a deep breath before she followed.

The room was painted in the maroon colors of sunset streaking deep reds across the wall. It was a cozy space with a modern bathroom to the side with a tub that had Vini itching to hop into it. She ignored the thoughts of what else could happen in a tub of that size and continued into the room. The bed was large with fluffy pillows and a thick white duvet.

Wait. One bed?

She had been so caught-up in how nice the place was, that she hadn't logged that the first time. It somehow didn't translate in her brain that Jessica had said each room had a king. *One* king. There was only one bed. For the two of them to sleep in. Dani knew this and she'd still pushed them together.

"If it's a problem, I can always call down and see about getting us a room with two queens." Vini looked up from the temptation that was the king in front of her. Jessica was setting her things down on the desk across from the bed. If it were anyone else, Vini would say she was relaxed, but she could see the subtle tension in Jessica's shoulders. How had she gotten to the point that she could read the other woman's body language? Was she really that tuned-in?

That was a question that she dismissed as soon as she thought it. She had been tuned-in to Jessica since the first moment they touched. She could tell Jessica was waiting for her reaction, and for that reason Vini forced herself to relax. If not for her sisters being around, she wouldn't even have hesitated at the chance to be alone with Jessica in a place as gorgeous as this. Then, with a start, she realized her sisters weren't around. They weren't even on the same floor. She wondered if that was a lucky coincidence or careful planning. The thought that Jessica might have wanted her alone filled her with warmth.

"Did you plan this?" Vini had to know. She set her bag beside the bed and walked over to where Jessica was still standing in front of the desk. When she was close enough to touch, she did. There was no one to hide from here. No one to see Vini's need to be as close to Jessica as possible. She watched the reflection of them in the mirror. When Jessica finally looked up, her gaze locked with Vini's.

"Yes. Though, I had thought you and Dani would room together."

Vini nodded, pleased with Jessica's answer. She leaned up on her toes and brushed her lips over Jessica's cloth-covered shoulder. "So you hadn't planned on inviting me back to your room after everyone was asleep?"

Jessica blinked slowly before turning. Vini released her hips but curled her arms around Jessica's waist once they were standing face-to-face. Light slanted over Jessica's eyes, making them seem to burn with an inner fire Vini wanted to warm herself on.

"I might have had a few thoughts about it," she admitted before wrapping her arms around Vini's shoulders and drawing her closer. The air seemed to shimmer with tension, and Vini took a few deep breaths. She still didn't understand how Jessica could affect her so quickly. Just the thought of her planning things in the hopes that she and Vini could have time together was enough to have her fanning herself. Vini knew they probably shouldn't risk it, even with Dani seemingly giving her stamp of approval. There was still Ava to worry about. But with every second that ticked by with Jessica so close, Vini's cares about getting caught fell away.

"Would you have been open to them?"

Vini dipped her gaze down as Jessica's lips formed her words. Her own tingled at the thought of pressing against them again. She wanted, and she had no desire to ignore that. Not when they could give in so freely.

"I'd be open to a lot of things," Vini admitted. "All you have to do is ask."

She let herself fall into the sweet tug of surrender. Their mouths met briefly in fluttering kisses that left her aching for more. She could feel Jessica smile and met her next kiss with a grin of her own.

Sixteen

"This place is bougie as hell." Vini coughed lightly to cover up her laugh. She had to admit that Dani wasn't wrong, though.

They had spent a couple hours relaxing, or in Vini and Jessica's and probably Grace and Ava's case, breaking in the bed, before they met up downstairs and headed to the restaurant. The Creamery sounded like a posh ice cream shop, so Vini was surprised when they walked in and were escorted to a private booth. Low light seemed to be the theme, though the candles on the table gave the evening a pleasantly warm glow.

"I know, right?" Jessica replied as they got seated. She was on the other side of Dani which was too far in Vini's opinion. But Dani and Ava had gotten in flanking Vini. She hadn't said anything, thinking it would probably seem weird if she was concerned about sitting next to Jessica but not Grace. The taste of Jessica on her tongue and the memory of Jessica's fingers buried deep between her thighs would have to tide her over until they could once again retreat to the safety of their room.

"It seems super stuck-up, but the food is amazing, and they don't scam you on the portions. It's the right mix of grown and sexy, and the drinks are to die for." Vini tried to focus more on Jessica's words and less on the plunging neckline of dress she was wearing.

They had all dressed to impress that evening. Vini had been happy to see that her leather pants still fit, and when she had held up two different blouses, Jessica had immediately told her to go with the emerald green one to pull the whole look together. When they had met the others, she and Grace had chuckled at how similar their styles were. The biggest differences were color, with Grace's blouse and the heels she sported being navy blue. Vini had never been one for uncomfortable footwear and had settled on her nice loafers to pull the outfit together. All in all, she thought she looked pretty good. The look Jessica had given her before they left the room seemed to confirm it, and for a moment Vini wondered if they would even make it to dinner. It had been tempting even with the knowledge that their absence would have caused questions that might have shone a light on their relationship.

Not that they had one. They were having sex. Sure, she and Jessica also talked, so sex wasn't the only thing they did, but calling it a *relationship* implied longevity, and Jessica was only around for so much longer. If Vini occasionally wondered if Jessica was out meeting other people when she wasn't with her at the shop, that was no one's business but her own. It also wasn't anyone's business how the thought of that had Vini's chest tightening.

"A toast." Dani's voice pulled Vini out of her musings, and she looked around the table. Glasses were raised so she did the same with her own. Dani looked over at her. "To our dearest Lavenia. Happiest of birthdays."

"My government name? Really?" Vini rolled her eyes when Dani snickered, but she clinked glasses anyway and smiled. "Thanks y'all."

Grace smiled and nodded at her. "Happy birthday, Vini. Thanks for letting us celebrate it with you."

Vini shook her head. "This was all you guys. I would have been just as happy having a small dinner at home, but I'm grateful." She looked over at Jessica. "And thank you, Jessica, for putting this all together."

Jessica didn't say anything, but she raised her glass with a small smile. Vini had to fight to shift her gaze away before she got light-headed. She leaned her glass over the table, and they clinked glasses right before the waiter arrived with their appetizers.

Vini had trusted that Jessica knew how to pick a place with good food, and now it was confirmed and then some. Cooking wasn't Vini's main talent. She could throw a meal together if needed, but she was never going to be a master of the culinary arts nor did she want to. But the food they had started off great and finished out amazing. They had settled on a couple appetizers including the deviled eggs with hot honey bacon, calamari that she was surprised to find she enjoyed and artichokes that made her rethink say-ing she didn't like artichokes. By the time the entrées came, they had split a second and third bottle of wine, and Vini was feeling relaxed as she enjoyed her steak and listened raptly to Jessica's story.

"So I go into the shop and the lady at the counter is talk-ing so much shit about me. I think she assumed I didn't speak any Korean."

"Does that happen often?" Ava asked. Vini had been pleased to see the two of them in the same space without an ounce of tension in the air. "You said you still had fam-ily in Korea, right?"

Jessica nodded. "I do. Most of my mom's side of the family is there, and we visit a couple times a year when my parents have time." Her smile went soft, and Vini al-most melted into her plate. "And not really. I mean, it's like here. Sometimes you have people who will talk so much shit about you, thinking you can't speak English. All you can do is laugh at them."

"Did you tell her you understood her?" Dani asked. Grace let out a huff of laughter before chiming in.

"Oh, I'm sure she did." She looked up at Jessica with a wide grin. "You did, didn't you?"

Jessica's smile went wicked, and she tossed her thick curly hair back over her shoulder. "You bet your sweet ass I did. I wandered over to the counter, and when she asked me if I needed help, I answered back in Korean. You should have seen her face."

Vini chuckled. She could imagine the scenario clearly,

and she was glad Jessica stood up for herself. Vini hadn't been out of the country yet, but she was hoping to go somewhere soon. She needed to hire a new person before she could up and leave for longer than a couple days, but she was looking forward to eventually getting the shop to that point.

"For the most part, people in Korea correctly assume I'm half Black and half Korean and will switch to speaking Korean to me," Jessica finished before taking a sip of her wine. "My mom was adamant about me and my brother Jason learning Korean. I hated having to spend my Saturday mornings in language classes when I was younger, but I'm glad now that she made us do it."

"I didn't know you had a brother," Dani said leaning her chin on her hand as she looked at Jessica. "Are you two twins? Is he hot?"

Jessica fake-gagged, and Vini giggled. "He's older than me," Jessica replied. "We look enough alike that I know we're related, but I definitely got all the sexy in the family. He's a goblin."

Everyone laughed, and Vini doubted that. She couldn't imagine anyone related to Jessica being anything other than wildly attractive. Vini had known Jessica had a brother, but she hadn't seen pictures of him so she couldn't be sure. She wondered if he knew about her. It made her stomach flip uncomfortably at the thought of him not having any idea she existed. But that wasn't the type of question you asked someone you were only sleeping with, right? She wasn't sure, but it didn't feel like she was allowed to give a damn if Jessica's family didn't know Vini existed. She and Jessica weren't in a relationship. Hell, they weren't even dating. Not really.

"He's actually meeting me in Atlanta in a couple weeks so we can fly out together to see our parents. They decided to hang out in Italy for the spring before Mom has a few auditions back on the West Coast."

"Italy," Ava said her voice full of barely hidden envy. Vini knew Ava had spent a few months in Europe when she was in undergrad, and clearly she wanted to make a return trip. "I visited Sicily once and always said I would go back one day."

"You should," Jessica insisted. "I can give you a few places to think about when you plan your next trip. They are super nice and not too pricy, since I prefer to spend my money on food and train trips to as many places as I can while I'm there."

Ava smiled widely, and Vini knew her night had been made. "That would be great."

They finished dinner and ordered one of each dessert to try. When the last bite of warm bread pudding was finally consumed, Vini dropped her spoon and leaned back against her seat. She was stuffed. The pants that had been such a good idea before the feast they had just devoured were now digging into her hips. Still, she couldn't deny that every bite was worth the slight discomfort.

"I can't eat another bite," Grace said tossing down her spoon and leaning back in a similar pose. She leaned her head back and closed her eyes. Ava stared unashamedly, her eyes trained on Grace's neck as if it were the next thing she planned on devouring, and that was more than Vini needed to see. Clearly it was time to wrap things up.

"I don't know about y'all, but if I am going to have the energy for our plans tomorrow plus going dancing, I need to turn in now." The others agreed with Vini, and Jessica signaled for the check. When the waiter brought it over and placed it on the table, Jessica snatched it up before anyone else could. Vini frowned.

"How much is it?"

Jessica opened the book before smiling and closing it again. "Don't worry about it. I've got it all covered."

Vini protested, but nothing she said seemed to work. Jessica signed the receipt, and when the waiter came back, she handed it to him with a smile. Vini was grateful, but she didn't want Jessica spending so much money on a place that obviously charged a pretty penny. She tried speaking up again, but Jessica waved her off.

"You have been a saint with trying to help me understand the difference between a brake pad and period pad, so I think you deserve a bit of spoiling," she replied. Ava barked out a harsh laugh, and beside Vini, Dani slapped her hand over her mouth but not before a snort of laughter leaked out. Vini wanted to scowl, but she couldn't deny the warmth in her chest at the thought that Jessica wanted to spoil her, especially not when everyone else at the table seemed to agree that Vini wasn't allowed to pay.

"Fine," she eventually conceded. "But I am buying you lunch tomorrow. You arranged all of this, and you paid for dinner. It wouldn't be right if you paid for everything."

Jessica shrugged. "It's your show, birthday girl. If it will make you happy, I'll let you pay for lunch and breakfast tomorrow."

Dani frowned. "Isn't breakfast free at the hotel?"

Jessica grinned. "Oops."

Vini knew she had been had, and she let a slight smile twist her lips as everyone else chuckled. It was fine. She knew exactly how to pay Jessica back, and once they got to their room, she wasted no time in pushing the issue.

"Damn, babe, I thought it was oysters that got people horny, not calamari."

Vini chuckled against the warm skin of Jessica's neck before placing a sucking kiss over the rush of blood she could feel right below the surface. Jessica's groan was subsonic, sending vibrations across her skin and into Vini everywhere that they touched. It had been easy to get back to their room without Ava being the wiser about the room situation. It helped that not only were Ava and Grace the first ones to get off the elevator, but also that Ava had been so noticeably distracted. Vini knew she and Jessica weren't the only ones feeling the effects of the night.

With a push, Vini backed Jessica up until she fell back on the bed. Her dress hiked up, baring more of her thighs and making Vini hungry in an entirely different way. Her shoes and shirt had been discarded already at the door. Jessica's shoes had been tossed as well, and Vini slid her hand over bare skin, following her desires until she was comfortably between Jessica's parted thighs.

"If you could only see yourself," Vini whispered. She

rested her palms on Jessica's thighs, sliding them up and taking the fabric of her dress with them. There was no hesitation, only desire, as she ran fingers over the lace-front panties that separated her from Jessica's pussy. She wanted them removed even if they were beautiful against the warm tan of Jessica's skin. She slid a finger under them brushing against wiry hairs and damp skin. Heat wafted up warming her face and beckoning her closer. Ignoring the pull wasn't even an option.

The groan that heralded the first touch of her tongue against Jessica's pussy lips was enough to send Vini's confidence soaring. It was a bone-deep sound that seemed to rumble up from everywhere and nowhere. Fingers slid over her cheeks guiding Vini in. She didn't need the encouragement, but she did enjoy it. She had no desire to leave before they were both satisfied, and for Vini, that meant having the essence of that flavor embedded into every memory. She flicked her tongue, pushing back the moist lips and aiming for that pulsing hole. Jessica's scent grew stronger, and her wetness seemed to multiply with each drag of Vini's tongue.

"Didn't even let me get my clothes off," Jessica panted. Her voice was soft, and the strain of arousal threaded through each word.

Vini looked up. She knew her expression was heated and probably more than a little smug. She was right where she wanted to be: between the thighs that beckoned to her all night. If not for being at the table with her family, she might have launched herself at Jessica, public be damned.

"In." Jessica's hands gripped pulling Vini in further. "God, deeper. Want to feel you deeper inside."

Not one to deny a plea as pretty as that, Vini brought a hand up and reached forward, letting two of her fingers join her thrusting tongue. She enjoyed the give and stretch as Jessica's cunt shaped itself around her. Her walls were slick and so very tempting, and she let herself taste more. Hips raised up, and Vini went with the motion, adding another finger when she pulled her tongue away. She let her fingers take over, thrusting them forward and twisting them just to feel Jessica shiver. Her thighs were spread wide-open now with her knees resting on the bed. It left her bared to Vini's ravenous gaze.

Vini looked up Jessica's body, loving the way her breasts moved with each panting breath. When her gaze met Jessica's, the heat there was enough to set the room aflame. Jessica's cheeks were fully flushed, the red matching the deep rouge of her kiss-bitten lips. Vini twisted her fingers just to see the way Jessica took it, throwing her head back and letting out a soft moan at the ceiling. It was enough to have Vini going in for the kill.

She leaned back in, this time paying attention to the engorged bundle of nerves that she had so far ignored. Jessica's breath hitched when she brushed the tip of her nose against it, and Vini chuckled. Gently, she flicked her tongue, her mind reeling when she felt the jerk of Jessica's body. A switch flipped, and suddenly all she could think about was making Jessica come right now.

Like a woman possessed, Vini wrapped her lips around

Jessica's clit, careful to keep her teeth away. She matched her motion with a hard thrust of her fingers, picking up speed each time she pushed in. Slick sounds and hitching moans weaved a symphony through the air, and Vini was barely hanging on just from the knowledge that it was her making Jessica light up this way. It was Vini who had Jessica crying out her release, and it was Vini who Jessica reached for, crushing Vini against her chest as she sought out her own flavor on Vini's tongue.

"Fuck," Jessica said as she slowed her breathing. They were forehead-to-forehead, both sharing heated breaths as the scent of sex settled over them. "I hope you don't think we're done."

Vini smiled as a pulse of arousal flooded through her. "I would expect nothing less."

Seventeen

"You're staring."

Jessica looked over at Grace with an unamused expression. The morning had been going so well, but leave it to Grace to rain on her fucking parade. Last night's fuck fest with Vini had her waking up over the moon. As soon as Jessica had opened her eyes, she knew the day was going to be a good one. When Vini joined her for a very handsy shower, that fact was pretty much confirmed. They had barely managed to stop at one orgasm, and if not for having made plans to meet everyone in the lobby to head out for a brunch tour, Jessica would have tumbled Vini back on the bed, wet or not.

"I'm not staring," Jessica replied, not wanting to give Grace any ammunition, regardless of how right she was. Jessica was staring, but Grace didn't need to call her out about it, especially not when Vini and her sisters were only a few paces in front of them. "Don't make it weird. The morning has been going so well."

Grace's snort was unnecessary, but being that Jessica was an adult, she opted to do the mature thing and ignore it. As good as the day had been so far, it wasn't without its struggles. Mainly the way she could hardly think about anything other than Vini. She had gotten Jessica bent into positions she had only ever dreamed of. It was an amazing and terrifying revelation that the past few weeks had been the best sex she had ever had in her life. And for the first time, she was realizing that she was going to miss Vini in her bed.

Jessica had had plenty of sex in her lifetime, but never had someone gotten to know her body so well so quickly. Is this how all small-town, corn-fed lesbians got down? Because if so, she might need to visit a few more small towns to check them out. Or…maybe she just needed to see whether or not it would be possible to stop in Peach Blossom maybe once or twice a year just to catch up and get her back blown out. Or maybe she could offer to fly Vini out once or twice a year to wherever Jessica was for a little impromptu vacation.

People did that all the time, right? Sure, Vini had her business, but surely she took time off sometimes. Jessica wasn't too proud to admit that not only was the sex fire but she had also been enjoying the enthusiasm that Vini showcased outside of the bedroom. Their conversations were always lively, especially once Vini had gotten over her shyness. She could argue with Jessica about everything from the price of gold to whether or not macaroni and cheese was an entrée or a side dish. Jessica's assumption that their conversations would taper off into nothing after a week or two had been so wrong it was almost laughable. They may have come from different worlds, but they were getting along just fine. It was part of the reason Jessica had taken charge for Vini's birthday.

She had come up with an entire brunch plan that allowed her to show Vini another side of life. Specifically, Jessica's life. All the places on their stop were places Jessica enjoyed and that she thought Vini and her sisters would as well. She had spent a few hours asking Dani what they liked and asking Grace to ask Ava what she liked as well. It had taken some searching, but Jessica had done well judging by the Williams sisters' responses. The wide smiles on all their faces had Jessica calling the morning a great success.

"Everyone is getting along and having fun."

Grace held her hands up. "I never said they weren't. And I'm not trying to make it weird."

Jessica rolled her eyes. "It sure seems that way, considering you're on my ass about staring at Vini."

Grace put her hands down with a crooked smile. "So you were staring."

She opened her mouth before closing it again. Jessica narrowed her eyes as she realized Grace had gotten her to admit to it. "Maybe I was. Is that illegal now?"

"Of course not. I'm just saying, the way you're staring at Vini with hearts in your eyes is making it obvious what's going on between you two. You said you guys were only in a situationship, but from where I'm standing, it looks like a whole lot of something else."

Jessica grabbed Grace's arm and stopped her in the middle of the sidewalk. When Ava, Dani and Vini turned to look at them, Jessica smiled and waved them off. "Grace and I just need to have a quick conversation about the plans for later on. You guys go on ahead, and we'll meet you at the next location."

Ava raised an eyebrow as she looked between Grace and Jessica. Vini at first appeared to have no expression, but slowly Jessica began to see concern bleed into her gaze. There were questions there too, questions that she had to ignore. Dani, on the other hand, just looked amused by whatever was going on. Jessica still couldn't get a lock on Dani's thoughts or feeling about a lot of things, and it was slightly unnerving. The woman should join the circuit with that poker face. Jessica had no doubt she would be able to fake people out with the best of them.

She was also surprised by the fact that it didn't seem like Dani was interested in snitching on her and Vini. Jessica didn't doubt that Ava would have flown off the handle if she knew just how close Jessica and Vini had been getting, so clearly she was still in the dark. She could understand Ava's desire to keep Vini from getting hurt. Vini was an awesome person, and Jessica was self-aware enough to know she wasn't girlfriend material. Hell, it wasn't like she was trying to be. But she just couldn't figure out what Dani was getting from keeping her mouth closed about it. If she were anyone else, Jessica would've assumed that she wanted something, and yet no demands had been made. If she had come to Jessica with some blackmail-type shit in the beginning, Jessica would have never let things go as far as they had. Now though, she could admit she would give in to Dani's demands, had she made any. Jessica was woman enough to admit that.

This whole family was confusing in ways Jessica had never experienced. Things with Jason and her had always been so straightforward. It's not that he had never acted protective of her, but they were enough years apart that they had hardly overlapped even in school. When Dani, Ava and Vini turned and continued down the sidewalk without Jessica and Grace, Jessica waited for a moment before speaking up again. She didn't want any part of their conversation to be overheard.

"Okay. Explain to me exactly what your problem is. It's been weeks, and we already hashed this whole thing out once before."

Grace jerked her arm out of Jessica's hold. "My problem is that you're still doing the same shit. You and Vini are out galivanting, thinking you're being all stealthy, but I know what's going on, and it's eating away at me to keep this from Ava."

Jessica groaned and looked to the sky as if for guidance. Surely someone was up there who could help her deal with Grace and her misguided conscience.

"First of all, this thing with Vini and me is not your secret to tell. I don't know why I have to say this all over again when we've already had this discussion." She couldn't believe they were still having the same conversation after all this time. "Second, it's not like we're having sex right in front of you. We're discreet about it."

"That's not the point, Jess."

"Yes, it is," Jessica insisted. "I'm not telling you to lie to Ava, because none of this is her business to begin with. Plus I'm only here for like another week. Then you won't have to worry about keeping anything secret."

Grace didn't look convinced, and Jessica was quickly coming to the tail end of her patience. "Has Vini seemed off at all to you?"

"What do you mean?"

"I mean, has she seemed upset or emotional?" Jessica waited for Grace's answer while also thinking on that question herself. She couldn't call to mind anytime Vini had seemed unwilling or apprehensive about their situationship beyond acting shifty at Dani's recent acknowledgment.

"No," Grace answered finally. "But that doesn't mean it's a good idea."

Grace's sigh sounded way more put-out than it had any right to, and Jessica readied herself for another round of arguments. Grace really could be stubborn as hell when she got an idea stuck in her damn head. It normally didn't bother Jessica, but then again, normally Grace's relentlessness had nothing to do with her.

Finally, Grace threw up her hands. "You know what? Fine. I won't worry about hurt feelings anymore. You're right. You're both grown-ass women, so when this explodes in both your faces it's on you."

Before Jessica could say anything else, Grace turned and

stomped her way down the sidewalk. Jessica would have found it amusing if not for their conversation. She watched Grace for a moment before letting out a heavy sigh and following in her footsteps.

"What was all that earlier?"

Jessica sat down on the bed, sighing at finally getting off her feet. The afternoon had been a lot of fun, but it had been a while since she walked that much. After her third mimosa, she had switched to water, so she wasn't feeling as intoxicated as she probably would be if she had attempted to keep up with Ava and Dani. Grace had practically had to carry Ava the last few blocks back to the hotel. It would have been amusing if not for the previous conversation between her and Grace still rolling around in Jessica's brain. The pushback she was getting from Grace had her rethinking things.

"Grace is still giving me shit about us."

Vini frowned. "Us?"

"You know," Jessica replied before making a crude gesture. "*Us.* She's upset about it because of Ava. I keep telling her it's no one's business but ours and to just let it go."

Vini nodded slowly. Her expression went thoughtful, and Jessica was left wondering what was percolating in that pretty head of hers. All of a sudden, a thought stopped her in her tracks. What if Vini thought Grace was right? What if she decided they shouldn't see each other anymore? It wasn't something Jessica had even entertained until now. It wasn't a pleasant thought. Far from it.

"You don't think she's right, do you?"

Silence, uncomfortable and still, met her words. Vini didn't say anything, and so Jessica waited. She had no idea what she would say if Vini agreed with Grace.

"No."

The amount of relief Jessica felt from that one word should have given her pause. Instead, she smiled feeling lighter than before when Vini smiled back. She didn't stop to think about how worried she was that Vini might have called for an end to this thing they had stumbled into. She hadn't, and that was all that mattered. A knock at the door had them breaking gazes, and Jessica frowned when she looked over at it.

"Did you call for room service?"

"No," Vini replied shaking her head. "I didn't even know that was an option."

"Of course it is. It's your birthday." Jessica walked to the door and peeked out of the peephole. "It's Dani. I wonder what she wants."

When Jessica opened the door, Dani sauntered in like she owned the place. She looked around for a moment, and Jessica and Vini exchanged looks.

"Dani, what do you want?"

"Can't a girl come say hello to her baby sister?" Dani asked with a wide smile. Jessica didn't trust that innocent expression for a second, and by the look on Vini's face she didn't either.

"If all you wanted was to say hi, you could've just sent me a text. So again I ask, what do you want?"

"You're no fun." Dani rolled her eyes before continuing. "I just wanted to come say hello and let you know that Ava and Grace are keeping to themselves tonight. They called me and told me Ava is probably not moving from the bed anytime soon."

Jessica raised her eyebrows. "She was pretty sloshed."

Dani laughed. "That is putting it mildly. Sis was passed out when I went by. I almost feel bad for Grace for having to take care of her, but then again, I told Ava to stop after the fourth mimosa, but she didn't want to listen to me. Serves her right."

Jessica snorted but kept most of her thoughts to herself regarding Ava and her drink tolerance. "So what's the plan, then?"

"Well, I plan to meet up with a couple friends who I haven't seen in a while. I don't know what y'all plan to do, but whatever it is, enjoy." Dani gave them a mock salute before turning back to the door. Jessica was going to let her go, but the niggling thoughts in the back of her mind had her reaching out.

"Wait," Jessica said. Dani paused, her hand on the doorknob. "You know about Vini and me, don't you?"

Dani turned with an arched brow. "Do I?"

"Cut the shit, Dani," Vini said.

"You first, little sis." Dani didn't say anything more, but there was something there, a tension that Jessica could feel. When she glanced back at Vini, she knew she was missing something very important, but she couldn't figure out what. It was the kind of wordless conversation that was unique to siblings, and Jessica was on the outside looking in. When Dani finally left, Jessica stared at the door trying to gather her thoughts.

"So that was interesting."

Vini gave her a look. "*Interesting* isn't exactly the word I would use."

"True, but at least we know we have the night free. We can go wild." Vini raised an eyebrow, and Jessica knew exactly where they should go. "In fact, let me make a call."

"Should I be worried?" Vini asked. "I don't know if I like the look of that smile you have on your face. I'm not trying to end up in jail."

Jessica snorted before she grabbed her cell phone. "I'm not sure what you're thinking of, but if handcuffs come into play at any time tonight, it won't be because we're being arrested, that's for sure." Vini's wide-eyed expression set Jessica off into giggles.

Tonight was going to be one to remember. She would make sure of that.

Eighteen

Vini felt silly. She knew Jessica said she looked great before they left the hotel, and she wasn't doubting the honesty of her words, but it didn't make her feel any less like she was at a party she wasn't invited to. She had put on the same tight black pants from the night before and this time paired them with a crimson blouse that she knew looked good against her dark brown skin. But compared to the other people here, she might as well have been wearing a potato sack.

The club Jessica had taken her to wasn't one she had ever heard of even the few times she had gone to Atlanta. It was posh compared to the bars Vini normally frequented, with dark velvet walls and dim lighting. The room seemed to pulse with a deep, heady energy echoed by the moves of the people out on the crowded dance floor. From high in the booth they were in, she could see the mass of people shifting like some massive living creature. Occasionally the strobe lights would wash over them, and Vini could make out features of people, some occasionally locked in an embrace that was definitely not dancing.

"This place is really something."

Jessica laughed. "Isn't it, though? My friend bought this place a few years ago and completely overhauled it. She's doing the same thing to a couple places in Houston." Her smile was wide and so open it was almost childlike as she looked around. "It's kind of amazing that she created all of this from scratch and manages to keep the place full night after night."

Vini could understand how impressive that was. She didn't know the first thing about running a club, but she knew that staying relevant and busy was a struggle no matter the industry. But it was still all a bit much for her. Everything was loud and crowded. She could understand the appeal, but it just didn't really appeal to her. She had never really been the clubbing type and being here now just confirmed it.

"Jessica!"

A new voice came out of the crowd, and by the time Vini turned to greet the newcomer, she was already there sweeping Jessica into a hug that was enthusiastically returned.

"I haven't seen you since that night in Ibiza. When I saw your text, I knew I had to make sure I was in the city to say hi."

Jessica's laughter hit Vini, and she felt her smile slip. She quickly rallied and reached out, the manners her dad had instilled in her finally manifesting. "Nice to meet you. This place is amazing."

"Oh, shit, I'm sorry, Madeline," Jessica said moving back to Vini's side. She placed a hand against the small of Vini's back, and Vini couldn't help but feel a thrill skirt up her spine at Jessica moving back to her side. "This is my good friend Vini. It's her birthday we're out celebrating."

The woman turned to her, and Vini found herself not knowing how to react to Jessica's introduction. She fixed her expression before her face betrayed her thoughts. She had no reason to be upset at only being introduced as a friend. Jessica had made it very clear from the beginning that what they had was not an actual relationship. As much as Vini found herself slowly wishing that their conversations meant more, the reality was that they weren't together. They weren't girlfriends, and they never would be.

She came out of her head in time to see Madeline reach out. "Good to meet you, Vini. Any friend of Jessica is a friend of mine." Vini blinked quickly when she saw Madeline give her an obvious once-over. Did that look mean what she thought it meant? She glanced over at Jessica in time to see her raise her eyebrows.

"Don't even think about it," Jessica said with a sharp smile. Madeline held her hands up and laughed. When Jessica's arm slid around Vini's waist, Vini tried to cover her surprise with a soft cough. "Hands to yourself, woman."

Madeline put said hands on her hips. "I should say the same to you. Really? Both of them?" She shook her head but didn't say more, and Vini wished she had continued. What did she mean *both of them*? Both of who? Vini wasn't sure if she should even ask. She wasn't entirely sure if she wanted to know.

Jessica shook her head but didn't say anything. When Vini glanced at her, she could see a strain in Jessica's smile that hadn't been there before. It didn't help her feel any less out of place with the whole conversation. She looked around, wondering the best way to exit. Jessica must have had the same idea.

"Vini, we should check out the dance floor."

That was not what Vini had in mind when she thought about exiting. Her idea had consisted of getting all the way out and heading back to the hotel, but before she could voice that, she found herself being pulled along past the other tables and toward the mass of gyrating people. Panic sharp and painful welled up in her. Dancing was not something she felt confident about. Hell, she preferred bars for a reason. Whoever thought that all Black people could find the beat had never had the unfortunate experience of watching her try to move. Still, she followed, eyes glued on the soft sway of Jessica's hips. People seemed to part for them as Jessica guided her deeper in until they were surrounded. When she turned, Jessica's lips were parted, and now Vini's gaze was caught again by the desire to delve between them knowing just how good they would feel and taste.

"Why do you look so nervous?"

"I'm not nervous," Vini replied quickly. She looked around hoping that everyone else was too into their partners to pay her any mind. When she looked back at Jessica, she could tell the other woman didn't believe her. She was relieved, though, when Jessica didn't call her on it and instead pulled her closer.

The beat was slow—slower than it had been when they first got to the club. Vini's eyes were wide as Jessica eased her into the heady beat. She almost didn't know what to do with herself but finally raised her arms, resting them on Jessica's shoulders. This was new—being out around other people and not hiding. It was more intoxicating than the slow, gentle grind they seemed to settle into. Vini's eyes never left Jessica's, not caring who was around them or who might be watching.

"See?" Jessica said, her voice barely carrying with the volume of the music. Vini had to lean forward to hear her clearly, which was fine with her. It put them even closer together, and she could almost feel the air from each of Jessica's words. "No reason to be nervous."

"You weren't at my prom." She hadn't meant to say anything, but once the words came, Vini knew she had to let them continue. "I think they decided to go ahead and crown the king and queen just to get me to stop dancing."

Jessica giggled and shook her head. "I'm sure it wasn't that bad." Her hands slowly slid up Vini's back before sliding back down again and settling on her hips. "I didn't even have a prom."

"You didn't?"

"I finished high school in Korea. My school had a lot of festivals, but we didn't do prom. I thought it was a myth until my cousins from Chicago showed me pictures."

Vini smiled. She hoarded each little bit of her life that

Jessica volunteered. "If it makes you feel any better, most proms are overrated. I mean, I had fun because I was with my friends, but I didn't go with a date or anything." Feeling a little emboldened by the fact that they were still swaying together and no one's foot had gotten stomped on, she continued. "For what it's worth, I would have asked you to go to prom with me."

"Yeah?" Jessica's smile widened, and it was like a spotlight had been turned on high. Vini felt almost weightless in the sight of that grin and before she could second-guess herself, she leaned forward, removing the space between them to press her lips against Jessica's.

The kiss was soft and almost hesitant but that didn't last long. Jessica's hands went from resting to gripping Vini's waist, and when Vini parted her lips to suck in a gasp, Jessica's tongue followed. Sucking kisses sent syrupy drops of pleasure sliding down Vini's spine, and she curled her hands over Jessica's shoulders in an effort to pull her even closer. They weren't close enough in her opinion. In fact, what she really wanted was to go back to their room so they could fall together without the barrier of clothes and common decency.

"Can we go?" Vini asked when they briefly parted for air. She didn't move far from her, not wanting to be without those sinful lips pressed to hers.

"Are you not having fun?"

"I am," she insisted before cupping her palm around Jessica's cheek. "But I want to get you out of those clothes and show you how much more fun we could have with just us two."

Jessica blinked slowly. "Jesus," she said breathing out loudly. "I definitely would have gone to prom with you if you asked like that. Let's go."

She pressed one last hard kiss against Vini's lips before grabbing her hand and leading them off the dance floor. It was a bit more difficult getting to the exit, especially when the music's tempo changed again. It took a few stops and starts, but finally they made it out of the crush of people. They were almost at the exit when Jessica's name was called. Vini groaned when Jessica stopped and turned to two women coming toward them.

"I thought that was you," one of the women said. She was a little taller than Vini with lightly tanned skin and almond-shaped eyes. Her hair was pulled back in a tight ponytail that hung over one of her shoulders. Vini tried not to let her eyes drift down at the woman's barely there outfit. The bodysuit was almost painted on, and it had cutouts that showed off more skin than Vini was used to seeing. "Madeline said you were here, but I didn't believe it. I thought you were headed to Italy."

"Patricia." Jessica didn't let go of Vini's hand as she addressed the woman. "I am in a week. Decided to hang out with a friend for a few weeks before shipping back out."

"Oh?" The way Patricia said that had Vini's hackles rising. Arousal warred with the need to just get away, and Vini squeezed Jessica's hand. Patricia looked down at their hands and raised an eyebrow. "Seems like more than just friends. I didn't realize we were getting serious about people after—"

"It's great to see you, Pat, but Vini and I are kind of in the middle of something. I'll reach out when I get back from Italy." With another tug, Jessica guided Vini around the woman and her friend. When they finally found themselves outside, Vini took a deep breath in, enjoying the fresher air and lack of people encroaching on her space. Jessica dropped her hand and reached for her phone. "Fucking hell, some people just can't take a hint."

Thoughts whirled in Vini's mind as she watched Jessica tap on her cell. Who was Patricia to Jessica? What was Madeline hinting about? Did it have anything to do with Ava saying Jessica wasn't relationship material? Vini tried to think back to the conversation they'd had a few weeks ago. She knew there was some kind of scandal that had gone down involving Jessica, but Vini figured that was not her business. Ava had mentioned it didn't have anything to do with cheating, and that was enough for Vini to dismiss it. But now, she was wondering if she should have asked more questions.

When Vini really thought about it, she had never heard about those two women in the entire time she and Jessica had been together. Jessica talked about her family easily enough, especially her brother, Jason. But rarely did she mention anything about friends outside of Grace. And definitely not by name.

"Okay, the Lyft should be here in a couple minutes," Jessica said. She reached back down and threaded her fingers between Vini's, and Vini let her. Her mind was still going a mile a minute, but she was also doing battle with the thought that it didn't matter who those people were. Jessica had made it clear that this was just for fun. After a week, they wouldn't even be on the same continent and the past few weeks would be like a wonderful dream that fades away at the first sign of consciousness. Did she really want to spend the last bit of time worrying herself into a migraine about people she would probably never see again?

"Good." Vini didn't waste time. She pulled Jessica to her, tilting her head up and pressing a firm kiss against Jessica's lips. She didn't want to regret squandering the time they had together.

Jessica's lips moved against hers with no hesitation. Madeline. Patricia. None of those other people mattered. Not now when Jessica was firm and solid in Vini's arms. The only thing that mattered was taking pleasure in the present. A vibration between them had Jessica leaning away. She lifted her phone.

"Car is here." Her eyes crinkled on the sides at her wide smile. "Let's take this to a more private location."

Vini nodded, keeping their hands locked tight as she followed Jessica to the gray Honda that was apparently their ride for the night. She slid into the back seat not bothering to keep any space between them. The driver nodded but said nothing else as they made their way back to the hotel. Vini was almost vibrating with need by the time they pulled up to the entrance, and after getting out, it was her pulling a laughing Jessica along.

"Eager to get in my pants tonight?"

"Among other things," Vini replied not wasting energy playing coy. She jabbed at the button in the elevator and was relieved when no one followed them in. As soon as the doors closed, she pressed Jessica back against the wall, covering her lips once again.

This kiss was desperate as she poured all her feelings into it. Seven days. That's all she had left before her life went back to the once-familiar existence that was before Jessica. It should have been comforting to have no more ambiguity. No more questions. Instead, it was terrifying. Somehow it had only taken five weeks for Jessica to get so thoroughly embedded under Vini's skin that she was no longer sure how to be without it. And worst of all, she couldn't say anything.

When the elevator dinged announcing their floor, Vini pulled back but kept Jessica close with a hand cupping the back of her head. Walking down the hallway was difficult when Vini could hardly make it a few steps before pulling Jessica's lips against hers again. She was surprised Jessica didn't ask about the change. This was not how Vini usually was. She was not this needy, desperate thing, and yet here she was unable to stand the thought of not having Jessica's skin against hers.

"Jesus, Vini." The soft utterance of her name in that heated tone had Vini smiling wickedly. She wanted more of that, over and over, until they fell together exhausted and unable to do anything but sink into the arms of sleep. How they managed to finally get into the room was anyone's guess, but when the door closed behind them, sealing them away from any potential prying eyes, Vini felt the last chains holding back her desire fall away. She surged forward, pressing Jessica against the door and taking control of the kiss again.

Hands wandered, both sets tangling in fabric and causing the occasional strain of a seam or two. When Vini felt nothing but warm skin beneath her fingertips, she knew it was time to get horizontal.

"Come on," she groaned against Jessica's neck her tongue darting out to get another hint of salty skin. She felt the rumble of Jessica's agreement, and they slowly weaved a tangled jumble of limbs to the bed.

The sheets were initially cool to the touch, and Vini smiled when Jessica arched her back away from them. They quickly warmed, though, soaking in the heat pouring off their bodies. Vini bore down, trapping Jessica's writhing form between her and the bed. It was thrilling to be on top of her, thighs between hers with the molten presence of Jessica's pussy lips smearing fragrant slick over her skin. Jessica hadn't been able to keep her hands off Vini when they were getting dressed earlier, but now it was Vini who was in charge.

Jessica's head was tilted back, inviting Vini to press more sucking kisses against the exposed skin. Each one had fingers digging into the skin of Vini's back, and she marveled in being able to affect Jessica so much that she seemingly forgot herself. When Jessica opened her eyes again, Vini raised an eyebrow in challenge.

"Take a picture, it'll last longer."

Vini chuckled at Jessica's snark, now seeing it for the foreplay that it was. She skimmed her hand up Jessica's side. The skin pebbled in the wake of her touch, driving Vini higher with the need to push for more. She wanted Jessica to lose herself to the pleasure so much she forgot her own name. Vini's hand finished its journey at Jessica's flushed cheek. Her skin was silky soft, and Vini couldn't help running her thumb across lush lips that just begged to be plundered again.

"I just might," Vini replied finally. "Don't tempt me."

She wasn't lying. Taking a snapshot of Jessica like this— laid out with her cheeks stained with red, her lips slick and swollen from their kisses and her chest heaving with each breath was an image Vini wanted to burn into her brain.

"If I could," Vini continued, "I would."

Jessica smirked before wrapping a leg around Vini's waist. "Sounds kinky. I'll think about it."

Vini chuckled and shook her head. She paused for a moment as she stared down at Jessica. When Jessica noticed her attention, she turned her head, an inquisitive expression sliding over her features. Vini knew she should say something, but she was caught in the admiration of where she was, how she got here and who she was with. The weekend was almost over, and yet she never wanted it to end. Reality meant going back to the norm, and the norm was not having Jessica with her.

"Vin?" Jessica said softly. Her hand cupped Vini's cheek, and Vini closed her eyes before leaning into that touch. The frenetic energy from before had somehow shifted and morphed into this soft thing that covered Vini like the most comfortable blanket. It made her sigh in contentment. When she opened her eyes, Jessica was still watching her, lips now turned up in a sweet smile that made Vini's fingers itch to trace. She had been joking about taking a picture earlier, but she was even more tempted now just so she could capture the look on Jessica's face.

"Thank you."

"For what?" Jessica tilted her head, her eyes falling half-closed when Vini nipped at her thumb before drawing it into her mouth. Vini hummed at the taste that was all Jessica. She shivered when the thumb brushed softly over her bottom lip.

"For tonight. For this weekend." *For everything.* She kept that last part quiet. It didn't seem the type of thing to say to someone you were only casually seeing.

Jessica shrugged. "Of course. You deserved to celebrate your birthday. Everyone does."

"I know," Vini conceded, feeling ridiculous for giving voice to the thoughts that had been swirling around in her head. She was clearly making a big deal out of nothing. Jessica was only being nice. She probably would have done the same thing for any of her friends, and here Vini was acting like it was some grand emotional gesture. Jessica was outspoken about a lot of things. Vini doubted she would keep it quiet if she did have those types of feelings.

"I know," Vini said again. She kissed Jessica's palm before shaking off her thoughts. She needed to get back the momentum that they'd had when they first fell into bed together. "And I am so going to reward you for it."

Jessica chuckled before drawing Vini's lips back down to hers.

Nineteen

The chill in the air matched the chill in Jessica's skin. She pulled the blanket around her shoulders to ward against the cold. It had been two days since they returned from Atlanta, and the weather had decided that it was time to get serious about it being winter. It wasn't that Jessica had never lived somewhere with an actual winter, but it had been a while. She and her parents tended to flee toward warmth, and Jason lived in SoCal. Winter wasn't a thing any of them did on a whim. Cold weather was something they planned out, so this abrupt dip into below-fifty-degree weather was enough to have Jessica's teeth chattering. It made her wish for warm kisses under even-warmer sheets.

"What are you doing sitting out here by yourself?"

Jessica looked up when Grace came out onto the porch. She was decked out in a thin jacket, but that was it. It made Jessica colder just looking at her and the lack of covering.

"Aren't you cold? Shouldn't you have more on than just that jacket?"

Grace shrugged and gave her a lopsided smile. "It'll be back in the sixties by the afternoon. Trust me. We're still early in winter for it to stay cold for long."

"This weather doesn't make any fucking sense."

"That's Georgia for you." Grace gestured to her car. "I'm headed to work. You sure you're going to be okay being in the house all day?"

Jessica smiled. "Aw, you worried about little old me?"

"Always," Grace replied with a shake of her head. "I'm sorry I couldn't take yesterday or today off. Testing days are usually a no-go unless your arm falls off or you vomit up your spleen or something. Robert would blow a brain cell if I called out."

Jessica waved off her excuse. She was fine. She didn't need a babysitter to get through the day. "Go and mold young minds, Obi-Wan. I can entertain myself well enough." Grace chuckled but nodded. When she got to the bottom step, she paused and turned back to Jessica.

"Maybe you should go visit Vini."

That had Jessica raising an eyebrow. This was certainly a change compared to the last few conversations that had to do with the mini mechanic. "Whoa. What is this? You're encouraging me to fraternize with the enemy?"

Grace rolled her eyes. "Vini isn't the enemy. I just fig-ured since we had a good weekend with no drama, maybe things are fine."

"It's about time you saw it my way," Jessica snarked. She

smiled when Grace rolled her eyes again. "Somehow, I'm enjoying this whole freezing-for-the-Southern-morning aesthetic. I'm going to sit out here for a little while longer."

Grace nodded. She gave Jessica one final wave before getting into her car and making her way down the driveway. Jessica watched until her car was out of sight before leaning back against the back of the couch she was lounging in. She wasn't lying about enjoying the aesthetic. The sun was slowly lifting over the tree line, gradually lighting the sky. Over the past five weeks, Jessica had come to enjoy the slow passage of time that was moving from morning to afternoon. It was weird to think that when she'd first got to Peach Blossom, she had been so worried that she wouldn't find enough to do here. Now that her visit was winding down, she almost didn't want to leave. She knew that was mostly due to one person.

"Fuck," she groaned, leaning her head back. It wasn't that she had never thought about Vini before, but now it was like she was all Jessica thought about. Her hands. Her voice. Her laugh.

Her smile.

Jessica stood up, barely managing to catch the blanket before it fell to her feet. She had planned on spending more time relaxing, but that seemed to be the worst plan now. She only had so many days left, and being alone for them seemed to be the worst plan by far. She wanted to spend it with Vini, and there was nothing wrong with that. Hell, Grace had just practically given her blessing. Jessica would be a fool to let that go to waste.

Now that Jessica had made her mind up about what she was going to do, nerves she hadn't known existed set in. She went through the motions of showering and deciding what to wear. In front of the mirror, she put one outfit in front of her before switching to the next, a frown marring her features. *It shouldn't be this difficult*, she thought to herself. It's just Vini. They had been hanging out for the past five weeks, so why was she making it weird now? With a moan she threw the skirt and shirt in her hands onto the bed before digging back in her suitcase for a comfortable pair of jeans and a sweater. She didn't doubt that Grace was right that it would be warm by the time the afternoon hit, so she put a camisole underneath. That way, if it got too warm, she could pull the sweater off and tie it around her waist. She pulled her hair back away from her face, turning her head before letting it drop back down over her shoulders.

"Oh my God, this is ridiculous," she hissed at herself. Vini never seemed to care what Jessica was wearing. In fact, the only thing she seemed to really care about was how quickly she could get Jessica out of her clothes. It was that thought that finally brought a smile to her face, and Jessica quickly braided her hair, securing it with a band before grabbing her purse and heading out the door.

It had been a couple hours since Grace left, but the temperature had already risen a few degrees. Jessica rolled her sleeves up before getting into the car. She hadn't mentioned to Vini about coming by the shop, but she figured the morning was probably not too busy. Just in case, she decided to stop at the diner in town and grab a couple of breakfasts to go, if only to bribe Aiden into making himself scarce for an hour or so if they weren't too busy.

Driving through town put a smile on Jessica's face like it always did. Peach Blossom really was an amazingly quaint town that, for its small population, still offered a fair bit. She had enjoyed wandering the aisles of Blank Pages Bookshop and sitting outside with a cup of coffee as she watched people go about their daily lives. It was almost more enjoyable than people-watching when she visited Jason in Los Angeles. There, people seemed to hustle and bustle from one place to the next, but here in Peach Blossom, people meandered as if just enjoying the fresh air and the lack of traffic. She could understand why some people wanted to make this place their home.

She parked her car, not bothering to lock it as she walked toward the diner. It was relatively empty, though that was to be expected for a Tuesday morning after the prework breakfast rush. Jessica decided to grab her own bite to eat and was quickly shown to a small table.

"It's been a while since we've seen you in here."

Jessica smiled up at Thomas, the owner of the diner. The first time she had come in, he had been her waiter, and when she'd mentioned being from out of town, they had gotten to talking. He wasn't the type to be overly chatty, but all the same Jessica appreciated the few conversations they'd had over the weeks, especially since he was also not originally from Peach Blossom.

"We just got back from Atlanta a couple days ago," Jes–

sica said before picking up the menu. "We went to celebrate Vini's birthday."

Thomas nodded. "Oh, that's right. I remember Brad saying something about Ava going up to Atlanta. If not for him coaching over the weekend, he probably would have convinced me to join you guys."

"That would have been a lot of fun, actually. Don't you still have a restaurant up in Atlanta?"

Thomas nodded. "I have a couple still up there, but I don't plan on going back anytime soon. My sister is running them for now, so I only go back and help out maybe once or twice a year. Plus I much prefer the slower pace of living down here in Peach Blossom. The traffic getting into town and heading home is incomparable."

Jessica knew exactly what he meant. The traffic in Atlanta had been horrendous no matter which direction they were headed. Even though they had left in the afternoon on a Sunday, there was still traffic backed up until they got past Peachtree City. She should be used to that kind of traffic, given she and her parents used to live in Seoul. But with the public transportation there, a car wasn't always necessary. Even though most of her extended family didn't live in Seoul, her parents maintained a condo in Gangnam that was free whenever they didn't have vacation renters.

"Are you getting this for here, or are you planning on getting it to go?"

"I plan on grabbing a bite for myself, and then I'll get a couple plates to go for Vini and Aiden. She promised to

look at my car one more time before I head back up to Atlanta to drop it off."

Thomas nodded before taking her order. A small smile
and a cup of coffee later and Jessica let herself relax back
into the booth. She wished she had brought a book with her
until she remembered she had downloaded a couple books
on her phone. She took her time enjoying her breakfast of
scrambled eggs, thick-cut bacon with a maple glaze and
the fluffiest Belgian waffle she'd had ever had. The first
time she had tasted it, she swore she saw the face of God.
Then again, it might have just been the culinary wizard
behind the kitchen door. You could fault the South for a
lot of things, but you couldn't fault them for some damn
good cooking.

The morning passed easily enough, and when it started
bleeding into early afternoon, Jessica grabbed the to-go
boxes and paid her bill before heading out the door. She
waved one more time to Thomas just in case she didn't have
time to stop back into the diner before she left on Saturday. She had already gotten his contact information and was
looking forward to being able to keep in touch with him.
She told herself it wasn't to keep a link with Vini, but at this
point even she didn't truly believe those words.

She slowly drove back through town heading in the direction of Vini's shop. The people and cars thinned out
until she was the only one on the road leading to that part
of town. Before long, she found herself pulling into the
shop. She swallowed hard against the lump that appeared
suddenly in her throat and tried to push away unhelpful

thoughts as she parked and got out. When she pushed open the door to the lobby, neither Vini nor Aiden were anywhere to be found. She called out looking around the corner to the back room.

"Vini? Aiden? You guys here?"

Rustling from the back room reached her, and then Aiden popped his head around a corner. His familiar cheeky grin lifted Jessica's spirits, and she marveled at how his golden-retriever energy was so potent that it picked her up without her even thinking about it.

"Why are you always hiding out in the back room?" Jessica asked as she placed the food bag on the counter. "I swear I have only seen you working on a car like once."

Aiden shrugged before his head turned up like he was sniffing the air. He looked so much like a curious dog right then that Jessica didn't even try to hide her giggling. She shook the bag at him.

"What's wrong? Did you not eat a good, hearty breakfast before coming to work?"

Aiden snorted before reaching for the bag. Jessica had no desire to tease him further and gladly let him pick up the sack so he could inspect what was inside. He groaned when the scent of bacon wafted up from the bag, so potent that even Jessica found her mouth watering again, even though she had already eaten.

"Are you sure you have to leave?" Aiden asked as he pulled out the two containers. He glanced at them before taking the one marked for him. It wasn't the first time Jessica had brought them food, so she knew exactly what he and Vini liked to get from Thomas's diner. "I know you have zero knowledge of cars, but we could train you."

"Why are you volunteering my shop for tutoring?"

Jessica turned, and Vini came in from the garage area. Jessica hadn't seen her out there when she pulled up, but there had been a few cars blocking her view, and with Vini's petite stature, she could have easily been eclipsed by one or all of them. When she saw Jessica, she paused so briefly that if Jessica hadn't been paying close attention, she wouldn't have noticed. As it was, she did notice, and she wondered what that was all about. Jessica tried to think back to whether she done anything to cause such a reaction with Vini. They had texted here and there since coming back from Atlanta, but this was the first time she had seen her since being dropped off. Jessica decided to go with it and pretend like everything was just fine.

"I thought I would bring you guys something to eat in case you hadn't already," Jessica said. "I know I missed breakfast, but I figured a good brunch couldn't hurt."

Vini nodded. "True. I didn't have breakfast this morning, so this is more than a little helpful." She glanced up at Jessica from beneath long eyelashes, and Jessica tried to pretend she hadn't lost her breath from that one look alone. The way Aiden smirked, she knew she wasn't particularly successful.

"Well, you know me. I live to serve," Jessica said, trying to stall for time while she attempted to reboot her damn brain. It wasn't fair for anyone to look that cute while wearing grease-stained overalls. "It seems like you guys are busy, so feel free to tell me to leave."

Aiden pointed at Vini. "You should probably stay and help that one get out of whatever funk she's fallen into. I thought getting out of town for her birthday this past weekend would have made her more agreeable, but she's been super grumpy."

"Anyone would be grumpy when they had to deal with your incessant off-key singing all morning," Vini shot back, giving Aiden a sharp smile.

"Hey, my singing is delightful." Jessica had to cover her mouth with her hand to keep the giggles in. She had heard Aiden's singing and readily agreed with Vini's assessment of it. She contemplated recording his singing to use as her alarm. If anything would shock her ass awake, it would be an unfortunately sharp rendition of whatever song Aiden was enamored with at the time. "Anyway, thanks for the food. Good luck with this one."

Aiden gave her a quick salute before grabbing his food and heading to the back room. Jessica watched him go for a moment before turning to Vini. "Well, I was going to suggest us going into your office so you would have privacy and time to eat. But since he's back there, maybe it's better if we just stay up here."

Vini nodded. "True. We could always eat out back."

Jessica tilted her head in confusion. "I thought there was nowhere to sit back there."

Vini shrugged before gesturing toward the back door. "I might have added a picnic table back there so we could have a little bit more privacy." She glanced up again, looking bashful, in a way she hadn't since that first week they met. "But we don't have to. We can always chill at the table in here if you want. Did you already have something?"

Jessica nodded. "Yeah, I decided to relax in the diner and talk with Thomas for a little while. I just wanted to bring you and Aiden some food." That wasn't completely true. Jessica wanted to see Vini again. She needed to take advantage of every moment possible for the next four days to get her fill of this place before she had to watch it fade away in her rearview mirror. "But if you have a picnic table back there, then absolutely, let's sit."

Vini gave her a crooked smile, the one that always made Jessica feel a little drunk. "What are you going to do, sit there and watch me eat?"

This time, Jessica answered with a sharp smile of her own. "Watching you eat is one of my favorite things to do." She knew Vini meant it in a different way than she did, but when Vini's eyes darkened with heat, Jessica knew she understood exactly what she'd meant. It was the truth. Vini was more than a little talented when it came to her eating technique, and just the thought of it left Jessica clenching her thighs with arousal.

"If I didn't have three cars to get out by the end of the day, I would give you a reminder of just how good I am." Jessica didn't have to be told to follow Vini out the door. She went more than a little willingly, her eyes glued on the way Vini's ass looked in her overalls. If she were a weaker woman, she wouldn't have been able to resist reaching out and touching.

Jessica sat across from Vini, unable to keep her eyes from

doing anything but following every movement as she un-boxed her food and took a first bite. When Vini's eyes fluttered, Jessica laughed knowing that she was milking her reaction just to get a rise out of Jessica. "You are something else."

Vini didn't reply as she dug more into her food. Normally Jessica would feel the need to fill the silence with words, no matter what the words were. And yet for some reason in the here and now with Vini across from her and only the sounds of birds chirping in the background, she was okay with not speaking. It reminded her of when she would walk into a room and see her parents sitting together quietly on the sofa, not conversing yet somehow soaking up one another's company. She had always found it strange before and would speak as soon as she came into the room, but now she understood. There was no need to say anything just to hear the sound of her own voice. The silence was not uncomfortable. In fact, it was quite the opposite. Vini seemed to feel the same way as she continued digging into her breakfast, not uttering another word until only a single strip of bacon remained.

"Do you want the last slice?" Vini asked looking up. She picked up the bacon between her fingers and held it out to Jessica. The scent drew Jessica in, but instead of taking the bacon from Vini with her own fingers, she leaned forward letting part of it rest on her lips before sliding it into her mouth and taking a bite. She hadn't planned the action, and yet she couldn't deny that she enjoyed the reaction it invoked.

Vini's eyes widened slightly, and she could feel the heat in them as they looked down at her lips. Vini's hand didn't move, still offering up the bacon as a sacrifice, one that Jessica planned on readily accepting. Something about it being from Vini's hands made it taste all the better, and Jessica didn't stop to think before leaning in for a second bite. This time she took a larger bite, letting her lips brush against Vini's fingers as she bit through the meat and leaned away. This time Vini's eyes were on hers, their gazes locked in a standoff as they waited for one of them to make a move.

The moment was electric, and Jessica felt it go through her like a zap of lightning. The day was cooler, and yet she could feel sweat starting to build on the small of her back. She needed Vini to move away because Jessica was no longer sure that she could be trusted not to try to take things further. She was almost disappointed when Vini seemed to hear her thoughts and pulled back. These moments, while few and far between, had been the most connection she had felt to someone in a long time. They were the reason why she pushed down her disappointment.

They had time.

Twenty

"How were things at work today? Anyone new come in that we should know about?"

Vini glanced at Ava. The question wasn't abnormal, and yet it made her think of Jessica. Most things these days did. It was like with each day that passed, her mind conjured more and more thoughts of Jessica that refused to be exorcised.

Three days. That's all she had left before she would drive out of Vini's life, probably for good. Vini didn't hold any illusions that Jessica would come back to Peach Blossom. She had practically said that more than once. This was a once-in-a-lifetime stopover for her before she moved on to places that more matched her large personality. Vini didn't blame her for that. She couldn't. She was too busy trying to put boards over the windows of her heart before the hurricane of sadness that came in the wake of Jessica leaving did its damage.

"No. It was pretty quiet," Vini replied. It was the truth. There hadn't been anyone new that came in. She had some routine work from the people in their town and the next one over. Jessica had come in again during Vini's lunch and though there had been the type of sexual tension that normally would have had them relieving it in the seat of Vini's car, they had spent the time talking. Just talking.

It had been a frustratingly wonderful past couple days, and Vini wasn't sure whether to be happy about the fact that Jessica seemed to like her enough to start really opening up or resentful over the fact that she was doing so now right before she left. The more Vini found out about Jessica, the more she liked her and the more she knew for sure it was going to hurt once Jessica was gone. She couldn't say anything, though, especially not to Jessica. This was the type of relationship she had agreed to. One that was nothing more than a few weeks of fun before she went back to the humdrum of normal life.

"So is Jessica still coming by the shop?" Ava asked. She phrased it nonchalantly, but Vini could hear a thread of something in her voice.

Vini paused cutting the vegetables and placed the knife down on the board before turning to look at Ava. "If you have a question, just ask."

"I'm just saying it's weird that that girl is always hanging around your shop," Ava remarked. She glanced over at Vini with a raised eyebrow. "It's almost like she's trying to get something from you."

Now Vini was angry. Sure, Ava actually wasn't far off,

in that both Vini and Jessica were getting things from one another, but the idea that the only reason Jessica was around was for sexual reasons didn't sit right with Vini. Why was it so hard to believe that someone like Jessica might have been interested in her for pure reasons? "And what if she is?" Vini asked voice going sharp. "I don't really see why it would be your business anyway."

Ava paused what she was doing and looked at Vini more fully. "It would be my business because you're my baby sister, she's Grace's friend and you don't know her."

"You don't know her either," Vini countered. "Seems to me that all you've got are some half-assed stories and some preconceived notions. I mean, Jessica was even nice enough to help throw me a birthday weekend, a weekend that you fully enjoyed, and yet you're still sitting here telling me you're suspicious of her for some reason. It's not adding up, so you tell me what your deal is so we can move the hell on."

Vini was growing tired of it. She had had a great few days, and she wasn't trying to spend the next couple days arguing about something that was no one's business but her own. Ava had always tended to overstep, especially when it came to Vini, but this was a new low. Never had she tried to get involved in Vini's relationships before.

"My deal is that you don't know the type of person Jessica is, so I don't know why we're even having to have this conversation. And why are you getting so defensive? You know I wouldn't ever do something to hurt you. Jessica is nice and everything, but she has a reputation, that's all. I'm just trying to look out for you."

"It seems like all you're doing is sticking your nose in business that doesn't pertain to you," Vini said. She looked down at the vegetables and sighed before taking a step back and wiping her hands on her pants. She wasn't even hungry now, and she definitely didn't have any desire to stick around while Ava was spewing this nonsense. "If you want to sit here and speculate on shit like this, you're more than welcome to do it by yourself. I have other things I'd rather be doing."

"Where are you going?"

"Out," Vini replied. She didn't bother going upstairs to get changed, instead grabbing her keys and leaving the house. She was halfway down the street before she dialed Jessica's number. She didn't know what she was doing, she just knew that she needed to get out of there. When Jessica answered the phone, she sounded like she was in a far better mood than Vini.

"Hey, Vin. What's going on?"

"Have you eaten dinner already? I'm kind of in the mood to get out of town for a little bit." Vini wasn't sure where she was planning on going, but she just knew she couldn't stick around. Not tonight. "There's a really nice Mexican place about thirty minutes from here, if you're interested."

She could hear talking in the background and wondered if she had interrupted when Grace and Jessica were busy. She felt tendrils of guilt slither in at the idea that she was once again monopolizing Jessica's time and eating into the days she could be spending with Grace. Especially since she'd come to Peach Blossom to visit Grace in the first place. It didn't seem like they had spent that much time together, and Vini knew it was because of not only her but also Ava monopolizing their time.

"Yeah, that sounds great, actually," Jessica replied finally. "I can be ready in about fifteen minutes if that works for you."

"Works perfectly. I'll see you in a bit."

Vini didn't stop to think as she made her way to Grace's place. She had barely pulled into the driveway when Jessica appeared at the front door. She moved quickly, striding down the stairs and over to Vini's car. She was in before Vini even had a moment to think about it, and she wondered if Jessica was as eager to get out of the town for a bit as Vini was. Vini looked back at the house and saw Grace looking out from the window. She wondered what that was all about but resolved herself to mind her business. That was what she said to Ava earlier, and it would be hypocritical for her to not do the same, no matter how curious she was.

"You are a cherry-flavored lifesaver," Jessica said blowing out a heavy breath. "Grace was driving me to contemplating homicide with her ridiculous questions and wanting to talk about my feelings."

Vini snorted softly. It seemed that they were both running, then. She could definitely work with that. "Well, glad that my chariot services came in useful." Jessica's laughter washed over her, and Vini bathed in the comfort of that sound as she turned toward the highway.

The car was quiet, both seemingly lost in their own thoughts. Vini wondered if Jessica and Grace were having the same conversation as she and Ava. Dani seemed to be the only one who knew how to mind her own business, and right now she was Vini's favorite sister. Even more so because she hadn't shown her face the past couple days outside of coming home to sleep before heading back out to work again.

"So tell me about this Mexican place," Jessica said breaking the silence between them. She didn't turn to look at Vini, instead looking straight ahead in the direction they were going. "When you say it's *amazing*, is it actually amazing or is it just the only option available?"

Vini laughed. "It's definitely not the only one available, but it is still one of the best in the area. Trust me."

Jessica nodded slowly and leaned her head back against the seat. She closed her eyes, and Vini had a tough time keeping her gaze on the road and not on the woman beside her. Still, the idea of getting to the restaurant in one piece won out, and she tightened her grip on the steering wheel as they continued down the highway. Twenty minutes later, they turned off the highway toward Valia City, a town even smaller than Peach Blossom. It didn't have much available in the way of entertainment, but of its three restaurants, the Mexican restaurant was the best. It also had amazing mango margaritas, and Vini was in need of one right now.

When they pulled in, the parking lot was half-full. The air was cool as was the norm these days. Mornings tended to be chilly with it heating up in the afternoon before the inevitable evening temperature dip. It was the kind of weather that people always joked about in the South.

"It smells amazing in here," Jessica remarked after they were seated at their table. She looked around, the small smile on her face making her seem years younger. Now without the need to keep the car straight, Vini could drink her fill of Jessica. She gazed across the table enjoying the excitement that practically leaked from Jessica's essence.

"If I had known you liked Mexican food this much, I would have brought you here weeks ago."

Jessica laughed. "I probably would have hopped in bed with you even sooner if you had." A waitress interrupted them before she could say more, and after a few suggestions, they were alone again with a margarita each and anticipation for the meal. Vini watched as Jessica tried the chips and salsa.

"So…" She waited for her to finish chewing. When Jessica's eyebrows shot up, Vini smirked.

"You are evil," Jessica said waving a hand in front of her face. "Why didn't you tell me that was the spicy one?"

"Aren't you half Korean?" Vini countered. "You bragged all about your spice tolerance when we were in Atlanta."

Jessica blinked away tears, her smile never leaving her face. "Korean spice and Mexican spice are two different things." She took a sip of her margarita, her shoulders dropping as she licked her lips. "Oh, man, this thing is amazing."

"Told you it was good." Vini took a sip of her own drink. She hummed at the familiar tang of the mango and the sharp bite of the tequila. It was a perfect combination after a long hard day at work. "I used to joke that this was better than sex, mostly because I wasn't having it. But now I know better." Jessica's laughter was contagious, and Vini found herself chuckling.

"I don't know about all that," Jessica said pulling her glass closer to her. She leaned over before looking up at Vini from beneath her kohl-dark eyelashes. "As delicious as this is, I think I would choose sex with you over it every time."

A thrill ran up Vini's spine, and she swallowed hard at the look in Jessica's eyes. She saw Jessica's lips moving, but all she could do was focus on the pounding of her heart. For the first time in a long time, she was regretting not having space of her own. She wanted to bring Jessica home and spend the night staring into those eyes as they dirtied every surface available. She wanted every corner of her place to be a reminder of her and Jessica and what they'd had.

That thought nearly stopped her in her tracks.

What *did* they have?

She and Jessica weren't together. Not officially. Not the way Vini wanted, and therein lay the problem. Vini had argued with Ava about not making assumptions about why Jessica sought Vini out, but was she totally wrong? Vini was quickly realizing that the comfort she'd initially had with her and Jessica's arrangement had somehow bled away in the past few weeks, leaving discontent and a gaping need to fill it. Vini had thought she was satisfied with how things were, but now she wasn't so sure. After having Jessica for the past month and seeing what a relationship could be like, how could Vini just let all that go? She knew she needed to tell Jessica how she felt, if only to get everything out in the open so they could deal with things.

Before Vini had a chance to say anything, Jessica's words reached her ears. "… And I can't wait to get to Italy. My parents spend every other Christmas there, so I've made some good friends."

"Oh?" Vini remembered Jessica talking about Italy a couple times, but she hadn't realized it was a place she went to frequently. "So you like it there, then?"

Jessica nodded enthusiastically. "It's one of my top three places. I bought a villa there a couple years ago for when I go stay. My friend, Gianna, lives there year-round and takes care of the place for me. She's always trying to get me to settle back there permanently."

At the sound of another woman's name, everything stopped. Logically, Vini knew Jessica had friends outside of Grace. Hell, she even knew that Jessica probably had other people she was seeing before she came to Peach Blossom. But with the idea of that right in front of her, she found herself shutting down. She hadn't expected Jessica to declare her love for Vini and promise to stay in town forever, but she hadn't realized Jessica was so eager to leave.

"Why haven't you?" It was a question Vini didn't want to ask, but she had to know the answer. "I've heard southern Italy is beautiful."

Jessica nodded. "It is. The beaches are nice too, but I'm just not ready to be tied down right now."

Vini nodded in agreement even as the fire of hope she had been reluctantly cultivating slowly dwindled. There was no way in hell Peach Blossom was competing with Italy. The two places weren't even on the same wavelength. Vini couldn't deny that it would be exciting to go and see something new. She wanted to travel, and it was in her plans for the future, but Peach Blossom was home for her. She couldn't imagine ever settling somewhere else long-term. Her life was the shop and building it into something she felt was truly hers. She had years before she could say that she had reached that goal.

"That's really cool that you have a place there," Vini said finally when she felt she could speak without her voice wavering. "I've always wanted to go to Europe. Ava visited in college and would always send us pictures. We were supposed to visit her over the summer, but life just sort of got in the way, and she came back to Peach Blossom before we could try to plan a visit again."

"You really should try to go," Jessica insisted. "My dad was stationed in Germany for a couple years, and my mom and I would always take train trips to the surrounding countries. I'm excited to see Italy again."

"I wish I could go with you," Vini said before snapping her mouth shut. She hadn't meant to say that. Making plans together that didn't consist of lunch or maybe a drive-in movie was not something they did. It went over the line of what they did. Peach Blossom was it for Vini, but for Jessica the world was wide-open.

Jessica opened her mouth, but before she could speak, their waitress returned with a platter of their food. Vini blinked away, pushing down the pain of realizing this thing between them was going nowhere. They were too different—too different to have a relationship work. Vini should have seen that from the start, but she was seeing it now. She had painted herself into a corner, and now she didn't know how to find her way out again.

Twenty-One

Jessica sighed and leaned back to relieve the pressure on her stomach. Vini hadn't been lying when she said the food at this place was delicious. The burrito she had ordered looked intimidating until Jessica's enchiladas were set down. With the miles of food between them, conversation took a back seat. Occasionally Vini would look up and smile between bites, but overall, they both ate in relative silence. She didn't know what Vini was thinking about, but Jessica's mind was on the fact that in three short days she would be away from all this, and the thought did not fill her with excitement. On the contrary. She was regretting not having chosen to stay longer.

Across from her, Vini looked just as sated, and Jessica whistled softly. "Damn, girl. You cleaned that plate good. Where the hell do you store all that?"

Vini chuckled. "It all goes to my hair, I guess." The waitress returned with the check, but before Jessica could reach for it, Vini snatched it up. "Don't even think about it. I asked you out, I pay."

A tiny thrill ran over Jessica at Vini's words. This wasn't a date, but if she ignored reason, she could pretend it was. If she ignored everything outside of the two of them and the circumstances they found themselves in, she could pretend that they were two people who just met and decided to actually try a relationship.

She could pretend she was what Vini needed.

"I don't remember seeing that rule printed anywhere," Jessica replied.

Vini pulled out her wallet. "Tough shit. You should have looked closer at the paperwork I had you sign."

"That was paperwork for my car."

"Was it?" The little smirk Vini sported did things to Jessica's insides that were unnecessary. She rolled her eyes to cover up just how ready she was to grab Vini and book it to a dark corner so she could taste that smug grin on her lips.

"You play dirty." When Vini's smirk only deepened, Jessica knew it was time to go. She had to get her hands on Vini right here and right now. "Where is the waitress? We need to go."

Vini cocked her head to the side. "Why are you so eager to leave?"

Jessica glanced around to make sure they couldn't be overheard before she pasted a sharp smile on her own face and leaned over the table. "Because dessert is needed, and you are on the menu."

She saw Vini's throat move as she swallowed. "I thought you were staying at Grace's until you leave?"

Jessica sat back down and leaned back. She crossed her arms but kept her gaze focused on Vini. "Are you telling me there are no motels anywhere from here to Peach Blossom?"

Vini blinked slowly as if savoring those words before she abruptly sat up and called out to a passing waiter. Jessica had to hide her grin behind her hand. She hadn't expected that reaction, but it was well worth it. Vini paid quickly, her hand moving swiftly as she signed the receipt before herding Jessica up from the booth and out of the restaurant. They were in the car faster than Jessica could make a sound, and as soon as her seat belt was on, she found her mouth taken in an ardent kiss.

Vini's lips moved like they hadn't just eaten, and Jessica loved it. She brought both hands up clutching Vini's cheeks, making sure she couldn't get away. They were in the parking lot in full view of anyone who happened to walk by the truck, but Jessica didn't care. The softly burning desire in her had cracked open, sending waves of molten arousal through her. She craved Vini's taste and touch, not being able to stop herself from pushing for more until Vini was almost crouched over her lap.

"Fuck," Vini gritted out, her hands gripping the loose strands of Jessica's hair. Jessica groaned as that hold tightened, pulling her head back as teeth closed over a sensitive spot on her neck. The air in the car was sticky, and when she slitted her eyes open, she could see her window was fogged over. She opened her mouth, attempting to say something, but all that came out was a tortured moan.

She couldn't give this up. Jessica had to find a way to keep Vini like this, but even as she thought that she wondered if it was fair. Jessica wasn't one to settle into a stable, everyday life, not like the one Vini had built. Vini was so secure and clearly knew who she was and what she wanted. The only thing Jessica was sure of was that she was sure of nothing at all. How could she tie Vini to her when she didn't even know what country she would be in in a month?

"Stop thinking," Vini breathed out against Jessica's cheek. The warmth of her breath spread over Jessica's skin, making it damp.

"Who said I was thinking?" Jessica asked. She wanted to protest as Vini pulled away, but she knew they shouldn't have let things get as far as they did when they were sitting in a parking lot. "God, Vini. Can we go somewhere? I really want to have sex with you."

Vini's body trembled, and when she pulled back, Jessica realized she was laughing. Jessica frowned. That wasn't the reaction she had been expecting. Then again, she hadn't actually meant to admit that in the first place. When Vini noticed her frown, she brushed her thumb over Jessica's lips.

"Don't look like that. I'm flattered," Vini said making Jessica frown harder.

"Being flattered is not what I was hoping for," she countered. "I was hoping for a little more *fuck, yes* and agreement."

"Oh, trust when I say I agree." Vini leaned forward again

brushing her lips over Jessica's. "And I know the perfect place."

She pulled back, leaving Jessica to chase after her lips until she was caught by her seat belt. When Vini chuckled softly, Jessica sulked and crossed her arms. She wasn't actually upset, but it was fun to play like this. This was a playful side that she didn't get to indulge in often. Most people who came into Jessica's life and her bed were fun, but she always had to be on guard with them. They knew who she was, but more importantly they knew who her mom was. Vini wasn't like that, and Jessica had not once tripped over a flag that would have made her take a step back. It was as frightening as it was refreshing.

Vini started the truck, and soon they were rolling down the road. Before Jessica could second-guess herself, she reached over and grabbed Vini's hand. The little smile that stretched Vini's lips was worth it even as Jessica's heart pounded. When they pulled into another parking lot, she sat up and took notice. It was a nice-enough-looking motel, though not one she remembered seeing.

"We are coming here to have sex, right? You aren't planning on murdering me and hiding the body in the woods?"

Vini snorted. "If I was going to do that, I wouldn't have taken you to my favorite restaurant. Too many witnesses."

Jessica followed Vini in. The bored-looking teen manning the front desk didn't bother looking up from his phone as he slid over a key. Vini wasted no time pulling Jessica along down the hallway. She quickly opened the room, and as soon as the door was shut behind them, Jessica took over crushing Vini against her and covering her lips with her own. No words were needed. They both seemed to feel the same desperation as they shared kisses that left Jessica trembling with desire. Vini's hands gripped her hips, and Jessica wrapped her arms around Vini's shoulders. She didn't want to let go, but they needed to get naked.

"Take off your clothes," Jessica whispered. She almost regretted her words when Vini stepped away but bit her lip when Vini slowly complied.

As dark skin was revealed, Jessica found her breath caught and she was unable to look away. Vini's hands never wavered as fingers swiftly undid buttons and slid off straps. Jessica found herself taken with a new type of hunger as dark pointed nipples were uncovered along with the flat plane of Vini's stomach and the dark *V* of hair that hid the sweetest fruit she'd ever tasted. Before Jessica could move, Vini was moving backward.

"Are you going to just stare or are you going to join me?" Jessica was speechless. Somehow this fae-like creature had fallen into her life, and now she was frozen with the need to capture it forever. Vini raised an eyebrow when Jessica didn't respond. "Jess?"

The sound of her name had Jessica moving. She threw off her shirt, not caring where it landed and did the same with her bra. Her pants were gone as soon as she reached the bed, and her panties followed. Jessica crawled up the bed loving the way Vini's eyes seemed to darken the closer she got. She paused between Vini's thighs, pushing them to spread them more fully as she slowly let her gaze meander down Vini's body. She soaked everything in, from the rapid rise and fall of her breasts as she breathed to the dip of her belly button. When Jessica leaned forward kissing it, she enjoyed the hitch in Vini's breath.

"I feel like I should give thanks for this meal."

Vini's snort morphed into a gasp when Jessica kissed lower. "Fuck."

"Gladly," Jessica replied before opening her mouth and licking a trail between the lips of Vini's cunt. The familiar musk of her had Jessica's mouth watering, and she knew without a doubt, that she would taste that flavor in her fantasies. Vini's little grunt of pleasure would star in the sounds of her dreams. The phantom grip of her hands in Jessica's hair would slowly drift from her consciousness when she awoke. She would remember everything and clutch onto those memories with everything she had.

"Please," Vini whispered, her hips slowly rising off the bed. Jessica followed the motion giving in to what they both wanted and pressing their lips together. Heat poured over her face as she glutted herself on Vini's pussy, tongue darting in and out between engorged folds. Jessica slid her hands up, loving the dips and curves of Vini's waist. She looked up and over the mound of Vini's pussy, and their eyes met.

Neither of them looked away. Vini's hands clutched at Jessica as her hips continued to undulate. Jessica sucked, wanting more of that sweet nectar that flowed from Vini's core. She needed that taste more than oxygen, and when a fresh burst of it coated her tongue, her eyes finally slipped shut. The sounds Vini made fell like raindrops on parched earth, and Jessica soaked them in. She pressed her tongue up against Vini's walls before changing her target to Vin's clit. Two of her fingers took up residence in Vini's cunt as she flicked the engorged nub with her tongue. She knew Vini was close when her sounds changed, and her grip became more desperate.

"Shit," Vini bit out. Her head went back, and Jessica stared at the bared skin that she planned to get her lips on as soon as she made Vini come. It didn't take much longer, Jessica adding another finger and pushing hard and quick. Vini's hips snapped up, and her legs fell open as she cried out in pleasure. The feeling of it washed over Jessica, and she shuddered as her own arousal flared. If it were possible for her to come just from hearing a sound, that would have done it. As it was, she barely held herself back when Vini shivered as Jessica withdrew her fingers.

Dark eyes watched unblinkingly as Jessica brought her fingers up, licking off Vini's juices with a soft hum. A shift of Jessica's legs reminded her of her wetness gathering between her upper thighs. She crawled up the rest of the bed and settled on her side beside Vini. While Vini came down, the hand not currently in Jessica's mouth drifted down before sliding between her own pussy lips. She moaned when she lightly brushed her own clit.

"Are you starting without me?" Vini asked. When Jessica opened her eyes, Vini was staring.

"Not without you," Jessica replied. "Just waiting for you to join in." Before her words were finishing, there was already another touch there as eager fingers joined her own. Vini's fingers moved firmly without pause, and Jessica spread her legs giving her full access. One finger and then two entered her, and Jessica leaned forward. "Kiss me."

It was a demand that was readily met. Jessica let Vini taste herself, her tongue seeking out Jessica's own. There was no talking then, just the slick sounds of their fingers dipping into Jessica's cunt and the smacks of their lips. The room was light enough for Jessica to see the sheen on Vini's skin before she closed her eyes. Her orgasm washed over her making her muscles clench and her teeth ache.

"You are so beautiful." Vini's words made her eyes burn, and Jessica had to take a deep breath before she could open them. Vini reached up cupping her cheeks between her warm palms. Their scents were mingled, creating an aroma of their own that was unique. Jessica wished she could bottle it for the nights when she was alone and wanting. Kisses were placed on her cheeks, and she couldn't help but lean forward and plant some of her own. They stayed soft, both of them trembling, though Jessica wondered whether from the cold or from emotions. She knew how she felt, or at least, she thought she did. What had started off fun and easy had swiftly morphed into something she had never experienced before.

Jessica let the heat of Vini's touches seep into her skin. It was addictive no matter how much she tried to fight. When she couldn't stand it anymore, she reached up and circled Vini's wrists. The feelings these touches invoked was too much for her. She needed time. She needed space.

"We should probably get some sleep," Jessica said kicking herself at not taking more advantage of the alone time they had together. She wondered what Vini's sisters would say when she didn't come home. She knew exactly what Grace would say, but she would deal with that when the time came. She knew Grace was watching her closely, and while she understood, she was tired. Jessica wasn't in the mood to be chastised like she was a child, not when she was also dealing with the fact that soon she would be on a plane heading thousands of miles away.

"Are you sure you're ready to go to sleep?" Vini asked. Her grin was sly, but Jessica could still see the tiredness behind her eyes. "I mean, we are outside of town, and we do have this big bed for just us two. I'm sure if we really put our minds to it, we could probably cover quite a bit of ground."

Vini's hands slid down Jessica shoulders until they rested on her hips. The grip was strong as Vini pulled Jessica against her. The way their curves melted together never ceased to make Jessica shiver. It had to be illegal for something to feel so damn good. It made it that much harder to fight against the desire that whirled within her.

"You have work tomorrow. Plus I have to start packing," Jessica replied finally. Her throat clicked, and she swallowed to get rid of the dryness. Jessica felt the room grow colder at her words, and as much as she desperately wanted to pull them back, she knew she couldn't. She had to create separation for her own sanity.

"You do realize I'm my own boss? I can open the shop late if I want."

Jessica pasted on a smile she didn't feel. "Oh? But what would your sisters think about that? And Aiden?"

"I'll text Aiden, and knowing him, he'll be jazzed to get to sleep longer," Vini replied. "As for my sisters, it's not their business, so they don't have any say."

Jessica nodded, not sure what else to say. She didn't want to stop. She wanted them to drown in one another until neither desired to come up for air. This was why she didn't do this. Deep down, she was too needy to be able to keep this up for too long before wanting more. She had short relationships built on mutual attraction and an understanding that things wouldn't last before flitting off to her next location. She didn't know how to stay still, and she still wasn't even sure if she really wanted to. What she wanted Vini couldn't give.

"Are you tired?" Vini's question gave Jessica an out, and she gladly took it.

"A little," she replied, faking a yawn. "I didn't get much sleep last night. Grace's guest bed isn't as comfortable as the mattress at the bed and breakfast I was staying at. I don't think she's changed it out since the last time she stayed in that house."

Her words had the desired effect, and Vini chuckled. It lightened the air in the room, and Jessica breathed out a silent sigh of relief. She wrapped her arms around Vini's shoulders and allowed herself one shoulder kiss. It was hard not to push things further especially when Vini responded so quickly. Her lips parted, beckoning Jessica inside, and it took everything within Jessica to not respond the way she wanted.

Instead of deepening the kiss, she kept it surface-level and promised herself that it was for the best. When Vini pouted, Jessica smiled and patted her cheek. "Come on, Vini. No long faces. You need sleep. I don't want you to be distracted and accidentally drop something on yourself in the garage. Aren't you sleepy?"

Vini paused her fingers, softly brushing the skin of Jessica's arm. She tried to ignore that touch even as it sent sparks along her nerves. "I am a little sleepy, but more than anything I'm excited to be alone with you."

Her words made something unnecessary flutter within Jessica's chest. There had been plenty of people who were excited to lie in bed with Jessica when it came to sex, but she had yet to have anyone say that they were excited to lie in bed with her just for the sake of just being alone with her. It made her soften to Vini's desires, and she let herself fall again as Vini's arousal enflamed her own.

Twenty-Two

Vini yawned, her eyes watering as something in her jaw clicked. She hadn't gotten to the shop until ten after dropping Jessica back off at Grace's house. They had spent the night trading slow kisses and heated touches until falling together in a heap sometime near dawn. It had been exhausting, and yet Vini had woken up feeling lighter than she had in a long while. They had barely been able to keep their hands off one another when they showered, falling into laughter when the water abruptly changed, pounding them both with drops of icicles. With teeth chattering, they had dried off and then put on their clothes from the day before and then checked out.

Vini hadn't bothered going home, instead changing into the extra clothes she kept at the shop. When Aiden wandered in twenty minutes after she arrived, he'd given her a knowing smile and a thumbs-up before greeting the day's first customer. Things had been steady all morning, and though Jessica hadn't come by, Vini wasn't upset. She knew Jessica was probably catching up on the sleep neither of them got. Hell, Vini would probably take an hour or so later for a catnap in her office.

By three, Vini was wide awake with a little extra pep in her step. She'd already finished an oil change and was working on another when Jessica called out from the lobby. With a wide smile, Vini stood up and grabbed the towel to wipe her hands. By the time she walked into the lobby, Jessica was already pulling out plates and setting them on the back counter.

"Seriously, Jess, you have to stop feeding Aiden, otherwise I'll never get rid of him."

"Ha ha. Funny," Aiden replied, rolling his eyes. He took the offered plate. "I'll make myself scarce so you two lovebirds can do your thing."

He left before Vini could say anything, but also she didn't want to deny it. Having Jessica alone was exactly what she wanted. "Sometimes I wonder if I could trade him in for a different model."

"How much would you get for him, really?" When Vini laughed, Jessica smiled. "Did you miss me?"

Vini's heartbeat quickened. "I saw you a few hours ago."

"Yeah, but you still missed me."

She shook her head but didn't deny it. Vini leaned in, meeting Jessica's lips and sighing at how right it all felt. She reached up, cupping her cheeks, and tilting her head up so they could press more firmly together. Vini was just getting into it, when a loud shriek cut through the air.

"What the fuck are you doing?"

Vini felt Jessica jerk back, and when she realized whose voice that was, her eyes shot open. She turned in disbelief to see Ava and Grace standing in front of the counter.

"What are you doing here?" Vini asked, confusion making her slow as her brain tried to understand what was happening. Ava's hands were balled into fists at her side, and her gaze was hooked on Jessica. Vini glanced over and saw Jessica standing there, mouth parted as if trying to think of the words to say.

"What am I doing here?" Ava asked loudly as she shifted to look at Vini. "What the fuck is she doing here? And why the hell did we walk in on you two kissing?"

"Ava, maybe we should—"

Vini cut Grace off. "She's here because she wants to be." Jessica was still silent, so Vini continued. "And because I want her to be."

"I told you to stay away from her," Ava said pointing at Jessica. "I told you she was no good for you. Jesus, Vini. Why would you get involved with someone who has no plans to stick around? That's just inviting trouble when you let the wrong people into your life."

"Who are you to decide who is good for me?" Vini asked raising her voice. "Who I want to let into my life is none of your business."

Ava narrowed her eyes. "It is when you lie to us. I can't believe you let her—"

"Vini didn't let me do anything," Jessica said, finally speaking up. She crossed her arms, and Vini was dismayed to see her expression shutter, giving no insight into what she was thinking. She looked like the same Jessica she met six weeks ago instead of the open person she had gotten to know.

"So you're saying you forced her?"

Grace stepped forward, putting a hand on Ava's shoulder. "Come on, Ava. Jessica would never force anyone to do anything. She's not like that." Ava whirled around, shrugging off her hand.

"Are you seriously taking her side right now? Did you know about this shit?" Her voice went shrill, and Grace winced. When Grace didn't reply, Ava's eyes widened. "Are you fucking kidding me right now?"

"It wasn't my busi—"

"Your friend was fucking my baby sister, and you knew about it and didn't tell me?" Her voice echoed in the lobby, and Vini wanted the floor to open up and swallow her whole. This couldn't be happening. Nowhere in her mind did she have this being a thing that would happen, and she wanted to rewind time.

"Actually, Vini is the one with the strap." They all turned to look at Jessica. Vini was torn between crying and laughing hysterically, mostly because Jessica wasn't lying. Ava, though, didn't appear to find it amusing as she launched herself toward Jessica. If not for Grace, she might have actually made it.

Pandemonium ensued with everyone talking at once. Vini's ears rang with Ava's yells, and her throat twinged when she yelled back. This was not how she wanted everything to come out. Aiden appeared, probably having heard the commotion, and after a few aborted motions, he and Grace managed to contain an almost vibrating Ava between them. Jessica had stepped back and was now leaning against the wall as she stared.

"Calm the fuck down," Vini said.

"'Calm down,' she says. You purposely got involved with someone who only came here because she got caught playing two other women. How does that scream *relationship material* to you?" Ava was breathing hard as she put her hands on her hips. "Was she the one who suggested keeping things on the down-low? Do you even like my sister, or were you just using her for entertainment?"

Grace spoke up this time. "Of course she likes Vini. How could she not?"

Vini appreciated the words even as something in her gut clenched, wondering the same thing. Surely Jessica liked her at least a little bit? She wouldn't continuously seek her out if she didn't. Vini glanced at Ava before hurrying to Jessica's side.

"Jess, I'm so sorry."

"It's fine." Jessica's tone was flat, and Vini knew just how not fine it was. When Jessica glanced down at her, her eyes were blank. There was nothing there to give Vini a hint at what she was thinking or feeling. Vini wanted to reach up, but now it was like there was a wall between them that she was afraid to penetrate. Something had shifted, and it made her want to cry out in anger.

"This is why I don't do this."

Jessica's words were soft, soft enough that Vini almost missed them. But she didn't understand what they meant. "What are you talking about? Don't do what?"

Jessica blinked slowly before pushing off the wall and moving away. "This. Relationships." When Vini tried to reach for her, Jessica stepped farther away. "I'm sorry, Vini, but I can't give you what you want. I can't do this."

Everything in Vini cried out, but the pain of those words stole her breath. She was frozen and helpless to do anything but watch Jessica shake her head. Vini's vision felt like it was darkening as she watched Jessica turn away. It wasn't until she was out the door that whatever spell had fallen over her broke and she stumbled forward, only barely managing to catch herself on the counter. When the door closed behind Jessica, sound filtered back in, and she turned to where Ava and Grace were loudly arguing.

"How could you keep this from me?" Ava yelled. "I can't believe you would lie to me."

"I wasn't lying," Grace countered, trying to reach for her. When Ava flung herself away, Grace's hand dropped back to her side. "Ava, please."

Ava scowled before stomping over to the door. "I'm not going to stay here and listen to this shit." She pushed the door open. "Do not follow me."

"Ava!" The door slammed shut, cutting Grace off even as she reached out. The lobby was plunged into silence, and Vini felt like her strings had been cut. The only thing holding her up was her grip on the counter.

Aiden looked between her and Grace as if he wanted to

say something but wasn't sure what. Vini didn't think there was anything that could be said that would save the shitshow that this day had become.

"I should go," Grace said finally. Her voice was quiet, and she didn't turn around. Vini saw her shoulders fall, but she was too locked in her own pain and anger to offer her anything. Aiden gestured toward Grace, but Vini said nothing. All she could do was fall back on the one thing that kept her going: work.

She turned, ignoring the food on the counter, and made her way back into the garage. She had a lot to do and wanted nothing more than to lose herself in the familiar movements of her work. Cars were much easier to figure out than people, and she could use a little easy right now.

"Vini!"

Absolutely not. She ignored Ava's voice and kicked her shoes off, preparing to shower and then fall into bed. She didn't want to talk, especially not to Ava. The rest of the day had passed by in a blur. She had faint memories of finally eating when Aiden had pestered her for the third or fourth time and of him finally pushing her out the door when the sun had gone down. But everything else was a blank. She barely remembered driving home, and now she wished she had just stayed away and booked herself a hotel room.

Vini turned toward the stairs and was halfway up them before Ava called out to her again, this time from right behind her.

"Vini, we need to talk."

"No, we don't." She continued up the stairs, ignoring the footsteps behind her. The rest of the house was suspiciously quiet, and she wondered where everyone else was. Did they already know? Well, Dani already knew what had been happening between her and Jessica, but clearly she hadn't told anyone else since this was all blowing up today. She closed the door behind her. When Ava came barreling through not a minute after, Vini gritted her teeth and tried not to show just how aggravated she was. "Ava, go away."

"Not until you talk to me."

Vini kept her back to her. "You did plenty of talking earlier."

"And you didn't do enough."

That had her finally whirling around. "Seriously? You think I have anything to fucking say to you after you walked into my shop and acted a fool in front of someone I—" Vini cut herself off with a click of her teeth.

"Someone you what? You like?" Ava narrowed her eyes at Vini's silence. "Vini, you can't be serious. You can't seriously think that Jessica is relationship material."

"And what if I do?" Vini countered, clenching her fists at Ava's know-it-all tone. "What the hell makes you think you know better about my life than me? Are you really that delusional to think I can't make my own choices about who I do and don't want to be with? Do you really think that lowly of me?"

Ava's eyes widened, and she dropped her arms from where they had been crossed over her chest. "Of course I don't think lowly of you."

"Oh, really?" Vini asked almost spitting out her words. "So explain, because from where I'm standing, all I hear is you telling me I need someone else to make decisions for me because I'm too stupid to be able to make them myself."

Ava shook her head, but Vini didn't believe it. "Vini, no. That's not—"

"Well, congratulations," she continued, not letting Ava get another word out. "You win. You've made the choice for me. I guarantee Jessica won't want a damn thing to do with me now." The burn of tears that had been threatening to fall was stronger than ever, and Vini knew she had to go. She wouldn't give anyone the satisfaction of seeing her cry now.

Before Ava could say anything, Vini went to push past her. She could find new clothes later, but what she couldn't do was stay in this house for another moment. Ava's hand shot out and gripped Vini's arm.

"Vini, wait."

Vini didn't hesitate to smack Ava's hand away. "Don't fucking touch me. You've done enough already."

"I'm just trying to protect you."

"You're trying to control me. There's a difference," Vini shouted. "You're not my mother, so stop acting like it."

The words fell like a stone sinking into water. The moment they left Vini's lips, she knew they would strike their mark, and when Ava's lip quivered that was confirmed. They were the truth, and yet Vini wasn't sure who was hurt the most by them, her or Ava.

"Hey. What's going on here?" Vini swallowed hard at

Dani's voice. She turned to glance over her shoulder. Dani was still in her scrubs, eyes crinkled with clear exhaustion as she looked between Vini and Ava. "Why are we yelling at each other?"

Vini turned her head, determined not to be the one to break the silence. Ava's silence seemed to be the same, but it didn't matter because clearly Dani already suspected.

"This is about Jessica, isn't it?"

"You knew?"

"Of course I did," Dani replied. Vini felt the air shift as Dani walked by. The creak of her bed had Vini sighing in equal parts annoyance and relief. Why the fuck did this all require a family meeting? If their dad showed up too, she would throw herself from the window just to get away. "Vini?"

With a sigh, Vini turned to look at Dani. She was sitting on Vini's bed with a tired smile on her face. She patted the bed beside her, but her sister didn't take her up on it. She wanted to be near the door in case she needed to make a quick escape. Dani shrugged before waving a hand at her.

"Yeah," she replied, "it's about Jessica. Ava burst into the shop today and saw us kissing."

"I didn't burst into the shop," Ava insisted. "I came by to talk to you."

Vini chuckled, but it held no humor. "Whatever. She came in and started a fight about shit that had nothing to do with her. Then Jessica broke up with me and left."

Dani nodded. "I thought you two weren't dating."

"We aren't—weren't." Vini paused and scowled. "We had an arrangement, but it was one that worked for us."

Ava scoffed, and Vini glared at her. "Vini, you are not the *arrangement* type, and you know it. You fall fast and hard."

"You don't know what the fuck I am because you never asked. You assumed and, instead of asking, ruined the best thing that I've had since Mom died." It was another low blow, but Vini was tired of skirting around subjects. Keeping things to herself was obviously not allowed, so she was going to let it all hang loose. "You keep acting like I'm this baby who needs to be parented instead of a grown-ass woman who would like to be able to talk to her big sisters without them flying off the fucking handle."

Ava reared back as if slapped though Dani didn't look surprised in the slightest. When Ava turned to look at her, Dani shrugged. "I love you, Ava, but she's not wrong."

"You can't really think Jessica—"

"It's not actually about what I think, sis. Or about what you think," Dani said cutting her off. "It's about what Vini wants."

Ava frowned as if she had never considered that before. The fists that had been clenched at her sides slowly opened, and when she looked up at Vini, her eyes were shiny. Vini looked back, not bothering to hide her anger or her frustration.

"Oh." Ava's voice was soft as she looked at Vini, and it seemed she finally *saw* her. "When did you get so old?"

Vini huffed out a breath, amusement bleeding through

her frustration. "We literally just celebrated my twenty-third birthday."

"I know, but…" It was like she was looking at Vini for the first time, and Vini was curious what she saw. "Fuck. I'm sorry."

The apology was so unexpected that it took Vini's anger with it. She could count on her hands the number of times in her life Ava had apologized to her. "Wow," Vini replied. "I had almost forgotten what it sounds like to hear you say those words."

"Shut up," Ava said before shaking her head. She sighed and walked over to Dani. "Scoot over. I think I need to sit down for this."

Vini rolled her eyes at Ava's dramatics. "There's nothing to sit down for. You apologized, and I accepted. All done."

"I know you don't think that's all." Dani raised an eyebrow. "We want to know all about how you feel about things with Jessica. Just because you're grown, doesn't mean we can't be curious."

"You didn't give Ava shit about Grace."

"Oh, yes she did," Ava replied, side-eyeing Dani. "This heffa cornered me when I was in the shower and grilled me until I was through. Every time I didn't answer a question, she flushed the toilet."

Vini grimaced. "That's just cruel." She sighed when she realized they wouldn't give up. "Fine, but there isn't much to tell. I told you, we had an arrangement. Friends with benefits or whatever."

Dani nodded. "But, you like her as more than just a

friend." Before Vini could respond, she continued. "That wasn't a question, by the way. That was a statement. Anyone who knows you and who doesn't have their head buried in Grace's cunt would have been able to see that."

"Hey."

Vini chuckled knowing that Dani was right. Maybe talking it out was what she needed to make sense of what to do next. "Fine, yeah. I like her."

"And you want a relationship with her."

"Yeah." The weight of that was heavy. As soon as she said it, Vini realized just how impossible it was. "But she doesn't. And before you get mad, she told me from the start that she doesn't do relationships, so I went into this with my eyes wide-open."

Ava glanced at Dani before speaking. "Then, why did you agree? And before you bite my head off, this isn't about control. It's about knowing you, and you've always said you wanted a relationship and marriage. Has that changed?"

Vini could appreciate Ava asking even if she didn't appreciate having the truth put so blatantly before her. "No. That hasn't changed. I thought I could handle just enjoying the time we had and then let her go, but I don't know if I can."

Dani nodded. "How long have you felt like this? Have you talked to Jessica about it?"

Vini ran a hand over her face, tired in a way she had never been. "I don't know. A few weeks maybe. And no, I haven't said anything to her about it. I was going to yesterday, but then she started talking about her plans for when she leaves, and she sounded so eager to go. I couldn't bring it up."

Dani and Ava exchanged looks, and Vini hated to see pity swirling in their gazes. "Then, what are you going to do?" Ava asked, and Vini could appreciate that she was trying.

What indeed? Vini knew what she *wanted* to do and what she *needed* to do, but how was she going to handle those two not being one and the same?

Twenty-Three

"I told you it was a bad idea."

Jessica sighed but didn't stop folding the shirt in her hand. She had been expecting Grace to come flying through the door as soon as she heard the familiar sound of those tires pull into the driveway. The knowledge that she recognized the sound of tires brought her thoughts back to Vini and the look on her face when Jessica had walked out the door. It had taken everything in her to get in the car and drive away when all she wanted to do was take Vini in her arms and tell her it was going to be okay.

"It wouldn't have been a bad idea if not for people flying off the handle for no reason," she shot back before placing the folded shirt in her suitcase.

"It wasn't for no reason. Ava is very protective of Vini. She has been since they lost their mom. It's the same as you being protective of Jason. Can you imagine how you'd be if you had to practically raise him or vice versa?" Grace put a hand on Jessica's shoulder, but she shrugged it off. "Seriously, you can't be mad at Ava wanting the best for her baby sister."

"And that's clearly not me." Jessica clenched her jaw before turning and giving Grace a withering look. "Are you saying I'm not good enough for Vini? She wants the best, and sorry, I just don't make the cut?"

Grace's eyes widened. "Don't put words in my mouth."

"Then, how about using your own instead of vomiting out whatever bullshit Ms. Perfect says? Or have you forgotten how to have an original thought of your own?"

"Now you're just being an asshole."

Jessica barked out a humorless laugh. "Yes, I'm an asshole. All of this is my fault and no one else's. I'm the bad person who fucks everyone over." She was on a roll now, and even though the words were designed to hurt her just as much as Grace, Jessica couldn't find it in her to stop. "Never mind the fact that Vini and I are grown-ass women who just happened to like one another."

"You do this all the time, Jess," Grace spat out. "Just because you're adults doesn't mean you should just go for it without thinking about the possible consequences. And I shouldn't have just gone along with it either."

"For fuck's sake, it wasn't any of your business," Jessica said. She turned and grabbed another shirt, flicking it out sharply.

"Well, now it is," Grace replied. "Sometimes when you do things, it affects other people, Jessica. It can hurt other people if it goes wrong. But I guess that doesn't matter to you as long as you get what you want. Right?"

Jessica whirled around. "If I had gotten what I wanted, Vini and I would have had a wonderful final week together, and then—"

"And then what?" Grace interrupted, voice raised. "And then you fuck off to Italy and leave us to pick up the pieces of Vini you left behind?"

Jessica frowned. "I wouldn't have hurt her. I like Vini."

"Well, clearly not enough to stick around," Grace said gesturing at the suitcase lying open on Jessica's bed. "Vini likes you enough to go to bat for you with her family, but when you're gone, then what does she have? You'll be gone, and she'll be here, alone. Think about that."

Grace sighed heavily, and Jessica realized how tired she looked. When Grace's gaze caught hers, instead of saying anything else, she shook her head and turned away. Jessica didn't know what to say, so she stayed quiet as Grace left the room. She turned back to her suitcase and looked down. It was halfway packed and suddenly she had the urge to dump it all out and pretend like it never existed.

She had to talk to Vini.

The thought took hold once she had it, and she threw down the shirt before walking away from the case. She was down the stairs and out the door before she even really thought about it. She didn't know exactly what she was going to say, but she knew she needed to say something. Vini deserved more than being left to pick up the pieces of them being found in such an unexpected way.

Jessica shouldn't have left her to deal with that alone in the first place.

When she pulled up to the Williamses' house, she saw Vini's truck was there. There were a couple other cars in the driveway, and she paused for a moment before getting out. She knew there was a chance Ava would be here since it was her house too, but Jessica was ready to deal with that. Maybe she had gone about all this the wrong way to begin with. If she had tried to get to know Ava, would things have turned out differently? Now she would never know, but she could do her best to fix what had gone wrong.

Jessica thought about what she was going to say as she walked up the drive and onto the porch. The house was quiet from out here which was a good sign. Unless they had knocked one another out with their words. She could only imagine an argument between all the sisters, especially when it really got heated. As much as she wanted to turn around and not have to deal with that, she held firm, raising her hand and knocking on the door. When no one answered, she tried knocking again, harder this time. This time, someone called out, and Jessica took a step back as the door opened.

"I wondered if you would show up."

Jessica cleared her throat before speaking. "Hey, Dani. Is Vini here?"

"That depends," she replied, looking Jessica up and down. "Did you come to apologize?"

"To who?"

"To Vini, for leaving her to duke it out with our annoyingly overprotective middle sister."

"Yes," Jessica confirmed, nodding vigorously. She could fully admit that she should have been united with Vini in telling both Ava and Grace that what was going on between her and Vini was nobody's business but theirs. Dipping out to leave Vini holding down the fort hadn't been the best move. There was a moment that she wondered if the door would be slammed in her face, and she held her breath as if waiting for her penance. When Dani smiled, she relaxed minutely.

"Then, yes, she's here." Dani took a step back inviting Jessica in. "Just so you know, Ava is out, so you can speak without worrying if your ankles are going to get bitten. Vini, you have company."

"Thank you, Dani."

Dani shrugged. "I want Vini happy, and if you're the one she chooses, then I'm on your side."

Jessica nodded at Dani, equal parts grateful and still confused about her. Her attention was taken when footsteps came from the stairs, and by the time Vini was in front of her, Jessica almost knew what to say. She vaguely heard Dani walk away, but everything in her was focused on Vini and the sadness clear on her face. Jessica had done that, or at least some of it, and she felt guilty.

"I am so sorry." Her words were out before she consciously thought to say them, but they were true. She hadn't handled any of the situation well, and she had a lot to make up for. She would apologize as much as she needed to in order to make things right. "I shouldn't have just left like that. It wasn't fair to you."

"It's okay."

Jessica shook her head and gave Vini a sad smile. "No, it's not. Both of us were in this relationship, and it should have been both of us taking the blame. Instead, I left you there to be yelled at for something that wasn't your fault, and I'm sorry."

Vini nodded though her expression didn't change. Jessica tried to search in her mind for something else to say to salvage things. They had been so good together, and just because there was an expiration date didn't mean things had to end less than amicably.

"Thank you for saying that," Vini said, sounding achingly sincere. "I appreciate it, I really do, but I think we should end things here."

Jessica blinked slowly. "You…what?" She frowned when Vini's gaze looked away. "Is this because of Ava?"

Vini looked back at her and shook her head. "No. This is because of me."

"But…" Jessica started, not sure what words would bring things back to how they had been. Things had been going so well between them. How did they end up going so wrong? "I thought we were having fun together."

"We were," Vini agreed. She took a few steps closer before stopping and crossing her arms. "Being with you was fun."

"Then, why—"

"Because I want more."

More. That word terrified Jessica almost as much as another four-letter word. Every time someone said they wanted more, she ended up with less. It was the reason why she kept things from getting too deep. Usually, it wasn't a problem. Others knew not to expect love and rainbows and enjoyed their time. Occasionally, when someone would express this same desire, Jessica could easily shut it down and move on. Now, though, was different. The fear was greater, as was her desire to run the other way.

Before she could speak, Vini kept talking. "And I know you won't give me that."

"Vini…" Jessica couldn't counter that. Vini wasn't wrong about any of this. "You're right. I can't give you what you're asking. I can't give you more than I have."

Vini looked up at her then, and her dark brown eyes were so enigmatic that there was no chance of Jessica turning away. "I didn't say you can't. I said you won't."

Jessica didn't understand the difference and said as much. *Can't. Won't.* They were different sides of the same coin, and it was clear that Jessica's biggest fear had come true. She couldn't give Vini what she was looking for.

"I'm sorry, Vini." She couldn't help repeating herself, not that it would do any good. She could see the determination in Vini's face, and the last thing she wanted to do was hurt her again. "I didn't mean for any of this to end this way."

"Me neither," Vini replied. She put her hands on her hips and looked down. Jessica willed her to look up again, but when Vini didn't, she knew the conversation was over.

Jessica took a step back, everything in her screaming to

stop and try again, but she couldn't. She liked Vini and re-spected her too damn much to hurt her again. What Vini wanted was important, and if Jessica couldn't give it to her, she knew she needed to step away and let her be with some-one who could. The idea of Vini falling into someone else's arms made her stomach roll, but she fought it down in favor of getting out as soon as possible.

"Bye, Vini." Pain lanced through Jessica as soon as the words left her mouth, but she swallowed it back in favor of leaving with the last bit of grace she had.

She wouldn't remember the walk back to her car or the slow drive back to Grace's house or ignoring Grace and Ava who were seated on the couch talking softly. Jessica walked in a daze, not stopping until she was back in the guest room, door shut behind her. She looked around, not sure how she had gotten there. Jessica walked to her bed, pushed the suitcase over to make space and lay down. She stayed there even as the room grew darker and her stomach growled with hunger until sleep pulled her under.

Twenty-Four

Vini stared at the door, wondering how it was possible to feel the need to run after someone and to stay at the same time. She felt the desire so strongly it almost split her in two. The look on Jessica's face when Vini had said they shouldn't see one another anymore had been too much for her, and she'd had to look away before she broke and took it all back.

Her conversation with Dani and Ava had been eye-opening in ways she hadn't anticipated. She hadn't realized just how much she needed to talk to someone about her feelings until they came pouring out of her like word vomit until she felt wrung-dry and exhausted. It had been worth it to get her feelings out and get some advice like she had always wanted but not been able to for the past few weeks. There were so many apologies that she never wanted to hear the word *sorry* again for a long time.

The end result, however, was the realization that she couldn't do this anymore. She couldn't keep seeing Jessica knowing that there were only a couple days left. She had developed feelings, and she knew she wouldn't be able to let her go if Vini continued to have her close. Vini couldn't keep going and pretend like she was going to be okay the day that Jessica drove away and out of her life. Already she was mourning the loss as if her partner was going off to war. When even Dani agreed that nipping it in the bud was the right thing to do, she knew she couldn't deny it anymore. Still, doing so had left her so emotionally drained that she quickly let Aiden know she would not be in the shop tomorrow and for him to take the day off.

Not wanting to stay in her room and wallow, Vini marched to the bathroom intent on standing under a hot stream of water until she couldn't feel anything. It partially worked until Dani pounded on the door and told her to not drain the water heater. She almost did it anyway, just to be spiteful, but she turned it off instead. She couldn't deal with anymore drama.

"Oh, hey, Dad." Vini paused before continuing into the kitchen. Her dad was at the table, nose buried in the paper like usual. He looked over his reading glasses before smiling. "Hey, kiddo. What are you up to? I thought you would be out tonight."

Vini frowned in confusion until she remembered having planned to take Jessica to the Christmas tree farm that was a couple towns over. The reminder of that nearly had her doubling over, but she kept her composure and gave him a brittle smile.

"Uh, yeah. A change in plans. I think it's just you and me tonight."

He nodded before turning his attention back to the paper. Vini sighed softly before walking over to the pantry and pulling it open. She didn't really have an appetite for anything, but she pulled out a can of soup and figured she could microwave it quickly before her stomach decided to rebel on her.

"You all right there, Vin? You're quieter than usual."

Vini nodded as she went through the motions of heating up her soup. "Yeah, I'm fine, Dad. Just tired, I guess. It's been a long day."

"Right," he replied, not sounding like he believed her story. "Just tired from work, huh? So you're telling me that the long look on that face of yours doesn't have anything to do with the woman you've been seeing?"

Jesus, does everyone know? Vini was quickly realizing that the only reason Ava hadn't known what was going on was more because she didn't want to see it and less because Vini was good at being sneaky. "What are you talking about?"

"I know you didn't think you was being slick." Vini sighed and turned to look at him. He had dropped the paper but was still looking at her over his glasses. "Really?"

"I wasn't trying to be slick, Dad. I just wasn't trying to put my business all out there in front of everyone," Vini replied.

He nodded. "I got that. It's why I kept my mouth shut. But don't you think it's about time to bring her over here so I can meet the poor woman? No need to hide her away, though I know your sister is a bit…"

"Overprotective? Controlling? Unable to mind her damn business?"

He laughed. "All of the above, silly girl."

She chuckled until she remembered that the point was moot now. She and Jessica were over. There was no need to introduce or reintroduce her to the family. "Either way, it doesn't matter. She and I aren't… She's leaving, so we decided…" Finishing her sentence was hard. It made the whole thing real to say it out loud. Vini swallowed hard before turning back to the stove and continuing to cook. It wasn't until the water started to boil that she spoke again.

"You met her already." When her dad didn't respond, she turned to look at him. "The woman I was seeing. You met her during Thanksgiving."

His expression didn't change, and Vini huffed out a quick laugh. "You knew then, didn't you? That I was seeing Jessica."

"I'm old child, not blind," he replied, making Vini laugh. "You spent most of the meal making googly eyes at that woman, just like Ava and Grace. Probably the only reason she couldn't see what was going on. That girl always did have a one-track mind."

More weight felt like it was lifted from Vini's shoulders, and she slowly realized that she didn't have to hide anymore. Dani knew. Ava knew. Hell, everyone in her immediate circle knew. She should have been happy that her infatuation was out in the open and she didn't have to keep it quiet anymore. But instead, she just felt sad. Sad that it had taken this long and yet she had nothing to show for it except a string of arguments and a broken heart.

"I shouldn't have started this thing, though," Vini said as she dropped in the dry noodles and started to stir. She let the motion keep her going as she gave voice to her thoughts. "I knew she was only in town for a short time and that she would be leaving. Who starts something with someone when they know they don't plan on sticking around?" She chuckled, though there wasn't any amusement in her voice. Vini was slowly realizing that she had set herself up for failure.

"What does that have to do with anything?"

The question threw her off. What did her dad mean? It had everything to do with everything. "Because she was only passing through, and I knew she didn't do relationships in the first place."

"Well, I can't speak on that last bit, but proximity means nothing if you want to be with the person. Hell, your mama was worth it, and I almost closed the shop for her when she got the chance to leave this place."

"What?" Vini turned, bewildered by the idea that her dad had even considered giving up the shop that had been in his family for generations. "You were going to sell the shop? But I thought you loved it?"

He nodded. "I did. Still do. But honey, I loved your mom something fierce, and if I had to move heaven and earth just to be with her, you bet I was going to do it." There was nothing in his gaze that gave Vini any doubt of his sincerity. "It was your mama who told me not to sell it and let my cousin, Terrence, run it for a bit while we checked out some other cities. He almost ran the damn thing into the ground, but after a year, your mama missed this place fiercely, so we decided to come back for good."

All of this was new to Vini, and she needed a moment to think. They were both silent while she finished cooking, and Vini let the information marinate in her mind. She loved the shop and hadn't ever known there was a time when it wasn't strictly in her dad's hands. The knowledge opened up whole new possibilities for her. But one blight still remained.

"But she said she doesn't want to be with me. At least, not the way I want to be with her."

"Well, that does present a problem," he agreed. "Normally, if someone said they didn't want to be with you, I'd say to hell with them. But I know it's hard for you when there's only so many potential matches available in this small town, so maybe you should give it another shot."

"Dad—"

"I know. I know. It sounds like I'm telling you to be desperate, but I'm not," he insisted. "I'm just saying, if you're this upset after only being with Jessica for a month, maybe there's something there worth fighting for. Think about it."

He reached over and put a hand over Vini's. She turned hers over and clutched at his hand like she had when she was a child and had nightmares at night. She wasn't sure if she would take his advice so soon after calling it quits, but she spent some time considering it and tried not to let the small flame of hope grow beyond what she could bear.

Twenty-Five

A soft knock on the door had Jessica blinking awake. Her mind was hazy, and her mouth felt like she had stuffed a handful of cotton inside. She slowly uncurled and groaned when her bones popped. Twenty-seven was too damn young to feel so old, and yet here she was snapping and popping her joints as she straightened. The knock came again, and she swallowed a few times so she could speak.

"Yeah."

"You want some breakfast?" Grace called out from the other side of the door. Jessica stared for a moment wondering if she should even bother answering. "Jess?"

"I'm fine."

She wasn't fine, but she wasn't ready to go out there and face anyone either. She was tired, more tired than she thought she had ever been before, even after the whole mess with her mom's coworkers popped off. That had been an annoyance, an aggravating diversion in the normal flow of her life. This was over and beyond worse.

"Did you eat anything last night?" Grace asked again. The doorknob turned, and Jessica's mind screamed out for her to stop. She didn't want to see anyone right now. Not until she could build back up the walls that had gotten her through the majority of her life unscathed. But of course, Grace couldn't hear her, and by the time Jessica had control of her voice again, Grace was already halfway inside the room looking at her with clear concern. "Are you all right?"

Jessica narrowed her eyes, glaring up at Grace and telling her visually exactly what she thought of that question. How could she possibly be all right when Vini had broken up with her? Or not broken up exactly, but said she no longer wanted to see her? How was Jessica supposed to bounce back from that?

"Right. Horrible question," Grace said, answering her own query. She twisted her hands before speaking again. "I just wanted to apologize to you about the things I said the other night."

Jessica gripped the sheets tightly as the memories of everything rushed back. She had enjoyed the dark oblivion of sleep and didn't want to rehash everything now in the light of day. Truthfully, she wanted to just skip past it all and wake up on Sunday morning in Italy where, for at least a little while, she could pretend that everything was okay.

"It's fine."

"No, it's not," Grace insisted in a weird parallel of her conversation with Vini that had Jessica blinking quickly.

"I was angry and hurt, but that didn't give me the right to blame you for that."

Jessica shrugged to keep from seeming so affected by Grace's words. "We both said some things that weren't okay. You were right about one thing, at least. I didn't think about the consequences if things were to go bad, not just for Vini and me but also for you, and for that I'm sorry." She looked up at Grace. "I'm sorry I messed up your relationship."

Grace shook her head as she stepped closer to the bed. "You didn't. I talked to Ava last night, and we both agreed that it was none of our business what you and Vini do. You were right that you two are adults."

The admission should have soothed Jessica, but all it did was serve as a reminder of what was lost. It didn't matter now that Grace and Ava knew and had agreed to take several steps back. Jessica and Vini weren't together anymore. Truthfully, they never had been, and the only person to blame for that was Jessica and her inability to commit.

"Anyway, it doesn't matter anymore," Jessica said looking down at the sheets. "Vini and I decided not to see each other anymore."

"What?" Grace asked in clear surprise. "Why not? I thought you guys were having fun."

Jessica sighed. "Yes, well, fun isn't all there is. We wanted two different things, and that made it impossible for us to continue."

"Aw, Jess. Please don't tell me you broke it off because you're leaving. Lots of people do long-distance relationships, especially with the ease of technology these days. You two could easily keep in touch."

That was a thought that Jessica hadn't even considered, but it still didn't matter. She wasn't the one who'd said they could go no further. She wasn't the one who had closed the door. "Vini broke up with me." She turned meeting Grace's gaze. "She was the one who said we shouldn't see one another anymore."

Grace's mouth opened, but no sound came out. She looked a lot like a fish, and if not for how damn depressed Jessica felt, she would have laughed. Or maybe thrown something at Grace to see if she could get it to land in her gaping mouth.

"What? Why?"

Because I can't or, rather, won't give her what she wants.

"Because it just won't work, and I respect Vini too much to try to change her mind."

Grace nodded in understanding. "Oh, well then, I'm sorry it didn't work out how you had hoped."

"Yeah, me too." Jessica truly was upset to be walking away.

"You need to get up. You can't just lie in bed all day feeling sad." Grace walked over to Jessica and leaned down taking one of her hands. "And you need to eat. You can't starve yourself."

"I can if I want." It was a childish answer, but Jessica didn't feel like being an adult right now. Still, she let herself be pulled up from the bed. She was still salty about her and Grace's conversation last night, but she had gone to bed without eating and she was hungry. "Fine."

"Good girl."

Jessica scowled but followed along. They parted at the steps with Grace running back to her room to finish getting ready and Jessica continuing down the stairs. When she got to the kitchen and saw Ava there, she almost turned around and made a beeline right back up the steps. She was not about to deal with this shit so early in the damn morning. Instead, she did what she always did when she was uncomfortable: held her head high and pretended she was unbothered.

"Oh, hello, Ava." Jessica was relieved to have her voice sound so steady, and she walked over to the stove to see a plate set out. She picked it up and walked over to the dining table, ignoring Ava completely where she sat at the kitchen island. Jessica could feel those dark brown eyes on her, but she didn't look up.

They sat together in silence save a few creaks from the upstairs floorboards. Jessica would have thought it was a setup if not for knowing how long it took Grace to get ready in the morning. She sedately ate her breakfast, not willing to look scared in front of Ava.

"I'm sorry."

Jessica crunched down on a piece of bacon and almost choked on it. She coughed softly into her hand before finally turning toward Ava. "Excuse me?"

Ava's eyes narrowed, but she repeated herself. "I said I'm

sorry. I shouldn't have gone off on you and Vini at the shop. What she does or who she does is none of my business."

Jessica frowned, wondering if this was a trick. She didn't trust Ava, especially since there were no witnesses. Still, she knew whatever she said would no doubt get back to Vini, and she didn't want to cause more trouble for her than she already had.

"I accept your apology. Thank you." Ava nodded curtly, and Jessica hoped that would be the end of it. Her hopes were dashed when Ava spoke up again.

"Grace told me…about the scandal with your mom's friends." Jessica clenched her jaw at Ava's confession. She wasn't surprised, but it still irked her to know that Grace had talked about it. If she hadn't, maybe none of this would have happened. "I shouldn't have let that cloud my opinion of you before meeting you. It's just hard to see my baby sister growing up and knowing that I can't really protect her anymore."

Weirdly enough, as a fellow sibling, Jessica could understand. There were a few times when Jason had been interested in people she didn't think were good for him. She hadn't gone as far as Ava, but she had had to catch herself from being overbearing about her advice to him.

"I can see how that would be hard," Jessica admitted. She wasn't going to give Ava a complete pass, though. She wasn't that nice of a person. "Vini is smart, though. I don't think you have anything to worry about."

Ava nodded. "True. She's probably the smartest of all of us," she said with a soft smile, and again Jessica found herself agreeing. "Listen, I know we will probably never be friends, but I just don't want to see Vini get hurt."

"Neither do I."

"I know that now. I really do," Ava insisted. "But I have to ask you, sister to sister, if you think you really can't be with Vini and love her the way she deserves to be loved, please just let her go."

The sincerity in Ava's voice almost cut deeper than her words. Jessica could hear the love there, the type of love that meant you would go to hell and back to make sure that person was okay. She empathized with it. She, too, would do anything to make sure Vini didn't get hurt.

Jessica didn't have a chance to reply. Grace walked into the kitchen, and Ava immediately jumped up to fuss with her clothing. Watching them joke and smile made the ache in Jessica that much more pronounced, and she knew what she had to do.

Jessica backed the car out of the driveway. She had spent the morning cleaning up and making changes to her travel plans. She was lucky enough to be able to find an earlier flight out of Atlanta that was leaving a little past ten that evening. It meant a seven-hour layover in Paris, but she was fine with that. There were plenty of shops she could wander around in and do some last-minute Christmas shopping as well as freshen up before the last leg of her flight. It did mean that she had left without saying goodbye.

She hadn't made the decision to leave early until after Grace and Ava had already left. There hadn't been a ton of seats left on the plane so she had to pick quickly before they were gone completely. Jessica had written a letter for Grace and also a note for her to give to Vini. Writing that note had been tough, and Jessica went back and forth with herself about leaving it at all. But it was done now. The letters were there, and she would let the chips fall where they might. Maybe she could come back to Peach Blossom in a year or two when the wounds weren't as fresh and see if they could start over. Maybe by then, Vini would be with someone new. Someone who deserved her affections. Jessica didn't doubt it would be tough for her to see, but it was what it was. Vini was a good woman, and Jessica had no doubt that once the right person realized that, they would never let her go.

Right when she put on her turn signal to merge onto the highway, her phone rang startling her. She took a deep breath before connecting the call. "Hello?"

"Sweetheart, what is this email I got from Delta about you coming to Naples early?"

Jessica sighed. "I changed my flight."

"But why? I thought you were planning on staying there longer."

"What gave you that idea?" she asked in confusion. "I never said anything about staying in Peach Blossom longer. Not over Christmas, anyway. Do you guys not want me to come visit?"

"Of course we do," her mom protested. "You know we love having you and Jason come stay with us. It doesn't feel like the holidays without the two of you with us." Jessica could hear her dad laughing in the background and the familiar sound lifted her spirits. "Oh, you hush. You know you miss the kids."

"I just thought it was time for me to come home. There's nothing keeping me here now that I know Grace is okay."

Her mom hummed over the line before speaking. "But I thought you were dating someone. You mentioned her all the time. Her name started with a *V*."

"Vini," Jessica replied before she could stop herself. She knew she had to clear up any misconceptions before she was forced to do it repeatedly over the holiday. "No, Vini and I were just friends."

"But all the texts about her and every time we called, you two were together or you talked about her. Truthfully, your father and I thought you might have decided to bring her with you. We were getting excited to meet her." That left Jessica's mind whirling. Had she actually talked about Vini that much? "Are you sure you two aren't dating? Maybe you just need to talk and tell her your feelings."

"Mom," Jessica started as she tried to think back to all their conversations. To her shock, she realized that after the first week, she had spent much of her time talking about things she did with Vini. She had no doubt that her text messages would show the same. "Oh, fuck."

"Sweetie, where are you?"

Jessica squinted and looked at the mile marker coming up. "Um, somewhere in the middle of nowhere headed to Atlanta. Why?"

"I suggest you turn your behind around and make your feelings known."

"Mom, I don't have—"

"Jessica Jae-eun Miller, I wasn't asking, I was telling. Now, I know you get your fear of commitment from your father—Calvin, hush, you know I'm right. How many cities did you move us to before I put my foot down? Exactly. Only thing you could decide on was me, silly man."

Jessica snorted at the familiar argument from her mom. It wasn't the first time her mother had brought it up, and she doubted it would be the last. Moving for their dad's job had become so familiar that she didn't think about it most days.

"Mom, it's not a fear."

"Oh, please. You took your father's commitment phobia and ran with it. But I know you also got some smarts from me. So trust me when I say if you don't face your fears and tell that girl how you feel, you will regret it for the rest of your life." Her voice was firm, and it had Jessica sitting up straighter as she thought about it. Had she really been so blind? She had been trying so hard to keep things a secret that she hid her feelings from herself.

"But she broke it off," Jessica said, her voice small and lanced with pain. "What if I can't be everything she needs? You don't get it, Mom. She owns her own business, and she's planning on expanding. She knows what she wants and where she wants to be. I barely know what I want to wear in the morning."

"Then, maybe she'll rub off on you a little."

"I'm not joking, Mom. What if she really gets to know

me and doesn't like me?" The thought was damn near im-mobilizing. Jessica had never thought she could have the type of love and stability her parents had. Her dad had got lucky. He had found someone willing to follow him and give up some of their dreams so he could achieve his own. "What if she realizes she doesn't want me?"

"Then, you feel proud that you put yourself out there and take it as a learning experience for the next time you find love." There was a shuffling sound in the background and suddenly Jessica's dad spoke up. "Honey, I know our lifestyle made it hard for you to feel like you could land on solid ground, but maybe you just needed someone to land for. You'll never know unless you let yourself really give it a try. Go get her, tiger. Put on the charm you got from your daddy. Ouch, Hillary, I'm just giving the girl a pep talk." Jessica smiled at the heated whispers over the line, before he came back. "Also, your mother said that she's canceling the plane ticket and we will see you sometime in the new year. Love you. Bye!"

Jessica didn't have time to say anything before the call ended and she was left staring at the phone. She doubted her mom would cancel her flight, but it didn't matter. She checked that the lanes were clear before she jerked the car over and cut across the median. She had to go back and give it one last try. This time, she knew exactly what she would do.

Twenty-Six

Vini leaned back in her chair, her eyes trained on the ceiling. She knew she should be out in the garage working on a couple cars that were in for basic service, but she had needed a moment to get herself together. She had gone over to Grace's on her way to the shop, hoping to talk to Jessica. She didn't know exactly what she planned on saying, but she had a rough idea. The conversation last night with her dad had given her the courage to face Jessica again and fight for what she knew they could have. There was something between them, and she knew it. She refused to let either of their insecurities or fears keep them apart. But when she got to Grace's house, no one was there.

Vini knew that Grace would be gone to work, but Jessica should have been there. She hadn't stopped to think about the driveway being empty with Jessica's car missing. She had been so focused on talking to her that she had missed the obvious. Jessica was gone.

Vini had knocked on the door a few times before letting herself in. Small towns came in handy when people didn't feel the need to lock their doors. Vini had gone inside and called out, but no one responded. In the kitchen, everything looked normal until she saw the sheets of paper on the dining table. One had been addressed to Grace and the other to Vini herself. She had picked it up, curious as to what it said, but after a few lines wished she hadn't.

Vini. I'm sorry. I was so busy trying to keep my heart from being hurt that I didn't realize I had already given it to you. I hope one day you can forgive me for being afraid and running away. You are everything. —Jessica

Vini wasn't sure how she had made it out of the house and into the shop before collapsing, but she did. Even now, those words were burned onto the back of her eyelids, and she saw them every time she blinked.

"If only I hadn't given her that stupid ultimatum," she hissed to herself. She felt the burn of tears and pressed the heels of her hands against her eyes until spots burst out. She wanted to go home and curl under the sheets until she felt ready to face the world, but she knew that wasn't an option. If she did that, she would never come out again. She didn't want her sisters to worry either. Knowing Ava, she would probably try to hunt Jessica down and then they would be right back at square one. No, there was nothing she could do but push forward.

A soft knock made her sit up. Aiden was at the doorway. He had been a rock for her this morning, taking charge and setting things up. She owed him a great deal more than just gratitude and planned to make it up to him.

"Hey, boss lady. You got a pick up out on Seventy-five South. Sheriff said it's a couple flats and maybe some underbelly damage."

Vini raised an eyebrow. "Underbelly damage? Did some fool try to U-turn on the median again?"

Aiden chuckled. "Probably. You know how those tourists can be. Want me to handle it or..."

She smiled in thanks. Getting out of the shop would probably do her a world of good right now. "Nah, I've got it. Thanks, Aiden."

"Of course," he replied before pushing off the doorway. "You know, I think it's going to be okay."

Vini tilted her head at his cryptic words but didn't have a chance to respond before he walked away. She glanced down at the letter on her desk before folding it and putting it in her pocket. She didn't yet know what she was going to do about Jessica, but she knew sitting around wasn't going to do her any good. She tugged on her boots and grabbed her tow truck keys before making her way to the back lot. By the time she was on her way down the highway, she was almost feeling good about things. Okay, that was a lie, but at least she wasn't crying.

She made her way up Seventy-five, slowing when she caught sight of the sheriff's car as well as the car with two very flat tires and grass tangled up in its front bumper. Her heartbeat jumped when she realized she knew that car. She had spent hours working on it weeks ago after towing it from this same highway.

Vini's hands shook as she eased her way around the emergency-vehicle shortcut and came down the other side. She slowed, moving her tow in front of the car before backing it up. She turned off the truck and took a moment to calm herself before she jumped to conclusions. When she thought she could get out without her legs crumpling beneath her, she opened her door. Immediately, that voice reached out to her.

"... Didn't mean to cut across. I don't know where my head was at, but I wasn't sure when I would be able to turn off and get back on."

Vini swallowed hard, the sheriff's response fading into the background as she closed her door and turned around. Everything seemed to move in slow motion as she stood there. Jessica was still looking at the sheriff and apparently pleading her case for cutting across the grass, but when her gaze finally landed on Vini, she stopped midsentence. Sheriff Patrick turned to look behind him and smiled when he saw it was Vini.

"Got a funny one for you, Lavenia. Seems she decided to blaze her own trail to turn around."

Vini nodded slowly, not looking away from Jessica. "It's fine. I got her, Sheriff."

He squinted for a moment before looking back and forth between Vini and Jessica. A sly smile split his face as he tipped his hat to them. "I'm sure you do, Vini. Enjoy yourselves, and please get home before engaging in any funny business."

Vin snorted but still didn't avert her gaze. "No promises, Sheriff, but I'll do my best." She didn't say anything else until he was in his car headed back down the highway. "I thought you were headed to the airport."

Jessica's throat bobbed as she swallowed, and Vini couldn't stop herself from moving closer. "I was, but then..."

"But then," Vini prompted as she stopped a few feet away.

"I realized I couldn't leave."

"Why?" Vini almost hated to ask, but she had to know. Writing it on a piece of paper was easy, but now they were face-to-face. If Jessica couldn't tell her now, Vini wasn't sure what she would do. She wanted this with a strength that was surprising, but she wasn't about to deny herself the possibility of finding someone she could see a future with. Still, she couldn't make this work on her own. Jessica had to meet her halfway.

Jessica bit her lip, and Vini's heart almost dropped before she looked back at Vini with a determined expression. "Because I like you. I like you more than I've ever liked anyone, and I can't leave without knowing if this thing between us is real."

Vini wanted to scream *yes*, but she knew she had to make herself clear this time. "I like you too, Jessica, but I can't be casual about this." Once the admission was out, it was easy to keep going. "I don't want to just be your friend or your benefit. I want to be your girlfriend. Your partner."

"You already were," Jessica insisted, closing the distance

between them. She stopped at the last moment when there was only a few inches between them. "You were the partner I didn't think I deserved, but I can't help but be selfish about you."

"What about Italy?" Vini asked.

Jessica smiled. "Italy will always be there. Maybe next time I can bring you with me. My parents apparently thought I was bringing you in the first place. They were disappointed when I said I wasn't."

It was Vini's turn to swallow hard. "You told your parents about me?"

"All the time. You were what I talked about most. Nothing I feel about you is casual, Vini."

"But won't you regret not going?" Vini had to lay it all out there. She didn't think she could handle if they tried again, and the same issues made an appearance. "I know Peach Blossom is boring compared to Italy, and I'm probably not as exciting as—"

Vini's words were stopped by familiar lips pressing against them. She couldn't think, only act, as she brought her arms up to wrap around Jessica's shoulders. Hands cupped her cheeks, shielding them from the cool breeze and keeping their faces close. When they pulled back slightly, Jessica rested her forehead on Vini's, the smile on her face softening her until Vini nearly melted into the grass below.

"You are everything I have been looking for," Jessica whispered, her words making Vini's chest burn with the feelings coursing through her. "Let's go home, okay?"

Vini smiled. "Do you consider Peach Blossom as home?"

Jessica brushed their noses together as she laughed softly. "You're my home."

Epilogue

Six Months Later

Jessica was nervous. Not that she would tell anyone that. Well, she was pretty sure Vini knew already, given the way she continued to squeeze Jessica's hand as the van bumped along the road. Scheduling this, a literal meeting of her two worlds, had taken some time. Truthfully, she had started planning as soon as she and Vini decided to give their relationship a real shot. She had known she wanted to introduce Vini to her family and show her some of her world as well. Italy seemed to be the perfect meeting spot for it all.

"Are those olive trees?" Vini's enthusiasm had Jessica relaxing. The flight over had been an experience. Jessica had pulled out all the stops, wanting to make this first hop over the ocean as pleasant as possible for her. Maybe it was nervous energy. This was the first time Jessica would be introducing someone she was dating to her family, and wasn't

that a trip. She was *dating*. She and Vini were in a relationship which was blowing her mind with how well it was
going. She thought she would feel confined or overly concerned with how things were going, but the sense of peace
she'd had since they officially labeled it was incredible.

"They are," Gianna said from the front seat. "There are
quite a few olive groves in this area as well as grapes and
figs. We grow some of our own as well."

Vini turned to look at Jessica, her eyes wide in surprise.
"You own an olive grove?"

Warmth infused her cheeks in the wake of Vini's impressed smile. "Well, technically Gianna oversees it. I just
bought the land and—"

"Don't let her be humble," Gianna cut in. "We just
bought another hectare of land to expand the grove, and
we're looking into another half hectare for our Monte-
pulciano."

"I don't know what any of that means, but it sounds exciting." Vini's smile was contagious, and Jessica found herself feeling shy for the first time in a long time. "You never
mentioned any of this before. It's seriously impressive."

Jessica had to fight the urge to shrug off the compliment.
She had been getting better about accepting them, especially
with how liberally Vini doled them out. Being appreciated
for something other than her skills in the bedroom was a
new experience for her. Sure, she had been complimented
when at work and on the occasions that she looked at re-
views from the audiobooks she narrated, there were kudos
sprinkled throughout, but this was different. This property

was her idea and one she had kept quiet about for years. Even her parents had only recently learned about the extent of it when the on-site bed and breakfast was finally finished and opened for business.

The forty-minute drive from the airport gave Jessica plenty of time to stew about what was coming next. Passing the familiar groves and vines she had come to love helped settle her, but this was still kind of a big deal. It wouldn't be the first time Vini met her family, but it would be the first time it happened in person. And they would all be together for a week which meant if things went wrong, leaving wouldn't exactly be an option.

"I can see why you love this place," Vini said catching Jessica's attention. "It looks so peaceful. It kind of reminds me of back home."

"You're not wrong." Jessica could see that, now that she had spent more time in Peach Blossom. It was a slower pace, similar to Abruzzo. How she hadn't seen that before was anyone's guess. "I always feel more settled when I come here."

The road was flanked by vineyards as they bumped down the narrow road leading to the main house. There were already cars parked, and Jessica's heart jumped into her throat. This was it. The meeting of the worlds.

She helped Vini out of the car, and they grabbed the bags from the trunk. The sun was high in the sky, and Jessica could feel herself starting to sweat. There was a light breeze that cooled the moisture on her skin, and if not for Vini grabbing her hand, she might have vibrated out of her body with nerves. The gravel under their feet crunched announcing their arrival, and before they reached the house, the door was thrown open.

"You're here!"

Jessica snorted at her mom's enthusiasm, but she didn't stop until she had those familiar arms wrapped around her. She let out a breath she hadn't known she was holding as her mom's familiar floral scent enveloped her. When she pulled back, her dad was already out and similarly had Vini wrapped in a tight hug.

"Look at you," her mom, Hillary, said with shiny eyes. "I feel like we haven't seen you in so long."

Jessica tried not to roll her eyes. "I saw you guys like a month ago."

"For a couple days. It's not the same." Jessica stepped back as her mom reached out to pull Vini in a hug. "And you didn't bring Vini. It's so good to see her finally."

Jessica's face hurt with the width of her smile as she watched her mom cup Vini's cheeks in that way only moms did.

"It's good to finally meet you too, Mrs. Miller."

"Call me Hillary, sweetie. Mrs. Miller feels so stuffy."

A snort from behind her had Jessica turning in time to see Jason come down the stairs. He looked good, relaxed in a way he hadn't seemed in a long while. He bumped Jessica's shoulder. "About time you all got here. I thought Mom was going to commandeer a plane and go find you guys herself."

Jessica chuckled. "Don't give her any ideas. We don't need her getting a pilot license." She looked over him, noting the slight strain still around his lips. "You look better. How are you holding up?"

Jason shrugged, but his smile didn't reach his eyes. Jessica wasn't surprised by that. They had been talking a lot more now than they had in a long while. "As good as can be expected, I guess. Have you talked to Alicia?"

Jason's ex-fiancée had blocked him after ending their engagement, and other than a few visits to get her things from his place, as far as Jessica knew they hadn't talked since. Jessica had tried to reach out a couple times, but when Alicia never responded, she stopped. It wasn't her business to get involved with what happened, as much as she wanted to for Jason's sake.

"No. You know she blocked me too," she said, and he nodded before running a hand over his face. "Is there anything I can do? I hate seeing you—"

"I'm fine," he said, cutting her off. Despite his words, he looked anything but. "This trip is for you guys. I'll feel better eventually. Getting away will probably help."

Jessica agreed but didn't say so. "You're always welcome to come visit us in Peach Blossom. Vini and I are looking at getting a place."

His eyebrows rose. "Cohabitating? That's a big deal." He latched onto the change in subject like Jessica knew he would. He wasn't wrong. Other than her family, Grace was the only other person she had ever lived with long-term. Even Gianna had her own house on the other end of the property. "So this is it for you, then? You're happy?"

Jessica looked over at Vini who was still talking with

their parents. Her rich skin glowed under the Italian sun, and her smile was wide and open. Jessica could feel the pull toward her, and the desire to taste the happiness that shone from her eyes.

"Yeah, I am."

Their eyes met, and Vini's smile grew so fond that Jessica felt her eyes burn. This was perfection.

★ ★ ★ ★ ★